NAKOMA AND THE PRINCE

THE PATEL CHRONICLES
BOOK ONE

MONICA SCHULTZ

For Mum and Dad.

Without your unwavering support for my earliest attempts at novels, this book would've remained a daydream.

ISBN 13 Paperback: 978-0-6459080-0-8

ISBN 13 eBook: 978-0-6459080-1-5

Cover art/design by Etheric Design

Editing services by R. A. Wright Editing

Proofreading by Magnolia Author Services

THE KINGDOM OF PATEL

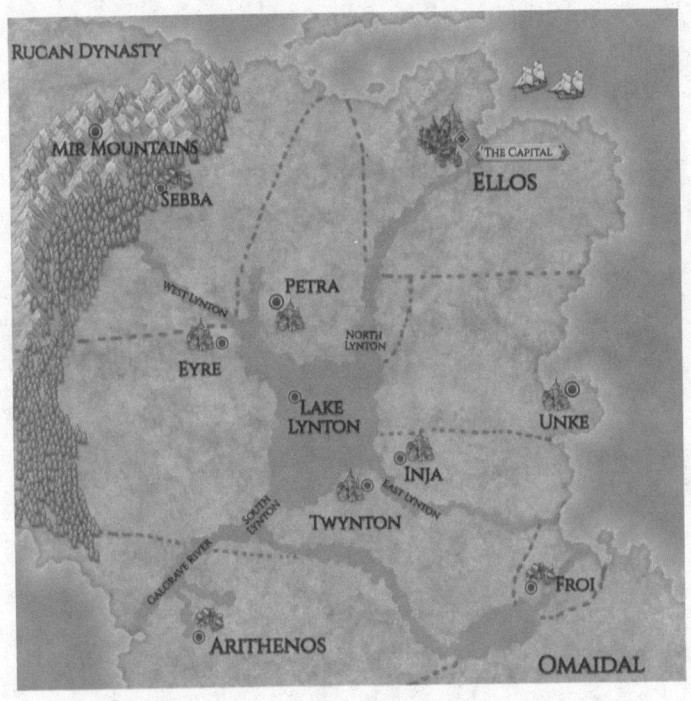

THE KINGDOM OF PAPER

NAKOMA AND THE PRINCE

Monica Schultz

NOTE:
This book is written with Australian English spelling.

CHAPTER
ONE

My first assignment as a guardian is nothing like I imagined. There are no enemies to fight. No countless miles of terrain to gallop across. Just hours of stillness, watching the crowds from the base of the temple steps.

Loose strands of black hair stick to the sweat on my face. I brush them away and ignore the drip of moisture sliding down my back. My focus must remain on the crowd, but I can't fight this restlessness. My eyes gradually drift towards Wish, my soul owl. She circles high above me, her white feathers glowing in the afternoon sun. Like me, Wish is also watching. She's waiting for a traveller. An eagle saw the lone man at daybreak, only miles from town. Rumours say he's from Ellos and seeks an audience with our chiefs.

I fidget in the saddle. Kato, my dapple-grey stallion, shifts beneath me. Neither of us are accustomed to hours standing still. Three years of training and another two spent in reserve led us to believe that every day is an adventure. Guardians are made for patrolling miles of empty plains or fighting off invading enemies. Apparently, we're also quiet watchdogs who twiddle our thumbs and wait for trouble to arise.

The common is busier than market day this afternoon. Dust swirls through the air as children play, ducking and weaving between groups of men who stand with their heads bent in conversation. Beggars keep close to these men, too interested in the talk to ask for spare coin. Women with babies tied to their backs and food rations in their arms slow down, trying to glimpse the traveller before returning home. Eventually, their patience pays off. The cry of an eagle pierces the air, announcing the traveller's arrival.

Every inch of me aches to crane my neck and watch the traveller as he approaches. My thoughts whisper that his clothes or gait might hold the secret of his intentions here. The last time someone from the Capital acknowledged our province outside of trading season, I was only a babe. Since then, the tension between Arithenos and Ellos has only grown. The commander warned us that people may take it upon themselves to find their own solution to Arithenos's current state of poverty.

Two fellow guardians, Omarion and Jai, flank the traveller dressed in brilliant purple. The crowd parts at the sight of them, but not without complaint. Aritheans spit at his feet as the traveller passes, and the air grows thick with their curses. Around the common, I notice others from my platoon adopt identical alert postures. We're all eager to prove ourselves if given the opportunity.

Sensing my tension, Kato flicks his ears towards me. I release my white-knuckled grip from my sword and rub his long neck to soothe us both. Still, my eyes never leave the traveller. He's young and has the build of a messenger boy, but perhaps it's a trick of the Capital. I almost wish he would pull a poisoned blade from his boot and give me a reason to display my skill with a bow.

My attention shifts to a merchant yelling obscenities that would make Mother blush. If he charges the traveller, I can intercept and restrain him with a length of rope like they showed us in training. But nothing happens. The extra guardians around the common are enough to calm any sparks of rebellion. Omarion and Jai pass with the traveller without incident, then disappear inside the sandstone temple that towers behind me.

With the messenger gone from sight, Wish descends gracefully. I flick my long braid off my leather shoulder guard so Wish can make herself comfortable. My skin prickles with the sensation of being watched. One glance around the common quickly uncovers the source. Torik, a freckled guardian from my platoon, stares at Wish with narrowed eyes. I acknowledge Torik with a quirked eyebrow and force my lips to smile before turning my back to him.

Most Aritheans have the decency to keep their eyes moving, but I've heard Torik whisper to anyone who will listen about how unnatural Wish is – *a fitting soul bird for*

3

an Arithean with blue eyes, he says. I grit my teeth, frustration bubbling to the surface as his gaze still pricks my skin. After five years bonded, I thought most Aritheans were used to seeing Wish around. I reach up and stroke the soft feathers that frame Wish's mask-like face. She leans into my touch, but her glossy, black eyes focus on Torik. A smile loosens my clenched jaw at the thought of a priestess catching Torik distracted and reporting it to the commander. I straighten my spine and return to my slow, watchful sweep of the common. At least one of us should have a chance to make it out of reserve tonight.

THE LAST RAYS OF DAYLIGHT DIP BELOW THE HORIZON, AND Wish departs on her nightly hunt. Without her pressed against my face, the night air sends a welcome shiver across my skin. Only a handful of bony strays and the beggars that shelter at the temple remain in the common. An apprentice priestess lights the sconces that hang from the seven gigantic columns around the entrance to the temple. The lanterns cast a flickering glow across the open space, transforming the joyous location of our rites of passage ceremonies into a hall of dancing shadows. Once the priestess has left and the air is quiet, I swing myself out of the saddle, landing in a crouch. I slip Kato's bridle off and comb my fingers through his mane.

Footsteps echo against the stone temple, startling me

from my meditative grooming of Kato. In one swift motion, I turn and face the newcomer. My lips twitch into a smile at the sight of Omarion striding towards me. He's the model of a perfect guardian – tall and muscular, with immaculate posture and a tidy beard. Between him and Kato, their combined height is enough to suffocate me, but Omarion keeps a respectful distance.

"Any news?" I ask.

I quickly scan Omarion's open face for telltale signs of excitement, but his dark-brown eyes are difficult to read without sunlight to brighten them.

"Hello to you too, Nakoma." Omarion chuckles.

I wave off his greeting with a flick of my wrist. "Do you know who the traveller is? What do they want?"

Omarion sighs wearily and rubs his neatly plaited beard. He's wearing the same uniform as me – khaki trousers and a loose scarlet tunic – except Omarion has embroidery around the neckline to identify his rank as captain. I slide my fingers across the empty neckline of my tunic and release a frustrated huff of air. At the rate I'm going, I'll be lucky to advance beyond a sergeant by the time I'm thirty.

"I suppose it won't be long before the whole of Arithenos knows," Omarion says. "The traveller came with an invitation to the royal palace in Ellos. Their precious prince has come of age and, as is tradition, must seek a bride."

My mouth forms a silent O. "He seeks a bride from Arithenos?"

"From every province—"

"He can't! The law declares a man can only take one wife."

Omarion rolls his eyes at me. "He's not going to marry all of them. It's part of an old pact designed to keep the peace in Patel after the last rebellions. The crown prince will meet a potential bride from every province before choosing. This way, every province has a chance of having their representative next in line to govern the kingdom."

"That doesn't make any sense," I interject, unable to hold my tongue. "The prince could simply travel to each province, take one look at a lady, and declare her met. Then he can be done with it and simply marry a lady from Ellos."

"The king does not include Ellos as an eligible province, since the royal family already lives there."

I shrug. "Then he can choose a different central province. They're all the same."

Omarion frowns, but the expression isn't half as fearsome as the commander's. His usually wide eyes still sparkle with mirth, even while narrowed into slits.

"Do you want to be told or not, Nakoma? I don't see Jai out here offering you information."

I flinch away from Omarion, surprised by the sting of his words. As the only woman in service, most guardians treat me with disdain, but not Omarion. He trusts that my femininity does not weaken my potential as a guardian. I'm lucky I ended up in his platoon instead of Jai's.

"Please, Omarion. Continue."

Omarion gives me a look, unsure of my sincerity. I mime locking my mouth and throwing the imaginary key over my shoulder.

"The prince has to do more than meet each lady. There must be a genuine attempt to know them as well. The king invites all the ladies to be guests at the palace for seven moons. They attend meals and parties with the prince, and he must spend time with all of them. Everyone gets a fair chance to have one of their own become the next queen."

I scrunch up my nose at the mention of parties. If parties were all it took to find a match, then my mother would throw one every day.

"It's still far from fair. The prince could choose a lady from the central provinces simply because the marriage would be more strategic."

Omarion cracks a smile at my scepticism. "It's not flawless, but it has kept the peace. Even if a lady does not marry the prince, the time in Ellos provides a royal education and the opportunity to meet other wealthy suitors. Many consider this just as valuable."

"So, I suppose *that man* wants one of our women to go back to Ellos with him?"

"Exactly. But the council is not in favour. A lot can change in two decades."

I nod slowly and let my thoughts wander. Time has not been favourable to our relationship with Ellos. Under the darkness of night, with only the stars and moon to light Arithenos, it's easy to ignore the creeping signs of poverty.

"Does the council see no gain for Arithenos if we send a representative?" I ask.

Omarion tugs on the ends of his beard in thought. I watch him silently, hoping to wait him out so he might speak his mind. Eventually, my patience pays off.

"Something like that," Omarion says. "The temple walls are thick enough to muffle their voices. Besides, Jai and I had to wait with the traveller while they discussed how to respond."

"Can we even trust Ellos with our lady?"

Omarion doesn't answer my question, and the lack of placating words is enough to tell me he feels the same way. After a few beats, Omarion's attention drifts away from me. I follow his gaze across the common to where another guardian patiently stands watch.

"Go home, Nakoma. The commander no longer requires your presence tonight."

I nod, understanding that Omarion has switched back into the role of my captain, not my friend. Omarion nods in return and strides off to deliver the message to retire for the night to the other guardians around the common.

I summon Wish to me with a sharp whistle that pricks Kato's ears. Moments later, she comes into view, a shadow against the stars, and together with Kato, we head home for the night.

CHAPTER
TWO

I rise early the next morning to the clatter of dishes and voices drifting upstairs from the kitchen. The smell of spiced bacon makes my stomach grumble. I slip into a lemon-yellow housedress and scoop my thick, black hair into a bun at the nape of my neck. The dress is faded and full of holes from Wish's claws, but it will do for breakfast.

Morning sunshine catches on the colourful tiles that decorate the kitchen walls as I make my way downstairs. Mother hums by the stove as she stirs a fragrant batter, ignoring the pile of dishes that soak beside her in the sink. Drops of food stain Mother's apron, but the dress underneath is still pristine.

Mother looks up as I enter the room and waves me over to the large wooden table. I sit across from my fifteen-year-old brother, Jakob, whose curly hair is as unkept as his temple uniform.

"You look well this morning, Nakoma," Mother says.

Jakob makes a face. "She means you look like a girl."

I roll my eyes at Jakob. "I *am* a girl."

"Yeah, but you *look* like one today."

"Jakob..." Mother warns.

Mother gives Jakob a stern look and places a heaped plate of breakfast in front of me. The smell of salty bacon and sweet porridge makes me salivate, but I don't pick up my spoon and fork. Mother has a plastered-on smile that spells trouble.

"Though ... it is nice to see you in something prettier than your usual clothes."

I sigh. Mother's voice carries the hope that I have finally given up my role as a guardian for something more feminine. I rarely allow myself a day to relax, but after the late night yesterday, I thought Kato deserved a rest from our usual routine.

"It's my day off."

Mother's smile drops, and she slams the rest of the breakfast dishes onto the table.

"You're going to give your poor mother grey hairs and wrinkles," she says, storming off to wash her abandoned dishes.

I ignore her outburst and shovel food into my mouth to satisfy my now growling stomach. As I eat, I watch Mother scrub a skillet, venting her frustration on the congealed grease and burnt patches. Even angry, Mother is pretty in her own way. Unlike the women of Arithenos, Mother has hair like golden thread and eyes as blue as the Galgrave River, which sustains Arithenos. Papa claims women in Ellos use ointments that burn their scalps just to have hair like Mother's. He even said women starve themselves to be as thin as Mother. I shudder at the thought.

The people of Ellos are crazy if they think fair hair and thin bodies are more beautiful than Arithean women. My curls appear loose compared to Papa's tight coils, but I've still inherited most of my features from him. Only my bright blue eyes give me away as not truly Arithean. Jakob and I share Mother's eye colour, but for some reason, my eyes appear startling in contrast with my face, whereas Jakob's cause all the girls in his class to swoon.

Jakob prods at my arm. "You've got that weird vacant look again."

I stand up and ruffle his mop of hair. After Jakob's latest growth spurt, while he's seated is the only time I can reach the top of his head.

"I'm just thoughtful, unlike some people."

Jakob swats me away and smooths down his hair. "You've put Mama in a mood."

"I know... I'll talk to her. Why don't you go to the common and fetch some honey from Yelena? She's supposed to have a fresh batch today."

Jakob grins. Honey always sweetens Mother's moods. Finished with my food, I take my plate with me to clean in the sink. Mother lets me take her place without comment and hands over the stubborn skillet. While I am no taller than Mother, years of archery have left my fingers strong enough to scour a pan in seconds. I move on to the next dish and search for something to say that might soften Mother as easily as the congealed grease beneath my loofah.

"Breakfast was delicious."

"Oh, so now you like my cooking," Mother says. "What happened to *Papa, your food is sublime! Papa, you should always cook!*"

Jakob snickers from the dining table, and I shoot him a dark look. It only takes a second for him to scramble out of the room on his errand.

"Mother, you know I love your cooking too."

"While your papa is out travelling and trading his goods, you know who is home, looking after you two? Who cooks and cleans all day?"

Mother punctuates her words with a wooden spoon, causing me to flinch.

"That's not what I meant..."

"And what thanks do I get? A son who makes tutors weep and a daughter who wishes she was a man."

The tray I'm working on drops into the sink with a splash of sudsy water.

"Mother! That's not fair! I do not wish to be a man. I am a woman, but I am also a guardian."

"How many guardians do you see raising their children?"

"Not everyone wants children," I spit, falling into our tireless argument.

"You don't know what you want. You're only seventeen."

I toss my hands in the air. Mother has a talent for

diminishing my dreams of becoming a legendary guardian in three words or less.

"Fine! Even if I want a family one day, I know plenty of guardians who have children."

Mother juts her pointed chin forwards and rests her hands on her hips. "Oh, do you now?"

"Yes! Many guardians have wives and children. They carry their locks of hair and always keep them close to their hearts."

"Exactly! They have wives. Do you think a man would do the same for you? Stay home and look after your children while you go on sentry duty for years at a time?"

"Guardians with a family are rarely called for sentry duty. Besides, who wants a man that can't look after his own children? I don't need to marry just to be complete."

"You'll regret that when you're old and lonely."

I roll my eyes. "I have Kato and Wish to keep me company."

"A horse and a bird," Mother scoffs. "It's not the same. Every woman needs a match. It's part of life."

"Arithenos is not the same as Ellos. Maybe the women there are too weak to think for themselves."

Mother's face falls. "Whether you like it or not, Nakoma, you are as much a child of Ellos as you are of Arithenos. You should be proud of your heritage."

"I'm thankful that I was born and raised in Arithenos. Arithean women are more than the man they marry. Female guardians may be unusual, but it does not mean giving up my life as a woman."

Mother reaches for me, but I flinch away from her touch.

"You do not have to be a guardian your whole life," Mother finally says.

I stare at Mother with disgust. "The High Priestess chose me to become a guardian at my welcoming ceremony. She saw my destiny."

Mother rolls her eyes. "She's not a god. It wasn't even magic. She saw an awkward child and told you something to make you smile."

I back away from Mother, my eyes prickling with the threat of tears. Mother is a nonbeliever, but I've never heard her be so cruel before.

"Why can't you be proud of me?"

I don't wait for her reply. Hot, angry tears already trickle down my face. I brush past Mother and run out the front door.

Outside, I am assaulted by the sweltering heat. Eager to escape the sun and prying eyes, I dart down the alley that runs beside our house. I wipe the tears from my face and watch the ground for wild prickle patches that threaten to prick my bare feet. Finding the gate that leads to the stables behind our house, I slip inside.

The family courtyard overflows with exotic flowers and fruits, filling the air with heavy perfume. I stand under their shade and take deep breaths until I stop sniffling. The plants transform our home into a treasure map of Papa's travels. Papa claims he brings the plants as gifts for Mother so that she can have the world at her fingertips, but it's Papa that tends lovingly to these gardens. As a little girl, I spent countless hours exploring this small space, feeling as if I was wandering an endless jungle.

These days, our courtyard seems cramped. After purchasing Kato, Papa renovated the space to include a private stable. It's enough for an overnight sleep, but Kato becomes restless if he doesn't get out to stretch his legs every day. Savouring the fragrant jasmine flowers, I sigh, letting my earlier frustration and anger roll off me. Kato wakes at the sound and nickers, startling Wish beside him. I smile in return and let the strong, comforting scent of Kato envelop me as I step inside his stall. I press my forehead into Kato's shoulder and try to match my breathing to his.

"What am I going to do with her, Kato?" I mutter.

Kato ignores me, nuzzling into the folds of my dress, searching for treats. I push his nose away and brush his speckled flank. As the dirt loosens, his white patches become glossy once more.

"I wish Papa never went to Ellos," I grumble. "Any Arithean mama would be proud to have a daughter work as a guardian."

Kato snorts in reply.

"Well, they would be far more accepting than Mother," I argue back.

This time, my only reply is the quiet, sleepy breaths coming from Wish. The rhythmic motion of brushing Kato allows my mind to wander back to the early days of my training. Mother's complaints started with comments about how my new calluses turned my soft hands ugly. Then it was how my growing muscles and broad shoulders ruined my silhouette. I'm sure she spent every moment of my training hoping I would fail so she could force me to act like a real lady. The memory alone is enough to send fresh tears sliding down my cheeks. I curse and breathe through my nose to try to stem their flow.

"I've got to get out of here," I whisper to Kato and Wish.

Wish regards me with a curious tilt of her head but remains on her perch. I switch brushes and comb out Kato's long dark-grey tail with renewed vigour as an idea forms. Sentry duty is notoriously boring, but it will get me away from Mother's nagging. I rock back on my heels and lean against the stall. Patel has been at peace with its neighbours for decades. I doubt I will encounter any trouble worth a promotion.

I push off the wall and pace within the confined space – back and forth, back and forth – until Kato flicks me with his tail. I roll my eyes at his backside.

"Don't worry, you'll come too. We just need to convince Omarion we're ready to go."

THREE

"**N**akoma! Are you out here?"

I jolt at the sound of Jakob's voice. Kato's tail slips from between my fingers, and my progress with his new braid is lost. I stand on my tiptoes to loosen the strands at the base of his tail, wipe the sweat from my brow, and step around Kato to face Jakob.

"There you are," Jakob says. "What have you done to Mama? She's angrier than a storm cloud."

My eyes flicker from Jakob to the young boy who has followed him into the courtyard. The child's feet are bare, and his arms are like toothpicks poking out of his oversized tunic. As Jakob speaks, the boy's ears twitch, listening for any intriguing snippets of conversation that might fetch a price on market day.

Shaking my head ever so slightly, I brush off Jakob's comment.

"Who have you brought with you?" I ask.

The boy nods at me in greeting. "The High Priestess sent me, ma'am. You're to come to the temple."

At the mention of the High Priestess, I straighten and dust off my dress. "Do you know what for? Should I bring Kato?"

"I don't know, ma'am. She just asked for you."

I stand dumbfounded, looking around the stable for equipment I might need to serve the High Priestess. My favourite bow and a full set of arrows hang from the back of Kato's stall. Behind them hides the bejewelled dagger I received from the High Priestess when she announced I would become a guardian. I can't bring either weapon into the temple, even if they comfort me. I dust off my dress once more and stare at my feet.

"Let me fetch some shoes, then I'll meet you out front."

THE TEMPLE TOWERS ABOVE ME AS I FOLLOW THE MESSENGER up the shallow steps. I pause at the top and tip my head back to marvel at the legends carved into the ceiling. Sunlight transforms the sandstone carvings into masterpieces that glow from within.

"This way, ma'am," the messenger calls.

I drag my eyes away from the artwork and hurry to catch up with the boy. Our footsteps echo in the grand hallway, though the temple is far from empty. Classrooms for all Arithean children and boarding rooms for the young priestesses are just some of the structures hidden behind these stone walls.

We find the council in a side room with few furnishings other than the long mahogany table they gather around. The council's varying shades of white clothes brighten their grey hair and soften their wrinkles. I bow deeply from the waist and wait in the doorway.

"Nakoma, I'm glad you could come," the High Priestess says.

She rises in greeting, and I am shocked by the amount of silver that now weaves through her hair. The High Priestess's slender arms sweep in a wide gesture, indicating I should take a seat with them. As she moves, the long sleeves of her robe billow around her, echoing her movements. One of the six council chiefs – Chione, Chief of Justice – clears her throat as I perch on the edge of a spare seat.

"Do you know why we gather today?" Chione asks, the wrinkles of her neck wobbling with each word.

I gulp. The last thing I want is to throw Omarion in the fire for disclosing sensitive information to his subordinate. I steady my hands in my lap, afraid to look like a fool.

"I have heard rumours..."

Sensing my unease, the High Priestess fills the silence. "You are not here to be reprimanded for idle gossip."

I bow my head in thanks and finally find my voice. "I heard the messenger wants Arithenos to send a representative to Ellos. So, I suppose you gather to discuss who it will be, if you send anyone at all."

"Exactly my point!" the Chief of Health bellows, slamming his fist onto the table. "Nobody should go. We are under no obligation—"

"Enough, Navid." The High Priestess's voice rings throughout the room, silencing the chiefs. "We have discussed this, and it will not do. Nothing shall change by us not partaking. We will never regain the treatment our people deserve by removing ourselves from the picture entirely."

Chione holds her chin high as she pointedly ignores Navid's glare.

"Some suggest we send you, Nakoma, as our representative," Chione says.

I gape at Chione. "Me?"

"Nakoma's commander has assured me she would be the ideal candidate," Os – the Chief of War – says. "She is the right age, perfectly capable of looking after herself, and has the status of a powerful woman in Arithenos."

I sit a little taller in my seat. This is the first time the commander has ever given me such high praise.

Os continues. "Once Nakoma is within the inner circle, she can assassinate their Minister of War and their generals. Destroy them from the inside out."

Eyes blazing, the High Priestess stands once more. "What good would that bring? You should know better than anyone, Os, that Arithenos would have the wrath of Patel upon it within a week."

Os folds his arms over his decorative chest armour

20

like a petulant child. "Arithenos is the backbone of Patel's military. Without us, there is no one left to fight."

"That is beside the point. Fighting will not put food in our people's bellies," the High Priestess says, and all bar one nod in agreement.

"We may have the most fearsome cavalry in the known world, but Arithenos is so much more than that," the Chief of Agriculture reminds the council.

Os glowers at the other chiefs, his beady eyes shining beneath a heavy brow.

"What would you have us do? Send one of your little priestesses in training?" Os demands.

The chiefs mutter, many shaking their heads in disgust, but the High Priestess remains impassive, unshaken by his jab.

"Need I remind you of our priestesses' devotion to prayer? They could not partake in this without losing their connection to the heavens," the High Priestess says evenly.

The Chief of Education, Damaris, raises her hand to gain the attention of the other chiefs before speaking. Grey curls frame her soft face and give her the appearance of a gentle demeanour.

"There are others, perhaps, who could fill the role. A young woman who is in line to become a future council member would be worthy of the title of lady."

"One cannot judge who will become a chief. It is experience that determines one's capability for the role," argues Navid.

"But we can see potential well before our youth become elders," Damaris retorts.

"If that is true, name me a worthy young woman," Navid challenges.

Navid smirks as the room erupts into chaos. Each chief yells to be heard as they pit the qualities of one lady against another. I pick at the pilling on my dress and shift in my seat to keep myself from frowning at them all. Plenty of the suggested young women are agreeable, but they will never choose a lady in this fashion. I clench my jaw to keep my mouth shut as a fire flickers to life within me. *You're only a trooper*, I remind myself. *Know your place.*

I lift my hand to my face and slowly rub the tension from my jaw as I look at the High Priestess. Like all our priestesses, she is the calm in the eye of the storm. Her lips whisper a wordless prayer to the ceiling that vaguely reminds me of Jakob's tutors. Then, as the chiefs' voices grow hoarse, she stands with her arms raised. Silence falls faster than a winter night as all eyes turn to her.

"Be still," the High Priestess says. "I have seen the path we must take. Os was right. Nakoma will represent our people. Who better than one of our guardians, the pride and joy of Arithenos?"

My eyes flicker across the table to Os. A smug grin fills his entire face, revealing several steel-capped teeth. "I will prepare our guardians for war."

"Not so fast, Os. Nakoma's mission will be one of peace. She will open a doorway so others will care to listen to our ambassador. Arithenos cannot continue to perform as King Alessandro's sword if he saps us of our strength with unfair taxes."

Silence falls over the council as each chief considers the weight of the High Priestess's words. I stare at them with mounting horror, suffocated by the thought of spending moons locked away indoors in ridiculous frilly dresses. They can't all agree with the High Priestess.

"Surely there is someone else?" I wince as I realise the words have slipped off my tongue.

"You don't believe you are the right choice?" the High Priestess asks.

My face heats, and with my eyes, I beg the High Priestess to forgive me.

"I did not mean to suggest you are wrong..." I stumble over my words. "...only that I find it difficult to believe fate desires me above all other Arithean women."

"Unlike other Arithean women, you swore to protect Arithenos. There is no better ambassador than one determined to fight till the last breath for their people, even if that fight is to ensure just treatment from their monarch."

The High Priestess's smile is as soothing as one of Mother's balms, but her words still cause my stomach to sink. As a lady of Arithenos, I'd become the laughing-stock of guardians – the silly, vapid girl only useful at gossiping. I keep my hands in my lap to hide their trembling.

"What of the king?" I ask. "Surely he would not accept a guardian living amongst their delicate ladies."

"This is true. To the central provinces, a guardian and

lady can never be the same. While in Ellos, you must represent us as a rich merchant's daughter."

I close my eyes against her words, slowly shaking my head.

When no one else dares to speak, the High Priestess continues. "Do not give us your response yet, Nakoma. Think about what you could do for all Aritheans. I know you will choose the right path."

FOUR

I walk home from the temple in a daze. The sun pricks the back of my neck, but I can't seem to make my legs hurry to escape the heat. My brain is too busy fighting itself to repress the memory of the High Priestess's request. Puffs of red dirt swirl around my feet as I shuffle along the road. Eventually, I stumble inside the front door.

"Nakoma ... is that you?" Mother calls.

I open my mouth to reply, but no sound comes out. If I tell her about the High Priestess's request, then I have to admit to myself that the council meeting was real.

"Nakoma?"

Mother's head pokes out from behind a doorway. Her blue eyes scan me from head to toe. She stops at my feet, and her face twists into a frown.

"I thought I told you and Jakob to stop walking dirt into the house," she says.

I glance at my feet. Dust clings to my sandals and leaves a copper trail behind me.

"The High Priestess has asked me to represent Arithenos as a chosen lady for the prince."

The words are out of my mouth before I have the presence of mind to suppress them. Mother's face smooths as a new light fills her eyes. My mind reels as it tries to take the words back.

"I'm not sure..."

Before I can complete the thought, Mother hushes me. There's a fierce look in her eye that I don't dare to argue with.

"There's much work to be done before any child of mine can step foot inside Ellos," Mother says.

"I have not..."

The sentence drifts into silence. Mother has already left the room. I unbuckle my sandals so I can follow her but don't make it through the first strap before she returns. Mother's stained apron is gone, and instead, she carries a coin purse tucked under her arm.

"Leave those on," she says. "We've got work to do if you are to be a true lady."

AUNT FIFI'S HOUSE IS STIFLINGLY HOT, DESPITE THE SHARP wind that blows through town. She has lowered the shutters across every window until only thin strips of sunlight filter into the house, yet Aunt Fifi refuses to open up. She insists that wind is the enemy of every seamstress, blowing about carefully placed scraps of fabric and scattering hasty drawings of the latest fashion. I doubt this is true. Most seamstresses do not have fabric piled on every spare inch of the floor until only thin pathways remain, nor do most seamstresses hang half-finished garments across the kitchen stools so that the guests have nowhere to sit.

"Ouch," I yelp.

I twist to escape Aunt Fifi's wrinkled hands, but the seamstress is faster. Aunt Fifi ducks under my elbow and pins another fold of fabric in place. Her shoulders hunch as she adjusts the bodice so it will fit snug around my curves.

"Be still, Nakoma," Aunt Fifi mumbles around a mouthful of pins, butchering my name so it sounds more like *Nickoma*.

I shoot a glance over my shoulder at Mother. She's perched on the bare edge of a cushion and watches Aunt Fifi's progress like a hawk, even though everyone in Arithenos knows Aunt Fifi is the best.

"This is unnecessary," I protest for the hundredth time. "I'm sure mothers in the Mir Mountains would not have half a dozen new dresses sown in a few short days."

Mother looks away from Aunt Fifi and folds her arms across her violet dress.

"Perhaps not in the Mir Mountains, but in Unke and Petra, they certainly would. And those ladies would not even need a new dress. They do not have closets filled with trousers and armoured uniforms that make a mother weep."

"I still don't know if I will even go," I argue, ignoring Mother's comments.

"You will do as the High Priestess asks, like you always do," Mother says.

I huff but keep my arms by my sides. The last time I tried to cross them over my chest, Aunt Fifi jabbed a pin into my elbow.

"Now, no more grumbling, Nakoma."

"I didn't even say anything!"

"And don't make Fifi waste any time wrangling you."

I glare at Mother over Aunt Fifi's head. Nobody, except the elders, calls Aunt Fifi by just her first name. Mother ignores me and brushes invisible dust from her dress.

"I must find Klue," Mother continues. "Her quick fingers will embroider a fine design onto your evening gown."

Mother hurries out of the room as if chased by flames. For a luxurious second, a breath of fresh air trickles through the open door before it closes and seals in the heat again. Mother is at least right about one thing; I can already see the wisdom behind the High Priestess's choice. Besides, the prospect of spending time in Ellos seems less daunting after my dreams of vanquishing bandits and thieves in the Capital. Maybe mercenaries will attack the palace and I'll save the day. The daydream is more than I can hope for in Arithenos.

Still, these thoughts don't make today easier. My stomach still churns at the thought of my usual breakfast of honey-sweetened porridge. Luckily, Jakob has hollow legs and was happy to switch bowls behind Mother's back this morning.

"Nakoma!" Aunt Fifi snaps her fingers in front of my glazed eyes.

"Sorry, the heat is making me drowsy." I mumble the lame excuse.

Aunt Fifi rolls her eyes and wags a finger at me. "You young people don't sleep enough, that's what it is. Down with the sunset, up with the sunrise is how it should be."

I try to keep my face as serious as possible. There's no point arguing with elders.

"Yes, Aunt Fifi."

"Well, quit standing around, then. Go have a look at yourself and tell me what you think."

I step off the wooden stool that acts as a platform and walk over to the mirror that leans against a far wall. My reflection is a little hazy, but it's enough to see the genius of Aunt Fifi's work. My legs seem to be surrounded by a voluminous skirt of brown tartan fabric. I shift into a squat and watch in amazement as the skirt splits into loose pants.

"This is brilliant!"

Aunt Fifi gestures wildly to the seat Mother vacated, causing her shawl to slide further off her shoulders. "Your mother said you could learn to ride side-saddle. *Bah!* Aritheans do not ride side-saddle!"

"Who is not riding side-saddle?" a voice calls from the front door, and I jump in surprise.

"Captain Omarion!" Aunt Fifi cries, rushing to greet him by the door. "You didn't tear through your trousers again, did you? I got a whole shipment of that fabric; I was so sure it would be right for our guardians."

Omarion shakes his head and straightens Aunt Fifi's shawl so it is no longer falling off her shoulders. Aunt Fifi blushes like a schoolgirl at his touch. I laugh behind my hand and follow the pair back into the main room.

"Don't fret, Aunt Fifi," Omarion says. "I'm not here for your services today. I heard Nakoma was on a mission to see how many dresses you can sew in three days."

"Hey, this is all Mother's idea. Don't blame me."

"Nothing these fingers can't handle." Aunt Fifi wiggles her fingers mischievously at Omarion, and I almost gag. "Now, are you thirsty? It's a scorcher today. I'll get you a glass."

Catching the look on my face, Omarion asks for one for me too before Aunt Fifi waddles out of sight. As soon as she is out of earshot, the laughter I've been fighting back escapes. It amazes me how charmed Aunt Fifi is by a man in uniform, even with the fine layer of dust that coats Omarion. He's not usually the type to draw attention from women. Omarion is the youngest captain in Arithenos and, despite his affable grin, women don't fawn over him like they do with other guardians. I assume it's because of his shaved head, or how his nose is crooked from one too many breaks. But to me, Omarion's good nature outshines these supposed flaws.

"It's true, then? They've asked you to become the lady of Arithenos?" Omarion asks.

"They've asked. I've yet to respond."

Omarion looks pointedly at the half-finished gown I am wearing. "But you will go."

I stare at the fabric that puddles around my feet, unable to meet Omarion's gaze. The High Priestess gave me the greatest gift of my life when she championed my training as a guardian. It's a debt I can't repay.

"I have to."

"But you don't want to. Nakoma, the High Priestess would never demand that you do this. It is your choice alone."

"I cannot deny her," I argue.

Omarion crosses his arms across his broad chest and waits for me to continue. The rest of my argument freezes on my lips. Omarion's brother died in a border skirmish when Omarion was a fledging trooper. To him, my longing for adventure must seem childish. I chew the inside of my cheek and look for a reason he will accept.

"You can't deny that I'm the perfect fit for this role. I'm the right age, Papa's business gives me the right status, and my training means nobody will fear for my safety. Besides, Mother has been preparing me to become a lady since the day she realised I was a girl."

"But could you marry him?"

I shrug. "He'll never ask."

"Don't be so sure," Omarion mutters under his breath as Aunt Fifi emerges from the kitchen.

Aunt Fifi hands us both chilled glasses of lemon water dripping with condensation. I gulp the drink down and sigh, cooled momentarily. Omarion finishes his drink just as quickly and hands the glass back to Aunt Fifi.

"Well then, I'll leave you lovely ladies to it," Omarion says. "If you are to have any hope of leaving before the new moon, we must begin preparations immediately. Who's packing your travel supplies? I'll check they're packing correctly. And let Kato rest for as long as you can. He has a long journey ahead of him."

I follow Omarion as he heads towards the door, nodding along with his orders.

"Heaven's speed with those dresses, Aunt Fifi. Don't make her too pretty. I need Nakoma back in the saddle come summer."

I roll my eyes at Omarion's departing back as Aunt Fifi fusses over him by the door. The wrinkles on Aunt Fifi's face gather into a deep valley as she frowns to herself.

"He could have stayed for a bite. In and out like a whirlwind, that boy," Aunt Fifi grumbles. "Anywho, we had better hem that dress before you trip and tear a seam. I've got enough to do as it is without having to start over with torn cloth."

"Of course, Aunt Fifi."

Aunt Fifi tuts and mumbles some more before leading the way back to the little wooden stool. Accepting her offered hand, I gather the long fabric in my fists, heft it up to reveal my calves, and step back into place.

CHAPTER
FIVE

The first full moon of autumn is a faint outline against the cerulean sky when we set off from camp. It's hard to spot amongst the abundance of clouds, but I'm still drawn to it. The moon is a reminder that we have only been riding for a few short days. Still, my backside aches like it has been a complete moon cycle.

"Do you know if we've crossed the border of Arithenos yet?" I ask Omarion.

I'm almost certain Omarion's answer will be no, but I can't help the questions. Despite insisting he will accompany me as far as Lake Lynton, Omarion has spoken less than a dozen words to me for the last two days.

"Not yet."

My eyes flick across to Omarion and find his usually open face stern and withdrawn. Perhaps he resents leaving the rest of our platoon behind for a mere escort role. Yazmin, his pinto mare, appears to enjoy the change of pace, regardless of her rider's disposition. Her white tail playfully flicks Kato if we venture too close.

"Do you think the prince will be a pompous layabout?" I ask to fill the silence.

I half expect Omarion to reply with nothing more than a grunt, but somehow, his silence is worse. I try to keep my attention focused on Kato and the steady motion of his walk. Instead, my eyes turn to the horizon. The plains of Arithenos are wide open farmland – perfect for flocks of grazing sheep and herds of cattle, not for an ambush. Still, Cedric believes a scout is necessary for any riding party. He looks ridiculous, riding only a mile ahead on clear ground. His scarlet uniform sticks out against the landscape like a sore thumb.

"You don't have to ride back here with me and Star," I say, nodding towards the pack horse tethered to my saddle. The chocolate-brown mare plods along beside me, my luggage exaggerating the natural sway of her body. The white patch that is her namesake shines between her eyes, even under a layer of sweat.

Omarion scoffs. "Of course I do."

Omarion is also wearing the red tunic, and it is just as bad up close. Usually sentries wear more neutral colours, but the Chief of War declared a lady of Arithenos should have a formal guard. Still, I'm jealous of Omarion's uniform. I know the tunic is thin and breathable, unlike the layers of fabric of my own riding dress.

"Really, I wouldn't mind if you want to act as a scout

with Cedric."

Omarion snorts at my last comment. I can only agree.

"You deserve company that doesn't shun your presence," Omarion says.

I roll my eyes. "Maybe you should have chosen someone to take your place, then."

Omarion finally looks at me. I fidget under his gaze, sure that he can see right through me to the nerves that have left me on edge for the last week. *What if the Academy traps attendees indoors all day, far from any hope of adventure? Or if the prince is insufferable and I still have to treat him with respect?*

Eventually, Omarion clears his throat and looks away. "I'm sorry. My thoughts have consumed me for too long."

I chew the inside of my cheek as the silence stretches between us. Every inch of me wants to bury my head in Kato's mane until I disappear completely. I should not have forgotten my place with Omarion. We've left the training fields of Arithenos behind, but Omarion is still my superior.

"We will cross into Twynton soon," Omarion says.

The corners of my mouth lift into the slightest smile as I repeat the name back to myself. I try to remember images of the province I saw in schoolbooks, but my mind comes up blank. All I can remember is that their soil is fertile thanks to their proximity to Lake Lynton.

I glance at Omarion. "So ... what's your verdict? Pompous layabout, or arrogant good-for-nothing?"

Omarion's lip twitches up, a ghost of his true smile.

"If the reports are true, then he's a layabout. Guardians say he flops about in his saddle like a fish on land."

I shudder at the thought. Playing the part of a docile merchant's daughter will be hard enough without watching some prince flaunt his limited abilities in a saddle.

"You're worried about what he'll be like?" Omarion asks, but the real question – *Why?* – remains unspoken.

My shoulders inch towards my ears, but Omarion deserves more than a shrug. "I have to spend seven moons with him. If he has a sense of humour, it might make the days less tedious."

"I thought you weren't going to marry the prince."

The sharp edge to Omarion's voice is enough to still my laughter.

"Of course not."

"But you hope he'll be decent enough to make you laugh?"

I roll my eyes. "Relax, Omarion. I'm not about to abandon our platoon for a couple of jokes in the Capital. Besides, I'm not the marrying type."

Omarion reins Yazmin in and comes to a dead stop.

"What did you say?"

I pull Kato around to face Omarion. The tense muscles of his forearms glisten with sweat in the harsh sunlight, and I imagine the rest of him is just as strained. A muscle jumps above his dark eyebrow, but it's the only sign of life in his frozen features.

"I will never marry. No man is worth jeopardising my career."

Omarion comes to life with a start and returns to my side.

"Who says marriage will be the end of your life as a guardian?"

I spur Kato on, eager to put this conversation behind us. Hundreds of times I've told Mother I won't marry, and her dismissive replies always harden my resolve. But Omarion is different. His genuine concern disarms me.

"It doesn't matter," I mutter.

"It matters to me."

I throw my hands up. "Fine. Nobody had to tell me. It's in our history. The only other female guardians both died on the battlefield without ever having taken a husband."

"You don't have to follow in their footsteps."

I laugh, the sound raw and brutal. My eyes turn towards the sky in search of Wish. Her white feathers are visible for a moment before she disappears behind the clouds on the trail of some prey.

"I'm already breaking enough unspoken rules with Wish."

"You're not the first guardian to bond with a bird other than a golden eagle."

"You're missing my point."

"Then explain it better."

"Married life just isn't for me," I growl. "I've seen how newlyweds fawn over each other, completely insensible to the rest of the world. Love like that would take weeks off my training."

Omarion chuckles at the thought. The sound is deep

and rich, like Papa's throaty laughter.

"A little time off wouldn't kill you."

"Easy for you to say, *Captain*. You were sixteen when you earned your place among the guardians."

A dark flash crosses Omarion's eyes, and I slam my mouth shut before I can say anything worse. Omarion's skills in hand-to-hand combat became legendary after he snuck into a camp of bandits to avenge his brother's death. It's a story the platoon whispers when Omarion is far from sight.

Omarion takes a deep breath before he speaks. "You don't need to prove yourself to anyone, Nakoma. You graduated from training with top marks, and now you're the best archer in our platoon."

"I still suck at hand-to-hand," I mumble.

"Training from dawn to dusk won't change the fact you're fighting guardians twice your size. Besides, a good platoon needs a range of talents."

I scowl at Omarion. "You sound like my mother."

Omarion shifts in his saddle and returns his attention to the land ahead of us. Slowly, his forehead smooths, and I know Omarion has decided to let the conversation rest. I reach forwards to scratch Kato's neck as a hazy strip of blue slowly unravels across the distant plains. I recognise it now as South Lynton, one of the twin rivers of Twynton. Until we cross it, we're still in Arithenos, and I have time to convince Omarion he's wrong about me. I'll always have to prove my worth as a guardian – right up to the day I die honourably on the battlefield, like the women who have served before me.

Sleep evades me for the second night in a row. The slow rock of the ferry as it glides across Lake Lynton seems to have a soothing effect on everyone except me. I pad across the quiet deck, the dim light of a candle guiding me towards Kato. He's tied to a post at the centre of the ferry with Star, surrounded by sheep and goats. I take a deep breath of their mingling earthy scents, chasing away the smell of mould that permeates my senses after attempting to sleep below deck. The smell doesn't bother the rest of the crew, but I doubt their noses work after years of eating nothing but chilli-stuffed fish.

The urge to wake Kato whispers at the back of my mind. He's the only company I have left, aside from Wish, who is absent on her nightly hunt. Without Star to slow them, Omarion and Cedric are probably halfway back to Arithenos by now, eager to return to more exciting duties. I sink to the ground and rest my back against a hay bale. The dry straw pricks my skin through my cloak as I squint at Kato with heavy eyes. Kato sleeps like a foal with a full milk belly, and I curse the heavens for gifting only one of us with sea legs. I pull my knees to my chest to ward off the ache in my stomach and unfold my most recent letter from Mother, full of her usual nagging reminders.

I mimic Mother's grating voice as I read the letter aloud. "Don't forget to comb rosemary oil through your hair before braiding each night."

Water splashes against the side of the ferry in reply. I jump at the sound and rush to the edge of the deck. The depths of Lake Lynton stare back at me, its fabled monsters hidden from sight. I scan the moonlit waves until I'm lightheaded with nausea and completely useless against any potential siren attacks. Defeated, I return to Mother's letter.

I imitate her once more. "Remember to use the beeswax lotion across your knuckles before the season changes to winter, or your hands will look like Aunt Fifi's."

I shudder and pull the tiny pot of wax from a pocket in my cloak. Mother will be furious when she discovers my riding gloves sitting on my bed. Her anger is enough to make me question my sweet papa's choice in a wife. Still, Papa insists it was love at first sight. He saw her across the marketplace in Ellos and would not rest until Mother agreed to defy her parents' wishes and become his bride. I roll my eyes. The fairytale marriage was sweet when I was five. Now it stings that Papa won't tell me the truth.

I scan the rest of the letter for any news about Jakob or Papa, but Mother only writes about Klue's daughter, who will marry in winter. The wedding details make my fingers itch to burn the page. The naked flame of the candle sings promises of erasing Mother's words. I sigh and tip my head back. The heavens are a spectacle of light, every inch covered in glittering stars. For a moment, it's enough to distract me from Mother's letter. I'll have to answer her eventually, but for now, I try to let my exhausted body drift into a fitful sleep.

THE SECOND FULL MOON OF AUTUMN IS NEARING BY THE TIME we cross the border from Unke into Ellos. I scour the midday sky for any sign of the growing moon. It's become my favourite game. Today, the wind has stretched the clouds into a thin barrier that hides the moon from sight.

I scrunch my nose in the general direction of the elusive moon and return my attention to Clay and Emmanuel, the men of my new escort. The two men bear the role of delivering me to the Capital no better than Cedric did. Their broad backs and the synchronised swish of their stallion's tails have been my constant companions since leaving Lake Lynton. Even now, they ride a good half mile away. Unfortunately, the distance doesn't save me from their crude conversations. The wind carries each word back to me as clear as an eagle's cry.

"If a woman doesn't have curves, she might as well be a boy," Emmanuel says.

I scoff as Emmanuel adds some hand gestures to suggest exactly where he likes those curves. At least they aren't laughing at my expense again.

"And if her shoulders are broader than her hips, she might as well be a man," Clay adds.

I grit my teeth as they both laugh. So much for the comments not being at my expense. I run a hand over my waist. My body forms a natural pear shape, but after years of archery, my shoulders have become broad and muscular. I tune out their voices by straining my ears for the shrill call of Wish on the hunt, but the only birds I can hear are ducks quacking downstream from us. Kato splashes through the man-made stream unique to the farmlands of Patel's central provinces. We've already crossed dozens of the waterways, but Star still pauses at each bank to consider her options. I cluck my tongue, and she plods forwards once more.

Clay whistles, and my attention snaps back to him. He's waving at the women working in the fields, and I can't help but cringe. Even at this distance, I can see them blush and elbow each other.

"Now she would make a fine wife," Clay says.

"Nah, more of a mistress. Who wants an Ellos woman when you could have the heat of Arithenos?"

"Maybe, but I bet they don't argue like an Arithean."

If I had any doubts about Clay and Emmanuel's

combined idiocy, they've confirmed it now. Mother fights like a rattlesnake when she's angry. Hisses like one too.

At least the women don't appear to hear them. They smile and stretch their bent backs, propping their baskets on their hips until we have passed the strawberry fields. Perhaps Clay and Emmanuel are handsome from afar. Their scarlet uniforms shimmer in the Ellos sun and create a striking silhouette for those who have never seen a guardian before. Their skin has not leathered under the sun, and they keep their beards neatly groomed, even while far from the Capital. Yet to me they are vanilla beans – sweet to the nose, but on closer inspection, bitter beyond compare.

Mounds of dirt in neat rows mark the next plot of land. Starlings saunter across the churned earth, pecking at unseen feasts until they still as one. Their warning chatter fills the air as Wish emerges from the clouds and swoops over the field. She's gone again in the blink of an eye, a mouse clutched in her talons, but the starlings don't settle. An enormous shadow flickers across the field moments before Trench, Clay's golden eagle, descends. Chaos erupts as the starlings flee, forming a cloud of black wings. I reach out as the mass of starlings envelops us, my fingertips brushing against feathers before they escape to the nearby trees. A bubble of giddy laughter wells within me. Prey birds are rare in Arithenos, with the abundance of eagles around. My eyes linger on the trees, waiting for another glimpse of the speckled birds, but they hold their positions.

"What do they even teach at the temple these days?"

My head whips around as the wind carries Clay's voice once more. His superior tone is enough to drop the smile from my lips.

"Exactly my point. These days, you're lucky if you can find a woman who can cook and clean," Emmanuel says.

"And the ones that can have a face like a donkey's arse," Clay adds.

That's enough. I spur Kato into a gallop, shrinking the distance between myself and my escort. Dust kicks up around me as I charge in front of Clay and Emmanuel, forcing their stallions to an abrupt stop. Their horses snort in frustration and stamp at the ground. Clay glares down his hooked nose at me, his nostrils flaring. The sharp angles of Clay's face give him the appearance of being years older than Emmanuel.

"You should be ashamed of yourselves," I hiss. "Women are not scraps of meat for your table."

Emmanuel's full lips shrink into a line. "I have nothing to be ashamed of."

Clay rolls his eyes and mouths a single word at Emmanuel. *Women.* My blood boils.

"You're despicable. You know that?"

Clay flicks a dark lock of hair out of his face and nudges his steed into a walk, skirting around me. Emmanuel follows his lead, but I refuse to let them go. Kato keeps pace easily, even as I gesture wildly to the women far behind us.

"You would be lucky if a woman spent more than a

minute in your presence and still consented to be your wife."

Emmanuel glowers at me, but with his round cheeks and wide nose, the look lacks all menace. "What would you know? I bet mummy still has to wipe your arse."

"That must be why she requires an escort. No real guardian is too weak to travel alone."

"You're here to make me look like a lady," I grind out.

"And you need all the help you can get." Clay sneers, his eyes lingering in a way that makes me want to cover myself.

"It will be a miracle if you can fool them long enough to meet the prince," Emmanuel adds.

I flinch away from Emmanuel, his words stealing my breath like a punch to the gut. Emmanuel and Clay move off again, and this time, I hold Kato steady. As the space stretches between us, arguments rise and fall from my tongue. *What if he's right? What if I fail?* If I'm caught, I'll be sent home in disgrace long before I can prove my worth as a guardian. I run my fingers through Kato's mane and scrunch my nose up at their retreating figures. I'd rather let Mother dress me up like a doll than let these two morons be right about me. If being a lady is what it takes to keep my place in the Capital, then I'll be the best lady Arithenos has ever seen.

SEVEN

"**D**id that bird of yours fail to find the king?" Emmanuel asks.

Clay snickers. In my head, I stick my tongue out at him in response. The mental image helps keep my temper in check. To stop my hands from betraying me with a choice gesture, I scratch Wish's downy chest feathers. Her talons flex over my leather shoulder guard in response. Together, we watch as the sun slowly turns the world to amber.

Clay nudges Emmanuel, his eyes glinting with mischievous delight. "It knows the palace is the largest building in Ellos, right?"

I wait until their laughter quiets before I bother responding.

"You've seen the return message, signed with the Patel crest. I suppose palace boys rise later than Aritheans."

Emmanuel's face drops and, with a huff, the pair

turns away from me, leaning in their saddles so they can whisper to each other. I roll my eyes. Such *boys*. They are lucky to be so far from home. The commander would have them on manure duty for a whole moon if he heard them make childish jabs within sight of the Capital.

I turn my attention back to the guards stationed by the enormous iron gateway to the Capital. The Capital rests in the mouth of a bay with hills encircling the lowland to protect it from outside forces. Atop these hills, the first rulers of Patel built an impressive stone wall with a single gate. Guards in royal purple tunics, armed with bow and arrow, dot the top of the wall, patrolling its length even while the road is empty of travellers. More guards with shining steel spears watch us quietly as we wait beside the main road. Unlike Emmanuel and Clay, they are stoic, their eyes slowly roving over the land.

Most of the guards hide their curiosity well, but every so often, I catch one staring at us. Arithean guardians rarely come into the Capital, and if we do, there is no need to wait for palace boys. I adjust the tartan fabric of my dress and try to remind myself that I am not a guardian in Ellos. To them, I must remain a lady.

By the time the sun is visible over the boundary wall, I can just make out a palace boy, clad in purple, darting between the trail of merchants entering the Capital. The child's orange curls flop against his face as he runs and catches each ray of sunlight. When he finally reaches us, the boy is panting.

"My apologies ... I was unaware ... of the hour ... I hope you have not waited long."

The boy's round, freckled face is red from exertion, and his voice comes out in high-pitched squeaks. This proves to be too much for Emmanuel and Clay to bear. The fools double over in their saddles from laughter. The sound makes the poor child's face brighter by the second.

I cast a sharp look at Clay and Emmanuel, but they ignore me. "My companions find your accent amusing. Please excuse them."

The boy smiles, revealing a wide gap between his front teeth. "It is of little consequence, milady."

I purse my lips, swallowing my laughter. The gap in the messenger's teeth transforms his Capital accent of elongated *s* sounds into a whistle. I shoot Clay and Emmanuel another warning glance before smoothing my features into a more serene expression. Mother says ladies do not glower in public.

"My name is Nakoma. Lady Nakoma, that is."

With an artful flourish of his hand and a smile, the boy bows.

"They call me Skip, milady. You are most welcome in Ellos, I assure you."

My stomach churns at Skip's excessive manners, but I keep a smile plastered on my face and wait for Clay and Emmanuel to regain their composure. Once they have calmed, Skip leads the way to the iron gate. The guards take one look at Skip and allow our small party to pass through; only a quick note of our names and weapons is necessary.

Beyond the Capital walls, people already crowd the cobblestone streets. They scurry to and from houses, never pausing at the breathtaking view of the ocean. The ships of the king's fleet sway on the sparkling water in a pattern that extends as far as the eye can see.

Skip deftly weaves his way through the crowd, disappearing out of sight before he stops and realises his mistake. Like all Arithean steeds, Kato can barrel down an oncoming army, but to gently push aside people in order to walk down a busy street is out of the question. Kato's nostrils flare, and his ears twist in every direction to capture the sounds of the crowd. Within a moment, Skip is back by my side.

"May I?" Skip asks.

Skip reaches for Kato's reins, and I reluctantly hand them over.

"Make way!"

Skip's voice carries surprising force for his slight frame. Under his guidance, Kato parts the crowd, allowing the horses to follow in single file towards the palace. I tilt my head and reconsider Skip. As a messenger of the palace, he must know more than the average resident of Ellos.

"Have you always lived in the Capital, Skip?"

Skip's pale-grey eyes widen as he watches me over his shoulder. "All my life, milady."

"Can you tell me about it – the Capital?"

Skip slows his pace. "What do you wish to know?"

I roll the question around in my thoughts, considering my options as we pass houses in every shade of yellow. The buildings crowd together, with thin alleyways winding between them. Flowers spill from each window, and clothes dangle from connecting lines. They flutter in the wind, transforming undergarments into strange flags. I peer beneath them down the alleyways, but there are no obvious rogues lurking in the shadows.

"Tell me about the people. Are they honest?"

Skip stops in the middle of the street. "Honest? Milady, are you concerned for your safety here?"

I gape at Skip. Pride demands I dismiss the question as ridiculous, but reason stills my tongue. A lady would be afraid in such an unfamiliar place, wouldn't they? Behind me, Emmanuel snickers, and my cheeks flame with the knowledge of what I must do. I purse my lips and choose my words carefully.

"I only hope to understand a little better what challenges I might face here."

Skip nods, and I sense I have passed some unwritten test. He continues up the cobblestone street, speaking as he walks. Most of his words are swallowed by the noise of the crowd and the clop of hooves against stone, but the message is clear: Ellos is a safe city. I sigh. The lack of roaming guards confirms Skip's assessment. I'll have to be constantly on the look out for a chance to prove myself.

The crush of people dwindles to a steady flow as we draw closer to the palace. White walls reflect the morning sunshine and cast the enormous castle in an ethereal glow. Brilliant yellow tiles glisten from every roof, and ornate, orange demon sculptures perch along elaborate arches. I resist the urge to mutter a blessing as we pass under their watchful gaze towards the timber gate at the side of the palace. Men and women with skin aged by the sun and clothes similar to Skip's give us wide berth as we enter the palace grounds.

I glance back at the simple gate as it swings shut behind us. "Why aren't we using the main door?"

"You will not stay at the palace, Lady Nakoma. Only your horse shall," Skip explains.

"What!?"

Kato comes to an immediate halt at the tone of my voice, yanking the reins from Skip's hands. Skip baulks and jumps away from Kato with his palms up.

"They didn't tell you?" Skip stutters. "All ladies reside at the Academy until the Spring Ball."

"Then Kato will stay at the Academy too."

Skip gulps. "I'm afraid not. The Academy has no stables. Ladies always arrive in carriages."

"Not always," I mutter through clenched teeth.

"What about the Arithean barracks? We have stables there," Emmanuel suggests.

I shoot Emmanuel a grateful smile and loosen my hold on Kato.

Skip's eyes stay glued to his feet as he replies. "They're full. His Majesty requested extra guardians to support the royal army while the Academy is open."

Emmanuel's eyes gleam with excitement. "Do you really think—"

"You cannot house an Arithean horse with the regular mount!" Clay finishes for Emmanuel.

For the first time in days, I actually agree with them. Acid sours my tastebuds at the thought of leaving Kato with strangers, yet the fear in Skip's pale-grey eyes is enough to soften my temper. He is only the messenger boy.

"How far is the Academy from the palace?"

Skip blinks up at me. "Not far. I promise. You'll probably think the distance is nothing compared to your travels to Ellos. You can even see the Pink Palace from here."

Skip turns and points to another grand building in the distance. I shut my eyes and breathe deeply through my nose to calm my churning stomach. Skip is correct. The Pink Palace is less than half a mile away. Still, the distance stretches before me like Lake Lynton.

"Kato must have the best care possible," I say. "They can't keep him locked up all day. I must be able to visit often."

Skip nods so fast I worry his head might fall off. "Certainly. I can arrange anything your Kato might need."

"Ha! Then arrange for a new stable to be built alongside the Academy," Emmanuel suggests, earning him a scowl from me and a smile from Clay.

Skip's voice trembles again as he addresses my escort. "Anything but that, sir."

I turn my face towards Wish so that only she can hear my command. "Up, Wish."

Wish takes flight in an instant, her soft feathers brushing my cheek as she launches from my shoulder pad. Her wings tilt, catching an updraft that allows her to hang over our heads. Unburdened, I roll my tight shoulders before dismounting Kato in one fluid motion. I land on silent feet beside Skip, who startles and trips backwards. I bite the inside of my lip to hide my smile and smooth the wrinkles from my dress until Skip can regain his composure.

"I can fetch a stablehand to unsaddle your horse while I show you the way to the Pink Palace." Skip's eyes are already searching for a lad to take Kato away before he can finish the sentence.

"No."

Though I am only a head taller than Skip on foot, he cowers at my raised voice.

"No, milady?"

"I will stay with Kato while he settles in," I explain, checking my tone. "You needn't stay. I'm sure I can find my way without you."

"Unfortunately, we cannot delay," Skip says, wincing as he speaks. "The Academy begins today. All the other ladies have already arrived."

I press my fingers to my brow to stop the skin from creasing. "Of course they have."

Skip apologises profusely, but I don't listen. Instead, I lean into Kato and draw comfort from his familiar scent. I run my fingers along his dapple-grey coat and watch as his skin shivers under my touch. Eventually, a shadow falls over me. Clay's stallion towers by my opposite shoulder, his hoof pawing at the cobblestone.

"We'll see him settled," Clay says.

I scan Clay's face for any trace of humour – some sign that he really intends to do Kato harm just to see me suffer. To my shock, Clay beats his fist twice against his breast in a show of loyalty to his fellow guardian. My fingers curl into a fist, ready to return the gesture, but a glance at Skip's furrowed brow stills my hand. Instead, I offer Clay a genteel nod and untether Star from Kato's saddle. Pressing a kiss to Kato's velvety nose, I bid him farewell and hand his reins to Clay.

"We can't stay all day, but we'll wait with Kato until Star has delivered your luggage."

I nod, lost for words. A simple *thank you* is too mild to express the ache that settles in my heart at the thought of leaving Kato with a stablehand, but I say it anyway.

"Thank you."

Without waiting for further direction, Clay nudges his stallion into a walk and leads Kato with him. Skip splutters and flags down a nearby stablehand to take them to the correct stall before Clay and Emmanuel can disappear. Like stones placed in the centre of an ant's nest, Clay and Emmanuel disrupt the flow of workers with no effort, each person scurrying out of their path. Though they have been a thorn in my side for the last few weeks, the sight makes me swell with pride for Arithenos.

CHAPTER
EIGHT

With only one horse in tow, Skip and I weave through the dwindling crowd with ease. Oblivious to Skip's attempts to hurry her along, Star plods beside me at the same steady gait she has maintained our entire journey. Eventually, Skip resigns himself to a slower pace, though he's always five steps ahead of us.

Skip leaves us at the foot of the Pink Palace. As soon as he is gone, Wish returns to her perch on my shoulder and presses herself against me. I welcome the familiar weight and scratch the space between her dark eyes, but Wish does not shut her eyes in contentment like usual. She watches the door, her posture stiff and alert, a warning that a priestess is watching.

I chew my lip and stare up at the bright peach walls that loom over me. The Pink Palace is a glorified mansion compared to the main castle. Its large clear windows extend two stories high, and minimal edge details decorate its facade. I loop Star's rope around a pink marble pillar and check the straps securing my luggage to her back. Before I can cross to Star's opposite flank, Wish hoots softly. The sound stills my nervous hands. *Has my hesitation already disappointed the watching priestess?* Gathering my courage, I leave Star behind, climb the front steps and knock on the grand oak door. Footsteps echo from within, and the door glides open on well-oiled hinges.

A gentleman with a thick black moustache answers the door, his eyes gleaming with curiosity. He bows from the waist, one white-gloved hand resting on the door to support his weight. Instinctively, I stand in my best guardian's pose, shoulders thrown back and feet square. Wish squawks in alarm, flapping her wings to keep her balance.

"You must be the lady from Arithenos," the man says, his Capital accent stretching out the *s* in Arithenos.

I nod. "Lady Nakoma, sir."

The man smiles, and it softens his entire face.

"You may call me Perriwick. I am the Academy's butler for the next few seasons."

I peer past Perriwick into the depths of the Academy. From this angle, all I can see is the white marble floor of the hallway.

"Shall I send a man to fetch the rest of your belongings? From the palace, perhaps?" Perriwick asks, each question punctuated by infuriatingly high pitch.

I bristle. The two trunks strapped to Star dwarf her frame.

"No need. It's all there."

"My apologies, Lady Nakoma." Perriwick bows again, and I'm close enough to hear his knees creak.

Perriwick pulls a bell by the entryway, and a maid materialises behind him. Her black A-line dress extends to the middle of her calves, and a white apron accentuates her delicate waist.

"Maria, find someone to help you transport Lady Nakoma's belongings to her room, and have Reynolds deliver her horse back to the palace stables."

Maria nods and soundlessly scurries off to complete Perriwick's orders. I watch the maid's progress until Perriwick clears his throat, diverting my attention back to him.

"You must be tired after your travels, though I'm afraid there is no time to refresh before class. The headmistress wishes to see you."

I look down at my sweat-soaked riding dress. It's the same garment I left home in four weeks ago. I rinsed my face and feet at the tavern last night, but my hair is greasy and full of knots despite its constant braid.

"Are you sure? It would only take me a moment to find something clean."

"My apologies, Lady Nakoma, but I must insist. The other ladies are already waiting in the classroom."

I flatten my flyaway hairs and run my tongue over my teeth. At least I did not have onions for breakfast to add to my travel aroma. Perriwick accepts my silence as complacency and leads the way past vases full of pink roses. The bouquets are so neat and orderly that I imagine someone using a measuring stick to space out each vase. Hanging above the flowers are portraits of grand women who watch my every step.

Perriwick stops outside of an engraved oak door and knocks. I hold my breath as we wait, my mind racing through various nightmarish versions of what could be on the other side. An eternity passes before a tall, slim lady answers the door. Her lips purse, and her keen eyes narrow as she inspects me.

Perriwick dips his head in the smallest bow. "Tutor Olga, this is Lady Nakoma of Arithenos."

"This is not a zoo," Tutor Olga says, her accent just as strong as Perriwick's.

"I didn't think it was." The response rolls off my tongue before I can think better of it.

"Then why is that filthy bird on your shoulder?"

I wince at Tutor Olga's voice and struggle to remember the words Omarion had me practice.

"This is Wish," I explain. "She is my messenger owl. I want to keep in touch with my family while in Ellos."

Tutor Olga's taught face wrinkles in disgust. "The Pink Palace has pixie doves for that. There is no need to bring your own creature."

"Arithenos believes owls are safer for long journeys."

I wring my hands behind my back, terrified Tutor Olga will see through the lie. It's true that pixie doves disappear more frequently in Arithenos than any other province. Still, the speed of the magic infused birds makes them worth the risk even for Aritheans. Tutor Olga's pencilled-on eyebrows twitch, but I can't tell if it is in disbelief. The poor brows sit high on her forehead, pulled back by her tight bun.

"Very well then," she finally says. "Perriwick can deposit your bird in your room so that we may go to class."

I glance from Wish to Perriwick's wary face. To his credit, Perriwick extends his arm towards Wish for her to climb aboard.

"Thank you, but Wish can follow you. Up, Wish. I will see you later."

Wish lifts off my shoulder and flaps awkwardly between myself and Perriwick until the butler has the sense to hurry down the hall. Tutor Olga scrunches her narrow nose at their departing figures.

"Come. The other ladies are waiting."

I stand rooted to the spot. "The other ladies? Aren't you going to talk to me first?"

Tutor Olga's murky eyes flick over me. "No. I've seen enough for now."

Her heels click against the marble hall as she strides off in the opposite direction from Perriwick. I hurry to follow her, my own soft leather boots soundless against the floor.

"Wait! What about the Academy? Aren't you going to explain how things work around here? What is our schedule like?"

Tutor Olga does not dignify my questions with a backwards glance. "I'll explain everything to the full cohort momentarily."

Tutor Olga leads me to a spacious room dotted with

ten desks and no windows. Only one seat remains empty. At the sound of our footfalls, heads turn in our direction, and I am once more scrutinised.

"Ladies," Tutor Olga greets, "this is Lady Nakoma of Arithenos."

I skim their faces, my mind struggling to acknowledge anything more than the varying shades of their hair. Ebony and ivory. Flaming scarlet and rich chocolate brown. Whispers echo off the stone floor and fill the room with noise as their gazes tear through my defences. Beneath their eyes, I am a commoner who dared to pretend her plain gown and scarred body was good enough for a lady.

"Ladies do not gossip or stare," Tutor Olga reprimands, her voice as brutal as a whip.

"Yes, Tutor Olga," the ladies reply in unison.

Tutor Olga stalks to the front of the room, her back stiff. The mirrored torches that hang from the ceiling stretch her shadow into a menacing creature.

"You'll have plenty of time to get to know each other over the coming moons," she says. "For now, our focus must be on education."

With a steady hand and artful letters, Tutor Olga writes *court life*, *manners*, *diplomacy*, *history*, and *arts* on the chalkboard at the front of the room. Nobody dares to speak as the chalk screeches against the fresh board. With a final flourish on her *s*, she turns, her lips forming a stern line.

"Do you require a personal invitation, Lady Nakoma? Sit."

I gulp and do my best not to scurry like a scolded dog to the empty chair.

"While you are at the Academy, you will study five subjects, each designed to transform you into a suitable bride for the future king. The arts include dance, music, embroidery, calligraphy, and painting. Two weeks prior to the ball, all students must attend dance lessons to avoid embarrassment, but until then, you may pick your preferred outlet."

My neck prickles from the stares of the other ladies. I squeeze my hands together to fight the urge to fidget under their gaze. Tutor Olga's disdain for Wish is enough to know I'm already on thin ice here at the Academy.

"You will take your core studies together, in this room, after breakfast and morning tea. After lunch, you will attend arts lessons."

"When will we have time to ourselves?" I ask.

Tutor Olga skewers me with a stare. "Do not speak unless called upon, Lady Nakoma."

My teeth grind together as Olga returns to the board without answering my question. Her words create a low buzz in my ears as she drones on about the importance of classroom manners. I hold my breath and count to three. The tirade continues, no mention of time off in sight. I fix a placid smile onto my face and raise my hand.

"I am not currently taking questions, Lady Nakoma," Tutor Olga snaps.

"Then when will you? Out in the hall, you said you would explain the schedule to the full cohort. I still have questions about it."

Tutor Olga's eyes narrow. "I don't appreciate your tone, Lady Nakoma."

Heat rushes to my cheeks. Silence permeates the air as the other ladies watch with bated breath. I know the expected response. Ladies are meek. We do not question the judgement of our elders. But I've seen Mother in action. I inject as much false sincerity into my voice as possible.

"My apologies. I did not mean to question your judgement."

Tutor Olga's taut lips pinch as if she has swallowed a sour berry. "Students have a free day on Saturdays, and afternoons where I see fit. If your lessons are not progressing at an adequate pace, I will revoke your right to leave the Pink Palace during personal time."

The thinly veiled threat is enough to steal the wind from my sails. I murmur my compliance and let my eyes fixate on the various embroideries of flowers that decorate the room. Each stitch is so precise that I wonder if ladies have gone mad while creating the artworks. I certainly will if I can't speak my mind in class without fear of losing the privilege of visiting Kato.

Tutor Olga continues her monologue about court life as if I hadn't interrupted her. Screeches of chalk and the random shrill flourishes of her Capital accent are the only sounds that punctuate her monotone voice. I squirm in my seat and try to focus on Olga. Understanding the royal court could be my ticket to a hearing for Arithenos. It should be my priority. Yet there's a nagging thought reminding me that no guardian has ever faced promotion for their ability to mingle within the royal court.

My eyelids droop as the lesson drags on. Boredom and stale air create a noxious mixture that makes my mind wander. I peek at the lady on my left and meet her gaze. Her dark eyes widen with horror as she realises I've caught her staring. She feigns interest in Tutor Olga, but the open book hidden beneath her desk tells me she was never interested in this lesson. Blood heats her cheeks as she shuffles a bookmark into place and closes the book.

My lips twist into a faint smile. There is something comforting about the tight weave of her twin braids and the soft slope of her nose. While her features differ vastly from the women of Arithenos, I can tell she is from an outer province. No jewels decorate her ears or neck like some of the other women in this room. I relax back into my seat, my shoulder loosening for the first time since entering the Pink Palace. At least Tutor Olga won't be my only companion for the next three seasons.

CHAPTER
NINE

The dining hall, located in the Academy's east wing, is full of enough tables to seat hundreds of guests. The ladies gather in clusters, nobody daring to claim the first seat or appear a glutton by rushing for the food. I roll my eyes at them and let my growling stomach lead the way to the serving station. The cook fills my plate with light refreshments of baked goods and fruit – a meal fit for a toddler's appetite. Still, I smile my thanks and find a place with a good view of the exits.

As I scan the room, the girl with twin braids catches my eye and inclines her head towards the two others with her. All three women have black hair and wear simple pastel dresses, but their similarities end there. The lead girl offers a hesitant smile as they join me at the table.

"Good day, Lady Nakoma. I hope our intrusion is welcome. May we share our meal with you?"

I swallow a grimace at the stiff formality of the lady's greeting and reply with my best Ellos manners. "You're very welcome here."

"I'm Lady Tia of Sebba," the one with braids says. "My parents are the leading silk producers in our village."

Tia has high cheekbones and a wide forehead that would give her a regal profile if it wasn't for her twin braids. Instead, she reminds me of a child dressing up in their parents' clothes. Still, she leads the way for the group and inclines her head towards the next lady so they will speak.

"I'm Lady Uri of Froi," says the next lady. "My family is not rich, but our elder chose me because I am already training to become an Ellos diplomat for Froi."

I raise my eyebrows at the matter-of-fact tone Uri employs for such a formal introduction. Uri meets my gaze with her own sharp stare as she studies my face. People usually consider Froi as Arithenos's closest neighbour, although we also share borders with Eyre and Twynton. From the way Papa talks about trade in Froi, I can imagine why Uri might want to become a diplomat.

"My name is Lady Hazel-Mae of the Mir Mountains. Pa is the village chief, so I was the obvious choice for a representative."

Hazel-Mae speaks with an accent so thick that I watch her lips to understand her. As I listen her *o*'s are clipped to *i*'s and her *r*'s roll into the next word. Her round, apple cheeks flush pale pink at the extra attention.

"Is it true Aritheans can communicate telepathically with their horses?" Hazel-Mae asks.

A surprised bubble of laughter escapes my lips before I can consider if I am being rude. "Do people really think that?"

Hazel-Mae shrinks in her seat and lets a curtain of her waist-length hair conceal her face.

Uri rolls her eyes at Hazel-Mae. "Don't be stupid. Only the priestesses can talk to animals."

I frown at Uri. "They don't *talk* to animals. Not really."

Every Arithean child learns about soul birds and their connection with the heavens in school, but it's still something I don't know how to explain. There are no laws of magic or science that soul birds follow. They're creatures manifested by the summons of guardian souls; they offer their eyes to the pure and faithful.

"The priestesses can only watch through soul birds. Sort of like a vision, but you choose the time and place."

Uri frowns, her thick eyebrows almost concealing her deep-set eyes. Everything about Uri's face is big—big hooked nose, big ears. The only exception is her lips and pointed chin. I watch as those lips form another question before Tia cuts her off.

"My sister can talk to wolves, but she says it's not like speaking words. More like thinking with other people."

Hazel-Mae's squarish jaw drops. "You don't mean the dire wolves of Sebba?"

"They're not as bloodthirsty as people think," Tia says.

"Not bloodthirsty? They make the alligators of Froi's swamps look like puppies," Uri says.

Hazel-Mae points at Uri with a slice of orange. "How would you know? Have you been to Sebba?"

Tia places a gentle hand on Hazel-Mae's wrist until she puts down the fruit.

"Enough about Sebba. Tell us, Lady Nakoma, how did Arithenos choose its representative?"

I shrug to hide the knot of fear Tia's question churns within me.

"Papa is a merchant," I explain, "and Mother was born in Ellos. Since none of our chiefs have an unwed daughter of suitable age, our High Priestess determined I would be the most suitable for the task."

Uri leans back in her seat. "Well then, that explains your eyes."

Hazel-Mae gasps, her mouth forming a petite O as she stares at Uri.

"You can't say things like that, Uri. How can you become a diplomat if you can't use basic manners?" Hazel-Mae says, but the impact of her words are diminished as each *you* transforms into a mangled *yi*.

"Well, I'm not one yet."

I open my mouth to add to their bickering, then just as quickly shut it. I can't forget myself with these ladies, even if their eyes are a spectrum of rich browns that reminds me of home. All it would take is for me to mention how the guardians say worse things than Uri for someone to realise I'm not just a merchant's daughter.

"So, what arts subject is everyone considering

taking?" Tia asks, effectively ending Hazel-Mae and Uri's argument.

Tuning out of the conversation as Hazel-Mae talks about watercolours, I turn my attention to the rest of the room. Across the dining hall, the other six ladies of the Academy have claimed two tables. They all sit with the stiff spines of awkward acquaintances, not unlike Tia or myself. However, at their table, only one lady is speaking. Everyone else watches as a lady with blond hair talks down her nose to them.

"Will you take calligraphy with me, Nakoma?"

I blink up at Uri, surprised by the question. *Is this a trick?* Uri has only just met me. Is it possible she already knows I'm hiding something?

"I haven't really thought about which art class I want to take."

"Surely not dance," Uri says with an exaggerated shudder. "I'll be avoiding that for as long as possible."

Hazel-Mae smiles dreamily. "Why? Don't you want to dance with the prince?"

Uri wrinkles her nose. "I've never seen him. I'm not sure if he's even worth dancing with."

I nod along with Uri but shovel food into my mouth to avoid adding to the conversation. Hazel-Mae shares a look with Tia, and I wonder if the pair travelled down to Ellos together.

"We saw him yesterday. He seems very charming. And so tall!" Hazel-Mae says.

"At least, we are fairly certain that it was him," Tia adds. "He wore very plain clothes for a prince."

"The prince?" Someone laughs. "That's as close as you'll ever see him."

I sit bolt upright at the Capital accent and stare into the face of the blond lady. Up close, I can see her hair is a dusty shade with highlights stripped of colour. It's twisted into elaborate braids and smells like rosewater, but I can see that it's as stiff and dead as straw.

"What's that supposed to mean?" I ask.

The newcomer's ice-blue eyes shift from Tia to me. I return her cool stare with squared shoulders until she eventually looks back to her friends for support.

"I only meant to point out the obvious," she says, her voice like vinegar with honey. "You may get to attend the same functions, but your connection to the prince will always remain distant. The royal family tends to gravitate to those similar to them... A little like how you've found each other."

I let the lady's words hang in the air as I watch each of her friends stand awkwardly behind her. The girls are all delicate-looking creatures with slim bodies that have never worked a day in their lives. Still, the lead lady is in a class of her own. With skin devoid of freckles or blemishes, she appears to have modelled both her looks and her personality off a statue.

I brush the crumbs from my fingers with painstaking precision before addressing the blond lady. "Your words were understood; now understand me. This table is full, and I am eager to finish my meal with friends."

The lady backs away from our table into her circle of

friends. "It was well meant," she sniffs before stalking away.

As soon as she is out of earshot, Tia's body becomes animated.

"That was Elisabelle," Tia says. "She's from Unke. Embry, Arabella, and Calypso follow her every movement."

"I tried talking to Calypso about her family's business when I first arrived," Uri says, "but it was like talking to a fish. I expect the other two are the same."

Hazel-Mae clasps a hand over her mouth to smother the bubble of laughter. I follow her line of sight to work out which of the three is Calypso, but it's no use.

"Which one is Calypso?" I ask.

"The redhead," Tia says. "Embry has the lighter brown hair and Arabella is the only one in the group without blue eyes."

I try to file away their names into a corner of my mind, but already the information is slipping through my fingers.

"So, you know everybody already? How do you possibly keep all their names straight?"

Tia shrugs. "We had formal introductions at breakfast today, though Hazel-Mae and I met most of them last week, when we first arrived."

I glance back at Calypso again and force myself to remember her face. Calypso's hair isn't red like Tia said. One of the other ladies has scarlet hair that burns with the intensity of a flame. Calypso's ginger tresses appear mundane in contrast.

"Do you also remember where everyone is from?" I ask.

"That's easy," Hazel-Mae interrupts before Tia can answer. "Calypso is from Lake Lynton. You can see it in her freckles, and her eyes are the same shade as the Lake."

Tia pouts at Hazel-Mae's interruption. "I was going to say I remember because her teeth remind me of pearls. Her family owns the largest pearl farm in Patel."

I squint at Calypso to see her teeth, but the only pearls I can see are the ones that drip from her ears and neck. A bell chimes, and I scan the room for the source of the sound.

"What does that mean?"

"Break is over," Tia explains.

I frown at the clock. "Already?"

My stomach growls in protest at the thought of lunch ending. I pocket the fruit off my plate and take the rest of the scraps back to the kitchen.

Hazel-Mae collects the other empty trays from our table and joins me. "Don't stress. Midday meal is better. Warm food, and we get enough time for a stroll in the garden."

I nod but don't empty my pockets. Together, the four of us make our way back to the classroom for another long session.

CHAPTER
TEN

Even as the clouds glow pink and the streets fill with brilliant orange lamplight, the palace grounds still swarm with people. Boys dressed in dull brown dart between stone pillars, lighting the halls of the grand palace for the night. With quick feet, I retrace my steps, following the cacophony of animals back to the stables. As darkness draws near, workers herd animals big and small from their grazing yards into the safety of pens. A trail of geese following a blond girl dutifully honk in greeting as the nanny goats trot past with their own keeper.

I step inside the stables to a riot of noise and a waft of sweat that almost knocks me off my feet. If I were a real lady, someone who hadn't trained with teenage boys who had no concept of personal hygiene, I would've turned tail and fled immediately. But I am no Elisabelle. With open arms, I welcome the musk of horses, cherishing it after a long day spent in the heady perfume of roses. My fingertips outstretched, I brush the nose of every horse that dares to poke its head out of its cosy stall. They blink back at me dozily, some with their mouths full of hay and others with stablehands bumbling around their sides with a brush.

Kato, however, does not poke his head out of his stall in greeting. A stablehand almost as tall as Kato stands before him. He holds his hands high and pitches his voice low to calm Kato.

"What do you think you're doing?" I demand.

The stablehand spins, his bright-green eyes wide with shock. A variety of stains cover his brown tunic and leave me questioning the hygiene of the stables.

"Just making sure he's comfortable, ma'am."

I shake my head, ignoring the warmth that creeps into my cheeks at the sound of his crisp, deep voice. Somehow, the elongated *s* of the Capital accent sounds less repulsive from his mouth.

Flustered, I wave my arms in a useless motion. "Well, don't. Any halfwit can see he doesn't appreciate your attention."

Kato huffs his approval.

"Halfwit?"

I roll my eyes. "Yes, you fool. Everyone knows not to turn their back to an Arithean stallion."

The stablehand chucks a quick glance over his shoulder, as if only now realising the difference between Kato and the regular palace ponies. He mouths a curse and flops over the stable door, landing with a puff of straw beside me. My eyes rove from his mud-covered boots to his wild black hair, unable to look at anything but him. The stablehand smiles sheepishly, and all my insults are sucked from my lungs in one swift motion.

I cross my arms, stalling for time as I struggle to find my equilibrium. "Who are you?"

The stablehand tilts his head, frowning. "You don't know who I am?"

I roll my eyes and look at Kato, who appears equally amused. These Capital people say the stupidest things.

"I wouldn't ask if I already knew."

"I ... just ... well ... I help around the palace?"

"You're not sure if you help around the palace?"

"We all have our moments of doubt."

"Well, you better go make yourself useful elsewhere."

I turn my back on the stablehand and let myself into Kato's stall. Kato greets me by nuzzling the folds of my dress in search of food. I murmur to him softly, reminding him he is good and strong as I slip him the slices of apple I pocketed at lunch.

"Who are you?" the stablehand asks.

I glance over my shoulder to where he leans against the stall door, watching Kato and me closely. He catches my eye and smiles. The expression is so effortlessly charming that my stomach flips. I turn back to Kato and busy myself with selecting a brush from his saddlebags that hang in the stall's corner. Surely, the stablehand will leave me alone if I ignore him for long enough.

"I don't mean to offend," the stablehand says. "It's not every day an Arithean horse is in our palace stables."

"Kato is my steed."

"Then you are an Arithean too?"

I tilt my head in a curt nod.

"That explains things, then..."

I fix the stablehand with a fierce look. "And by that, you mean...?"

"Your accent. It's very thick. Unlike anything you hear in Ellos."

The stablehand's Adam's apple bobs in fright, even as he steadily holds my gaze. I smile knowingly. Mother always complains about how rude Aritheans can be.

"You're a terrible liar."

The stablehand laughs, a deep, wholesome sound that warms my stomach like a hearty bowl of soup in winter.

"You're as shrewd as a hawk."

"Thank you. That's a fine compliment to an Arithean. Though I prefer owls." I face the stablehand as I speak, but continue to groom Kato, who watches us quietly.

"What is an Arithean stallion doing outside of the sentry's quarters? Isn't that where all your horses usually stay?"

"Usually, yes, but they're full, or so I've been told. The king requested extra guardians to monitor Ellos. The next best place for Kato is here."

"Then you're a wife of one of the newly sent guardians?"

I almost drop my brush. *A wife!* How old does he think I am? I turn my back, gritting my teeth to suppress my comments.

"I'm sorry. I didn't mean to offend again."

"Guardians do not take their wives with them on duty." I grumble as I walk around Kato's backside to begin work on his opposite flank.

"I didn't know."

"The people of Ellos know nothing," I declare, my anger clouding my judgement.

"Hey! I'm sure you're as ignorant to the ways of Ellos as I am to Arithenos."

I stop midstroke to stare down the stablehand. "Well, you'd be wrong."

"Oh, really?"

"My mother is from Ellos, and she would rather die than leave me uneducated about the ways of Ellos," I say, punctuating each word with Kato's brush.

The boy merely laughs. "And yet you still make assumptions about our intelligence!"

I shrug. "It's not an assumption. I speak the truth I see."

"Then you are not afraid to cause offence."

A smile creeps back onto my face at his assessment of my character.

"You could say that."

The stablehand shakes his head, causing dark locks to fall into his eyes. I watch entranced as he combs the hair back without smoothing a single strand into place. My fingers itch to fix it for him. Would his hair be soft? Or perhaps coarse like Jakob's?

The stablehand clears his throat, and heat rushes through me as I realise I've been staring.

"You still haven't told me who you are," he says.

"I am Nakoma, daughter of Barooch the merchant, chosen lady of Arithenos."

"Nakoma." The stablehand muses over my name, twisting it in his mouth, tasting the sound of it.

"Kato has to stay here because the other ladies do not have their own steeds. They arrived in carriages."

"Why didn't you travel by carriage? Surely it would be more comfortable for a long journey."

I scoff. "Aritheans are born in the saddle. It's where I'm most comfortable."

The boy frowns, and I rush to correct myself, unsure if he knows that few citizens outside of the guardians would own a horse like Kato.

"My father spoils me. I'm lucky to have Kato – a true Arithean horse – not some lady's pony."

No response. I work to fill the silence, worried he will see straight through me. I switch from brush to comb, untangling Kato's long mane and tail.

"Is it true that Arithean horses are magical?"

My head whips around to check if the boy is laughing at me. His green eyes watch Kato intently, and there's no hint of a smile on his lips.

"Legends say Arithean horses are ancient descendants of a creature that served as a mount for elves and orcs."

A crease appears between the stablehand's dark brows. "Do you believe that?"

I shrug. "No. Elves and orcs aren't real. I think Aritheans are just better at breeding and training strong bloodlines."

The stablehand doesn't reply. I peek over Kato's shoulder to check that he's still waiting by the stall door. He catches my eye and smiles.

"My name's Lars, by the way."

"So, Lars, surely you have something better to be doing than watching me groom Kato?"

Lars's eyes dart towards the stable doors before flicking back to me. He covers the flash of guilt with an affable grin, perfectly curated to put me at ease.

"I'll have you know this is time well spent," Lars says.

"And why is that? You've accomplished nothing."

"I learnt your name."

I blush at the comment. For not the first time, I'm glad to have my father's complexion, which hides both blushes and bruises equally well.

"Besides, now I know not to use the same brush for the mane as you do for a horse's flanks," Lars adds.

I laugh, caught by surprise. "You cannot be serious?"

Lars laughs too. "Believe me, I am."

"How could you get to be ... what are you, seventeen? And you still don't know how to groom a horse."

"I turned eighteen this past summer!"

I look at Lars again. Really look at him. He has the height of a man, I suppose, and broad shoulders. But his face is so smooth.

"I am used to beards on men your age," I admit, offering it as a weak apology.

Lars strokes his naked face and leaves a smear of dirt across the little dimple in the centre of his chin. The sharp lines of his jaw are visible even without the edging of stubble.

"In Ellos, the only men who do not shave are in the military, or the poor who cannot afford a razor. A beardless face is cleaner."

I shake my head. "Beards are a symbol of wisdom. The longer the beard, the higher your status."

Lars smiles at me, the torchlight sparkling in his green eyes. "It seems there is a lot you can teach me about horses and facial hair."

It's hard not to smile at Lars. "I'm well educated in both."

Kato nudges my shoulder, and I drag my eyes away from Lars. Around us, the stables have grown quiet, with only the gentle sounds of sleeping horses to keep us company. I stand on tiptoes to whisper goodnight to Kato before dropping the comb back into his saddlebags and exiting the stall. Lars falls into step with me, but I do my best to ignore his presence. I've chatted for long enough. Tutor Olga probably expected me to return to the Academy by now, even if she failed to mention a curfew.

A rush of cold air hits me as I open the stable doors. The sky has a softness that permeates the early hours of night, but the earth in Ellos does not retain its heat like in Arithenos. I pump my arms to keep warm and stride back through the palace grounds. Lanterns hang from posts spaced evenly along the path, lighting the way to the main streets of the Capital.

"Nakoma? Nakoma, wait," Lars calls after me.

With his long legs, Lars matches my pace easily.

"What?" I ask without slowing.

"You're not walking back to the Academy alone, are you? It's dark out. At least let me walk with you."

I shake my head and laugh inwardly. Of course, Lars must think I'm a soft little lady in need of protection from the dangers of the night.

"Compared to an Arithenos autumn night, it's as bright as day. I'll be fine."

"You're pulling my leg. Night is just as dark everywhere in Patel."

I stop midstride and frown at Lars. "Pull your leg? I've not touched your leg!"

Lars's mouth drops in surprise a moment before he guffaws in delight.

"Oh, Nakoma. It's merely an expression. I meant you must be deceiving me in jest."

"Oh." I double my pace to hide my embarrassment. "Well then, I assure you, it's quite bright here. We have lanterns in Arithenos, but not enough to light up the entire city."

"Still, it's not safe. Ladies shouldn't walk alone at night."

I roll my eyes. Lars's misplaced chivalry frays my already thin patience.

"I'll be fine. It's only a short walk down the street. Besides, I'm an Arithean. We're made of tougher stuff than you Ellos folk."

Lars sighs. "You should be careful. I'd hate to say I told you so."

I snort at the idea. "Goodnight, Lars."

"Goodnight, Nakoma. It was a pleasure making your acquaintance."

I pass through the palace gate, glancing over my shoulder in time to catch the quizzical looks Lars receives from the palace guards as he waves goodbye. He must be an oddity among the stablehands to remain on duty this late. I shake my head, erasing him from my mind as I stroll down the cobblestone street. One more turn and I know I'll be out of sight. A spike of adrenaline shoots through me as I poke my head down each dark alleyway, searching for a moment to prove myself. Nothing. Only an abundance of stray ginger cats lurk in Ellos after dark. With each empty street, I deflate a little more, until I'm back at the Academy and no closer to my dreams of a promotion.

CHAPTER
ELEVEN

Chalk scratches against the blackboard as Tutor Olga writes with elaborate flourishes. The curls and twists blend her letters together until the board becomes a meaningless mess of white against black. One more reason to hate manners class. Olga turns to face us and I'm amazed her black skirt is free from chalk dust.

"Who can tell me the correct way to introduce yourself to His Highness?"

Several hands fly up, each lady eager to impress Olga. Among them are Tia's and Hazel-Mae's. My eyes flick to Uri. I'm almost certain she also knows the answer, but Uri leans back in her chair, her slick black hair creating a curtain between us.

"Yes, Lady Jadera?"

Jadera's pale-grey eyes widen as the attention in the room shifts to her. She swallows hard, her hands trembling in her lap.

"Is it your name, the province you're from, then well-wishes?" she asks.

Olga tuts. "Lady Elisabelle?"

The moment Olga turns away, Jadera's thumbnail flies to her mouth to be chewed on. Elisabelle sits a little taller in her seat so we can all admire the curve of her neck and the cut of her signature pink dress as she speaks.

"It is name, province, *status*, then well-wishes."

Olga smiles at Elisabelle. "Very well done, Lady Elisabelle."

I roll my eyes. If I had a coin for every time Tutor Olga has said those same five words this lesson, I could afford to bribe someone else to take this useless class for me. Everyone in this room already knows how to be polite. Surely the prince won't notice if we forget to tell him our father's rank the second we see him. If he does, then I'm not sure I want to meet him.

I imagine executing a practiced curtsey that Olga would deem worthy of a prince. In my mind, he's athletic, with the blond hair and blue eyes that are prized in Ellos. I shudder inadvertently as I realise this prince is a male replica of Elisabelle. With a twist of my lips, I give my imaginary prince more warmth, like sunshine on the ocean. I hope it's enough for this fictional prince to not become a conceited blockhead like the representatives of Patel's central provinces are proving to be. Or maybe it's a trait that all the upper class are destined to have? If it is, Arithenos is doomed. There is no way someone set in their beliefs would give me the time of day to extol Arithenos's virtues. I force myself to shake off the thought. Imagining the worst won't make today easier.

Tutor Olga's voice continues to drone like the buzzing of a fly – irritating, but easy to drown out. My gaze drifts from Olga to one of the many embroidery hoops that decorate the classroom. The artist's lifeless rendition of a cluster of lavender and daisies is as dull as Olga's lesson. Surely manners tutorials are not what the High Priestess had in mind for me.

My only hope for escape is the classroom door. It's situated close to the chalkboard and would take a miracle to slip through unnoticed. Everyone would see me. Unless a distraction turned all their heads to the back of the room. If only I had Jakob's mind for mischief, but all his escapades relied on the use of a window to flee.

My mind ticks, but the stale air of the classroom stifles any spark of inspiration. Sweat drips down my spine and plasters my dress to my skin. I glance at the other ladies, but there are no sweat stains on anyone else's dresses. Even Embry's soft brown hair still floats around her shoulders instead of clinging to her skin. She reminds me of a rabbit, with her twitching nose and propensity to jump every time Olga punctuates a point with a scrape of her chalk. My eyes flick to the volume resting on each of our desks. If I dropped the heavy tome, would Embry cause enough of a distraction to mask my escape? I scoot the book back to the centre of my desk. More likely, Olga would zero in on me rather than

Embry. The last thing Arithenos needs is to be known as the troublemakers of Patel.

Sighing, I distract myself from thoughts of escape by imagining Embry as a lovesick fool, like Arabella. Those sad, distant eyes might brighten if Embry watched Calypso the same way Arabella does.

"Lady Nakoma?"

I jerk upright in my seat. Olga stares at me with one thin eyebrow raised in an expectant arch. Her left foot taps against the marble. I get the impression she has asked more than once.

I try to coat my voice with honey and ask, "Could you please repeat the question, Tutor Olga?"

I blink at her with wide eyes and hope the startling blue will help me appear innocent instead of stupid.

"In what order are meals served during a formal dinner at the palace?" Olga says.

I gulp at the sharp edge of Olga's voice. She's punished no one yet, but that doesn't mean I won't be the first. My mind races back to Mother's cooking during celebrations. Every year she complains when we try to eat the salad with the main meal or skip our soup in summer. My confidence surging, I focus on these memories as I reply.

"It is soup, salad, main course, then dessert..."

I pause. There's something else. I try to recall the late nights when Aunt Berna would join the festivities.

"After dessert, you move off to a drawing room for tea or coffee and another bite-size sweet. I don't remember the name of that meal."

Olga huffs. "*Petits fours.* You would know this, Lady Nakoma, if you paid closer attention to your studies."

Despite Olga's clipped words, the room doesn't fill with snide remarks and snickers from the other ladies. Olga turns back to the chalkboard, and I raise an eyebrow at Uri in question. Uri widens her dark eyes and mouths, w*hat just happened?* I shrug. Are *petits fours* already listed on the board amongst Olga's flourishes? I dare to sneak a look at Elisabelle. At the sight of her slack jaw, my confusion fades to pride.

THE SKY IS THE DEEP PURPLE OF AN OVERRIPE PLUM BY THE TIME Uri and I return to our room. Despite the enormous size of the Academy, Tutor Olga has assigned us all shared rooms to keep us out of mischief. The bedroom is big enough to fit two private quarters, complete with two closets, two canopy beds and a connecting bathroom.

Wish greets us from her perch beside my bed as we enter the room. Uri ignores her and drags me across the room to her bed.

"Okay, explain yourself," Uri demands, her arms crossed over her chest.

My spine stiffens at the tone of her voice. *Does she know?*

"Explain what?" I ask.

"Don't play dumb with me, Nakoma. I mean how you magically knew the answer to Tutor Olga's ridiculous question!"

I recoil from Uri's flailing arms as she gestures wildly. "So ... I guess Olga hadn't covered food yet?"

"Heavens, Nakoma, no. She asked that out of nowhere when your head slumped into your hands."

Pride unfurls within me once again. "That explains why Elisabelle looked like I was speaking in tongues."

"No kidding?"

I ignore Uri, kick off my shoes and climb onto her bed. "Right, sorry. Didn't I tell you my mother is from Ellos?"

Uri stills and blinks sheepishly as she processes my question. "Oh. That's right."

After a long moment, Uri follows me onto the bed and props herself up with a pile of cushions. "I assumed she was lowborn. I can't imagine someone like Elisabelle choosing to marry a man from one of our provinces."

"She is *not* like Elisabelle," I snap.

Uri holds up her hands in surrender. "I only meant in the sense of wealth and status."

I relax back into the bed and choose my words carefully. "She could be lowborn, I guess. It's not exactly something we talk about. But some of the ridiculous traditions she insists upon suggest a more affluent childhood."

"You're not close?"

I recoil from the question. Suspicions creep into my mind, whispering not to trust an outsider who pries into the life of guardians. But to Uri, I'm not a guardian. I take a deep breath and try to channel the open friendship that Omarion offers to the world.

"Mother has tried to shove Ellos's values down my throat since I was a little girl. I just want to be Arithean."

"She sounds like my pa. He thinks I should leave politics to the men. Thank heavens I don't have a brother. If he had a male heir, I wouldn't have a chance of avoiding marriage to the first man that asked."

"What about your ma? Does she support your diplomatic training?"

Tears collect against Uri's lower lashes, but she blinks them away before they can spill down her face.

"Ma died when I was seven. Swamp fever."

"I'm sorry," I murmur.

Uri brushes aside my comment with a wave of her hand. "I'm used to it. Besides, my grandmama is a force to be reckoned with. Pa is too afraid she will stop babysitting my younger sisters if he says no."

A bubble of laughter escapes me and sets off Uri's own snorting chuckle. I relax back into the cushions of Uri's bed and gaze at the gauzy fabric that shrouds us while Uri wipes tears of mirth from her face. The thin linen sways in the breeze and creates shadows that dance in the lantern light. We sit in companionable silence, listening to the ruffling of feathers as Wish stretches on her perch.

Lost in my own thoughts, I have no idea how long has passed before a sound causes me to bolt upright.

"Did you hear that?" I ask.

Uri frowns. Her head tilts to catch the noise. I jump off the bed and pad over to the door. Footsteps echo down the hall.

"Is someone there?" I call.

The only reply is Wish's echo of *whoo* before she swoops out the window on her nightly hunt. Uri joins me in the doorway and squints at the shadows cast by lanterns spaced along the hallway. Nothing.

Uri shrugs and shuts the door. "Whoever it was is long gone."

I nod in agreement but struggle to shake the feeling of being watched as we prepare for sleep.

TWELVE

As I enter the palace stables the next day, a waft of horse manure hits me, and despite the stench, I smile. The pounding of my head eases as my muscles unwind. There are no ladies here to act for. No manners lessons. Just the soft sounds of horses and the bustle of palace workers.

Each step towards Kato sends thoughts of today's dull lesson further from my mind. Wish flies ahead of me, startling a stablehand when she swoops to perch on Kato's stall. Kato pokes his head out to greet me and huffs with impatience. I roll my eyes at him, but my smile falters at the thought of him spending long days stuck indoors. With the same efficiency that earned me the top of my class in training, I saddle Kato and lead him out into the yard.

"Lady Nakoma!"

Lars waves at me from the door of the stables, afternoon sunshine cascading over him. A chestnut mare stands by his side, its reins grasped firmly in his hands despite its obviously docile nature.

"I must be the luckiest man in all of Ellos. Here I was, lamenting a ride with Blossom on the same tedious valley path, when you appear with Kato."

Lars's green eyes sparkle with the joy of a secret joke. Twin flames of embarrassment and longing to be included in his joke heat my cheeks and leave me uncomfortable in my own skin. The palace grounds seem to hold its breath waiting for my response, but I have no quip for Lars with so many people watching. I lift my chin and stride past him. In my mind, I only have to outrun his attention. But Lars follows, Blossom plodding along behind.

"Did I offend you?"

I glance over my shoulder before replying. "Everyone is watching you."

Lars shrugs, but his Adam's apple bobs nervously. "It must be my irresistible charm."

I pause at a fork in the path and peer at Lars. In the light of day, everything about him has a certain allure. His simple shirt and trousers no longer look like a commoner's uniform. The cloth alone would cost a week's wages as a guardian.

"Who are you?"

"Someone who is about to be scolded if I hold up my riding party any longer. Will you come with us? It isn't much for scenery, but Kato will enjoy it more than the training circle."

I stare at the dirt patch they call a ring and, beyond it, the horses grazing in a threadbare pasture.

"I wondered if that was the only place the king has for exercising his steeds," I admit.

Lars grins as I mount Kato in one swift motion. Although the extra fabric of my gown is a nuisance, I can't help but praise Aunt Fifi's genius. Anything is better than riding side-saddle. I do my best to act busy adjusting the skirt as Lars awkwardly yanks himself into his own saddle.

Once seated, Lars leads us to the outskirts of the palace grounds, where two men in palace uniforms wait astride matching cream horses. Lars introduces the men as Fredrick and Mikael. They offer the usual pleasantries but otherwise remain as bland as the Academy porridge. Before long, the two fall behind Kato's quick stride.

As the path widens, I ease Kato into a walk and wait until Lars is riding beside us. Wish slows with us, perching on the branches of elms and oaks as we pass beneath them. Salty ocean air sweeps along the path and sends goosebumps dancing across my skin, but I'm still sweating beneath my gown. The heavy fabric perfectly traps the humidity of the valley. I steal a furtive glance at Fredrick and Mikael. Despite our steady pace, both riders maintain their distance from us.

"What did you say your job was again?" I ask.

"I'm not sure I told you."

I frown at Lars's deflection. "I only ask because your friends appear even less like stablehands than yourself, though they're better horsemen."

"True. Well, you're right, they're not stablehands... They're more like supervisors."

"Because you're so bad at riding?"

Lars wheezes with barely concealed laughter. "I'm expected to practice my horsemanship daily."

I glance at Lars's broad grin and smile back at him. Warmth radiates through my chest, encouraging me to be bold.

"You must've skipped a lot of lessons as a child."

Lars puffs up his chest and looks down his nose at me. "I'll have you know I was a star pupil. Tutors wept for the pure joy of teaching me."

I frown at Lars until I notice the mischievous twinkle in his green eyes. "You're tugging my leg again, aren't you?"

Lars clutches at his chest. "You wound me, Lady Nakoma. I would never dare touch the leg of a distinguished lady."

I roll my eyes at him. Lars shares the same odd sense of humour Mother insists is sarcasm. He's not the only one in Ellos. The serving staff at the Academy make similar jokes when they are off duty, and I suspect Tutor Olga would as well if she wasn't so highly strung.

"How is the Academy?" Lars asks in a more serious tone.

"Dull as anything. Though everyone is looking forward to Saturday. The Academy is hosting a tea party that we will all attend."

"Oh? Is the regular food so bad at the Academy that you're starving for cucumber sandwiches?"

I smile at the thought of Elisabelle stuffing her face with food in front of royalty.

"No – it's the prince," I explain. "It's our first chance to meet him."

Lars glances over his shoulder at Fredrick and Mikael. "Are you excited to meet the prince?"

I scratch behind Kato's ears and watch the passing ferns that brush against his legs. A swirl of emotions bubble within my stomach. Meeting the prince will make everything more real. Impress him, and the burden of Arithenos's tax may lighten. Fool him, and no one will be the wiser about my life as a guardian. Yet, beneath all this, I harbour a spark of hope that he will also be kind and sweet. Someone worth knowing.

"Yes. I believe it would be impossible not to be. After all, one of us has to marry him, and I don't even know what he looks like," I finally admit, trying to keep my tone light.

Lars nods but says no more. My cheeks flush with embarrassment. Did I say too much? My mind races as I search for some thread of conversation to fill his silence.

"Have you met the prince?" I blurt out.

Lars pales. "I ... um..."

I draw Kato to a halt. A flustered Lars is surely better than a silent one. Besides, an early introduction to the prince could be Arithenos's ticket to an audience with the king. I press on.

"Or maybe Fredrick or Mikael has met him?"

Lars gulps. His eyes dart to Fredrick and Mikael.

"They've met him."

94

I tap a finger against my chin. "Maybe knowing a member of the king's council would do the trick?"

"What are you talking about?"

I turn Kato in a tight circle, an idea taking shape.

"If I beat you back to the palace, will you help me seek an audience with the king? For Arithenos?"

"The king?" Lars splutters. "Who do you think I am?"

"Well, maybe not the king, then, but you could help me meet someone important, right? You must know people if you take supervised rides on palace grounds."

Lars leans back in his saddle and gestures to Kato. "It wouldn't be a fair race."

"What if I make it back to the palace before you can exit the valley?"

Lars smiles. "Now this I would like to see. On the count of three. One..."

I lean over Kato's neck as Lars repositions Blossom.

"Two..."

Kato's ears flick back as Blossom stills beside us.

"Three!"

Blossom bolts into a gallop before Lars can yell the last count over his shoulder. I shout in surprise as I spur Kato into motion. Despite appearances, Blossom is no child's pony. Still, it doesn't take long for Kato to pass her. Fredrick and Mikael jump out of our way as Kato builds speed.

Kato's hooves pound a steady rhythm into the earth as we fly back up the valley. My heart soars. We move as one, the wind rippling in our wake. The trees morph from dense forest back into the scattered saplings that border the palace grounds. I glance over my shoulder. Lars and Blossom are far from sight. With a grin, I slow Kato to a trot and wait outside the stables.

Wish has returned to her perch on my shoulder when Blossom finally emerges from the tree line. I share a wicked grin with Lars, forgetting to act the part of a gracious lady.

"How did you do that?" Lars asks.

I pat Kato's neck. "Practice and a good horse."

"Blossom's no snail."

"Then you must need practice," I laugh.

"You should come riding with us more often. Apparently, I can stand to learn a thing or two from you."

Stablehands peer at us curiously as they walk their charges back from the fields. My tongue turns to lead under their eyes. *How many of them have seen a guardian in action before?* I dismount and hope Lars won't notice that my skill with Kato is out of place for an ordinary Arithean.

Lars follows my lead, mistaking my silence as a polite declining of his invitation.

"I'll see what I can do about the introductions, but I doubt I can line anything up for you before Saturday."

"Thank you," I murmur, but my heart isn't in it.

The possibility that I have blown my cover is enough to sap my confidence. Lars does his best to keep up a steady conversation as we wash Kato and Blossom, but as soon as they are clean and dry, I hurry back to the Academy.

~

BEFORE I CAN MAKE IT UP THE SANDSTONE STEPS OF THE PINK Palace, the great oak door swings open. Perriwick fills the doorway. Elisabelle stands behind him, shadowing Perriwick's every move.

"Lady Nakoma, Tutor Olga has requested your presence in her office immediately."

I gulp and glance at Wish. Whoever is monitoring Wish would be eager to follow me to Olga's office, but I know how much Olga detests Wish's presence at the Academy. There's no need to push my luck.

"Up, Wish. I'll see you later."

Wish blinks slowly, a sure sign that the priestess has departed before Wish obeys my dismissal. The thin remains of my high spirits evaporate as I follow Perriwick and try to ignore Elisabelle's knowing smirk.

An elderly man and woman rise from their seats on the couch as we enter Tutor Olga's office. Perriwick bows to them, then faces Olga.

"Will that be all, ma'am?"

"Yes, you may leave, Perriwick."

As soon as Perriwick is gone, Olga gestures for the elderly couple to resume their seats. The full teacups rattle on the serving table as the man bumps his knee. I wait awkwardly in the doorway, unsure if I am expected to sit with them or in one of the hard wooden chairs that face Olga's desk.

Before I can make up my mind, Olga speaks. "Elisabelle has introduced me to the honourable Klaus and his wife Yvette this afternoon. It has been a most interesting discussion."

I peer at the couple before returning my attention to Olga. *Is this some sort of test?*

"I'm glad you are having an enjoyable evening," I say, attempting to embody today's manners lesson.

Tutor Olga smiles without joy. "Do you not recognise them, Lady Nakoma?"

I resist the urge to answer Olga with a shake of my head. "No, Tutor Olga."

"I only ask because I believe they are your grandparents."

CHAPTER
THIRTEEN

I stare at the elderly couple. They're dressed in expensive clothes that could rival Elisabelle's collection, and they both have an air of arrogance. But my *grandparents*? Yvette has startling blue eyes like Mother's and silver hair that might have been blond two decades ago. An intricate bun with a golden pin keeps the silver strands neat at the nape of her neck. Still, Yvette's features only capture my attention for so long. Klaus returns my inquisitive gaze with the same intelligent spark that is ever present in Mother.

Tutor Olga clears her throat, breaking the silence. "Thank you for your assistance, Lady Elisabelle. That will be all."

Elisabelle freezes, her eyes darting between Olga and me. "Are you certain? Perhaps I can still be of help?"

Olga's eyes narrow. "I am certain, Lady Elisabelle."

Elisabelle's cheeks flush as she curtsies and scurries

99

from the room. Olga is quick to shut the door behind her and gestures for me to sit in one of the hard wooden seats by her desk. I perch at the edge of the chair, my heart hammering a frantic tempo. With the door shut, the walls seem to close in on me. I fight to keep my breaths from turning into shallow pants.

Tutor Olga makes a show of shuffling some papers at her desk, drawing Klaus's attention away from me. Age spots mark his wrinkled skin and give his cheeks a hollow appearance.

"Lady Nakoma, let us be honest with one another."

My focus snaps back to Tutor Olga, her words setting my frayed nerves on fire.

"I am not fond of wasting an evening," Olga continues, "so I will be direct. Is it possible that you have grandparents in Ellos?"

"Yes."

I keep my answer simple, wary of Tutor Olga and my apparent grandparents. Do they hate Mother for choosing a new life in Arithenos rather than one with them? Is Tutor Olga fishing for a reason to send me home? Or worse, does she already know I am a guardian?

Olga arches her brow. "You are here to represent Arithenos?"

"Yes."

"Was one of your parents born outside of Arithenos?"

"Yes."

"Lady Nakoma, I'm not sure what game you are playing at, but I would appreciate more than one-word answers."

I swallow the urge to reply with "Okay."

"My mother was born in Ellos. Papa was born in Arithenos."

Tutor Olga sighs and leans back from the table. "Then how, pray tell, did they meet?"

"Papa is a merchant. He travels all over the kingdom for his trade. He met my mother while at an Ellos market."

Tutor Olga nods thoughtfully. I glance at Yvette and Klaus to gauge their reaction to my brief version of events. Klaus's lips press together, and he crosses his thin arms over his chest. Yvette watches him too and rests a hand on his knee in either comfort or restraint.

"Do you have a daughter living in Arithenos?" Olga asks, her attention now off me.

Klaus exchanges a look with Yvette before speaking. "Our daughter Elaine left home at eighteen to marry an Arithean man. We did not remain in contact with her, for many reasons."

Yvette tuts. "Why hide the truth? We cut her off. Elaine was betrothed to a lord of Ellos. When she refused him, we were furious. I thought by refusing her a dowry, she might reconsider." Yvette's voice wobbles as she speaks, and her eyes glisten with unshed tears. Klaus pulls an embroidered handkerchief from his pocket and passes it to his wife.

"Elaine is stubborn," Klaus continues for Yvette. "She gets that from me. She was true to her word and never spoke to us again."

"Were you aware your daughter has children?" Tutor Olga asks.

Klaus winces at the question, and Yvette covers her face with the handkerchief. Their reactions are enough to make me second-guess my earlier assumptions of their appearance.

"I have a brother as well. He is two years younger than me," I murmur.

Yvette peeks at me from behind the handkerchief, hope blossoming in her eyes.

"I suppose our Elaine would have children by now, but I never imagined those children ... our grandchildren ... might be old enough to travel to Ellos," Yvette says.

Olga nods once more and stands behind her desk.

"I apologise if this interview has caused any offence. Let me assure you, the Academy and I hold you in the highest esteem. But it is my duty to investigate any suspicions over the eligibility of our ladies at the Academy."

My stomach swirls with unease. Perched at the edge of my seat, I watch each twitch of Olga's lips.

"It is clear Lady Nakoma is a stranger to the both of you, and thus has no unfair advantage from her relatives in Ellos."

Yvette smiles weakly as Klaus offers her his elbow. I stand as well, my chest tightening with every breath. My heart yearns to hold them close, to make up for the years with only one set of grandparents. But we've just met, and I never asked Mother about them before.

"If that is all, madam, we will be on our way," Klaus says.

They shuffle past the low table, leaving behind full cups of cold tea.

My voice rings out in the silent room. "Wait."

All eyes turn to me. I swallow down my pride.

"Tutor Olga, is it against the rules for me to get to know my grandparents now? I hadn't thought to find them before, but now they are here..."

Yvette's face lights up at the suggestion, but Klaus's remains a mask of indifference. I try to force myself to adopt the same expression as Klaus and fail miserably. My years of training have fled at the first sign that my grandparents might care.

Tutor Olga speaks with slow, deliberate words. "I see no problem with it. Part of the Academy's success comes from women such as Nakoma being introduced to the wider society of Ellos. The fact you are relatives does not change Lady Nakoma's past as a child born and raised in Arithenos."

I nod, not trusting myself to execute a curtsy. "Thank you, Tutor Olga."

"I will send a messenger with our details so we may arrange a suitable time," Yvette says. "I would hate to interfere with your lessons here."

Tutor Olga replies with the grace of a good host and summons Perriwick to escort my grandparents back to the front of the Pink Palace. I step outside the office with them and attempt to listen to their conversation even after Perriwick has led them away. Klaus's deep voice floats across the marble, but with it comes another sound. The soft patter of feet rushes down the hall to my left. A flash of Elisabelle's unmistakable pink gown and blond hair catches my eye before she slips out of sight.

CHAPTER
FOURTEEN

I take my time at the breakfast table on Saturday morning, hoping that if I slowly pick apart my bread roll, my appetite may appear. My stomach gurgles, and I force myself to swallow the food in my mouth.

"This is stupid," I grumble.

Uri looks up from her letter, her midnight hair falling across her face. Ink spills from her quill across the page where she has stopped midsentence.

"What's stupid?"

"I know I should be hungry, but this bread makes me want to gag."

Uri shrugs and turns back to the letter. "Get something else to eat."

I drop the remains of my bread roll back onto my plate. There is still some fresh fruit out on the sideboard I could try, but I doubt it will make a difference. I drum my fingers against the table.

"It must be last night's fish," I say.

Uri drops her quill back into the inkwell and blows on the parchment to help it dry. Her penmanship is enough to make Tutor Olga rage at our class about the qualities of a lady. Still, there's something comforting about how Uri scratches out a letter. Each word is as sharp as Uri's tongue during a debate lesson.

"I don't think it's the fish," Uri says.

I don't ask why. Uri will tell me soon enough. Instead, I watch as she folds up the unfinished letter and tucks it into her dress pocket.

"Your body is subconsciously helping you delay the inevitable."

"And by that, you mean...?"

"You don't want to meet the prince."

I shake my head no, but it is hard to deny when half the ladies have already returned to the dining hall in carefully selected gowns. Instead of answering, I watch as Jadera doubles over with laughter at something Quinn says. Quinn keeps going, her arms acting out a scene, only pausing to tuck her unconventionally short hair behind her ears. Uri takes my silence as confirmation. She pushes back from the table, taking the inkwell with her.

"Come on, we can't sit here forever."

I sigh and empty my plate into a bin. The room fills with excited chatter as more of our peers arrive for the picnic. My own dress is a bright green that reminds me of lemongrass. Hazel-Mae helped me pick it out last night and assured me it's fine enough for a tea party, but it still seems plain compared to Quinn's buttercup yellow dress. Or worse, Jadera's floral gown with matching petals pinned throughout her scarlet hair.

I drag my feet like a petulant child as Uri leads the way back to our room. *The prince is just a man,* I remind myself. *He can't read minds or predict futures. There is no way he will know you are a guardian by looking at you. Relax.* I pick up my pace and catch up to Uri as she swings open our bedroom door, releasing an odour so foul I double over.

Uri gags. "What is that? Did your owl bring in a skunk?"

I scrunch up my nose and step inside the room. The stench differs from dung or a carcass – it's like rotting fish and sour milk combined into one abomination. Wish's perch is empty, and I can't see any fresh remains beneath it, but still, I scan the room, searching for old bones I might have missed.

"I don't think Wish..."

The words die on my tongue. Thick goop drips off the ends of my lemongrass dress and pools beneath it on the bathroom floor. My jaw drops open, then promptly shuts against a waft of what can only be last night's dinner. A smear of creamy fish casserole covers the length of the dress, ruining the fabric. Nearby, Uri's mustard-coloured gown is untouched.

"Oh Lord," Uri mutters. "That's disgusting."

I reach out to stroke the dress, but my fingers recoil at the first touch of room-temperature food.

"Do you have another dress you can wear?" Uri says.

The question turns my vision red. As if I can ignore the nightmare in front of me. This is no accident. Someone must pay. I yank the dress from the hanger and ignore the splatter of food that falls off it. Holding it as far from my body as possible, I storm out of the room.

"Nakoma? Where are you going?"

I ignore Uri's question. She chases me down the hall, but I'm faster. My blood boils with rage, urging me to act now. The satisfying slam of the dining hall doors opening is the only thing that slows me enough not to shout at the top of my lungs. All eyes turn to me as I throw my dress onto the closest table.

"Who did this?" I demand.

The silence is deafening.

"Don't make me ask again," I grind out.

Uri appears behind me, her breaths coming in little puffs. I don't spare her or any of the outer territories a glance. Only a highborn brat would stoop this low. I glare at Elisabelle and her entourage. Only Elisabelle has the nerve to meet my eye. She wrinkles her nose and delicately lifts her chin towards my dress.

"I think, Lady Nakoma, you might need to be a little more specific if you want answers. I'm sure no one here knows what you're talking about."

Elisabelle's sickeningly sweet tone is enough to make the skin at the base of my neck prickle with fury. My fists clench at my sides.

"Somebody defiled my property. They know what they did."

Elisabelle's face is full of mock surprise, her lips forming a perfect O. My eyes narrow.

"Such a shame," Elisabelle says, with a hand to her chest. "I couldn't imagine who would do such a thing."

Tia pushes her seat back with a screech. "Maybe we can fix it. There's still a little time before the prince arrives."

Uri places her hand on my shoulder, but I shake her off. No one can fix this. At least, not in time for the party.

"Why fix it?" Elisabelle says. "The dress suits Nakoma now. A stench to match the cow dung of Arithenos."

The world around me fades. The only thing left is the smirk on Elisabelle's face. I launch myself around the table, shoving chairs out of my way.

"You'll pay for this!" I roar.

The words rip from my throat before I have time to consider them. Ladies scream and dart away from Elisabelle. She scrambles out of her chair and up onto the table, as if that will stop me. I grab her ankle and yank with all my might. Elisabelle falls with a loud smack against the table. She shrieks – whether with pain or fear, I don't care.

Uri shouts in my ear. Her hands pull at my shoulders, but I'm stronger.

"Nakoma! Get off her! She's not worth it."

"Security!" Elisabelle shrieks. "Get this savage away from me!"

Elisabelle's voice hits me like a slap in the face. I drop

her ankle, my hand going slack at my side. Uri keeps pulling at my arms until I stumble away from Elisabelle.

"She's not worth it," Uri says again. "Tutor Olga won't let you go to the tea party if she hears you've been fighting."

The rage inside me dims to regret. Tutor Olga is the last of my worries. I'm lucky Wish wasn't here to witness my complete loss of control. The High Priestess would be so disappointed. Omarion would be furious. We are guardians, not thugs who fight at any provocation. I put more distance between myself and Elisabelle.

"You attacked me," Elisabelle says.

She points her finger like the rest of the room didn't see it happen. Time stills as everyone stops and stares at the mess I've made. Someone will have heard us. It's a matter of time before the Academy staff arrives. My mind reels. I have to salvage this.

"I did not attack you."

Elisabelle opens her mouth to protest, but I stop her with a glare.

"You fell. If you did not fall, then you also claim responsibility for the destruction of my property. Everyone heard what you said."

Elisabelle's lips disappear as she clamps her mouth shut. Her eyes turn to steel.

"If I have so much as a bruise, I will—"

"You will do nothing, or Tutor Olga will also hear that I saw you sneak into the kitchens last night. Do you understand me?"

Elisabelle crosses her arms and manages to look

regal, even while sprawled on top of the table. Her eyes flick towards Arabella, Calypso and Embry. They hurry to Elisabelle's side and help her clamber off the table. Her feet have just touched the ground when Cook bursts into the room. Cook's three chins wobble with rage as she waves her wooden spoon wildly.

"What is all the fuss about?" she rumbles. "I've got enough to worry about with this party without having to babysit you lot."

Elisabelle puts on a smile so fake that I shudder.

"Sorry, Cook," Elisabelle says sweetly, "just a minor disagreement. It's all sorted now."

Cook grumbles some more and wipes her sweaty palms across her apron. Her beady eyes scan the room once more before she accepts Elisabelle's answer and waddles back out of the room. I follow her out. The moment I'm out of sight, I sag with relief. I can't let my temper escape me again. There's no story I can concoct that will explain why I don't fight like a lady – no hair pulling or scratching for me.

"Do you want to borrow something from my closet?" Uri asks.

Uri walks a step behind me and, judging by the smell, she has brought the dress too. I would hug her if it wasn't for that dress.

"No. I'd trip on the hem and make a bigger fool of myself."

"You're not that short."

I give Uri a look. There's no point in lying about something so clear to save my feelings.

"I know I'm short, Uri. Don't start acting like a central province on me."

Uri shrugs. "Well, there's no saving this dress. Not today, at least."

I stop and stare at my dress hanging limp in Uri's hands. My stomach churns at the smell of it.

"What you did... That was really dumb, Nakoma."

I pull my focus away from my dress and meet Uri's eyes. A shiver rolls down my spine. Every inch of me wants to hide from her stare, but I don't. The deep black-brown of her knowing eyes is enough to both terrify and comfort me. In them, I am a guardian again. And if she sees that too, Uri wouldn't say a word.

"It was dumb," Uri continues, "but I'll cherish the look on Elisabelle's face for the rest of my life."

Uri smiles, and I'm back to just being Lady Nakoma, daughter of a merchant.

"Thank you," I say.

I can only hope Uri realises I'm thankful for more than the offer of a dress.

CHAPTER
FIFTEEN

When Tutor Olga announced the Academy was hosting a tea party, I never imagined something so grand. The gardens are out of season, but there are still multitudes of roses decorating the pavilion and scattered amongst the refreshments. I gaze longingly at the decorative pastries. My mouth waters as the scent of rich chocolate wafts towards me on the morning breeze. I curse my appetite for returning now of all moments.

"Quickly, ladies, our guests will arrive any moment now. I want one perfect line from the pavers to the lawn in order of province to greet His Highness," Tutor Olga says.

Dark circles ring Olga's eyes despite the heavy powder she has covered them with. She's exchanged her usual stark black dress for a lighter grey that does nothing to soften her appearance.

"Remember — name, province, status, *then* well-wishes," Olga continues.

I join Uri at the end of the queue; Tia and Hazel-Mae are not far in front of us. I curl my toes in my soft leather slippers. If only it wasn't poor manners to walk barefoot at a party. Tutor Olga would have a conniption if she caught me out on the fresh-cut grass without something to protect my feet. I whisper my idea in Uri's ear, and she snorts with laughter.

Olga cuts us a look. Her frown deepens as she takes in my pale blue smock and gloveless fingers. Shoulders wound tight, Olga abandons the head of the line to address Uri and me.

"Lady Nakoma, what *are* you wearing?"

"A day dress," I explain. "Is it not in fashion in Ellos? They are quite popular in Arithenos."

I keep my eyes wide and innocent as Olga splutters. Uri warned me Olga would not like it, but it was the only clean dress I had left, and none of Uri's dresses fit my figure. They all pooled around my ankles and stretched to their limit across my shoulders.

"It is so plain. Next time, please consult with myself or Elisabelle so you are wearing something appropriate for royal guests."

Uri clamps her hand over her mouth to control a snort of laughter. Tutor Olga ignores the choked sound and hustles off to Calypso, who has styled her ginger hair in long, loose ringlets. At least Olga has the sense to ignore Uri's own unfortunate dress. It's tailored to the latest fashion, but the mustard gown does not complement Uri's complexion. Even I can see that. Uri's gloved fingers press the fabric flat over and over until I worry she will work a hole into the seam.

"You look beautiful," I tell Uri.

Uri rolls her eyes at me and continues to smooth her gown.

"You are also observant and clever."

Uri stills. "Thank you."

Guests file past us with polite nods on their way to the refreshments table. Thick rugs and pastel cushions decorate the lawn, but none of the courtiers dare to take a seat first. I watch them trickle in absentmindedly until a familiar face catches my eye. Lars stands with a cluster of nobles, dressed in finery that is not garish despite being an intense shade of purple. My eyes dart between Lars and the other guests. Men and women twice his age follow his lead in greeting Tutor Olga before turning to our queue. My stomach sinks.

I reach across Uri and give Tia a sharp poke. "That's the prince?"

"Prince Antonio Lawrence of Patel," Tia whispers, her voice trembling with nerves.

I squeeze my eyes shut and curse under my breath. Horror clouds my thoughts as I rush through every interaction I've had with Lars. *Lawrence*. What must he think of Arithenos?

My stomach rolls as Lars presses a kiss upon Elisabelle's knuckles. I tear my eyes away from him. Anger surges. I may be a fool, but Lars lied. He could have corrected me at any point. I stare resolutely at the jasmine hedge beyond the party set-up. My feet itch to run, but I force myself to stand with squared shoulders.

"Do you know him?" Uri murmurs.

I nod, the movement stiff with tension. Waiting for Lars to greet each lady before me is agony. I swallow hard to calm my raging stomach.

"He keeps looking at you," Uri says.

My eyes flick up the queue to check his progress. Lars bends over Tia's hand, using the movement to conceal a stolen glance. My cheeks burn. *Remember your training, Nakoma*, I scold myself. With deep, calming breaths, I do my best to ignore my surroundings and continue focusing on my best chance of escape. The jasmine hedges.

"My name is Lady Uri of Froi, Your Highness."

My nerves hum as Uri speaks to him, every inch of me aware of his proximity. I refuse to look, but I don't stop listening. Uri is saying the right things. The Academy manners we've all been practicing. I just have to do the same for a minute. Sixty seconds.

Lars steps in front of me. His eyes search my face.

"My name is Prince Antonio of Patel. Welcome to Ellos, my lady."

My eyes narrow. What game is he playing? Acting as if we have never met. I curtsy, but my hand hangs limp at my side. My mouth grows dry.

"My name is Lady Nakoma of Arithenos," I finally force out. "My father is a merchant."

Lars nods, waiting patiently for me to continue with the same bland words we were all taught to say. *I hope your family is well*. The phrase catches on my tongue.

"I'm not wearing gloves," I say instead.

A true smile tugs at the corners of Lars's mouth, but his eyes are still uncertain. "I can see that. I suppose it is a bit too warm for gloves."

My eyes shift restlessly from the food to the distant gardens. Sixty seconds stretches before me.

"Is that why you did not offer your hand, Lady Nakoma?" Lars asks.

"Among other reasons."

I meet Lars's curious gaze with my chin raised. His mouth opens to speak, but I don't wait for his reply.

"If you'll excuse me, Your Highness."

With a sharp turn, I march off towards the hedge maze. The green shrubs do nothing to cool my raging blood. I head deeper. The maze twists before me, but it is easy to follow the main path to the centre. It wouldn't do for the Academy to lose its ladies in a maze. My stride slows as the buzz of conversation dims to a distant whisper.

The world around me gradually comes back into focus, and with it, the sound of quick footsteps. I whirl around to face Uri.

"What are you doing here?" I demand.

"What am *I* doing here? What about you? Care to explain what that was all about?"

I deflate in the face of Uri's questions and cover my face with my hands.

"Was it really that bad?"

Uri pulls my hands away from my face and gently wipes away tears I hadn't realised were there.

"Come, sit." She tugs on my hand until my feet obediently follow her to a nearby bench. The seat is firm and unforgiving, but the cool marble helps me focus.

"I've met the prince before."

Uri doesn't speak, her silence urging me to continue.

"He told me his name was Lars," I explain. "He was at the stables, in Kato's stall, and I thought... I never dreamed that he was actually the prince."

"That's not so bad."

I shake my head. "I was so rude to him – to Ellos – and then far too casual."

"You saw him more than once."

"He invited me out riding," I confirm.

Uri nods slowly. "So, he likes you."

I jump to my feet. "What? No! He lied to me."

"Calm down, Nakoma." Uri yanks on my wrist until I return to the bench. "Whatever you've said to him in the past, he took no offence."

"How can you be so sure?"

"You weren't looking at his face," Uri says.

I cross my arms over my chest, ready to argue the point, but one look at Uri halts my tongue. A storm of emotions battle for control in my mind. Nothing makes sense.

"That still doesn't explain why he would lie."

Uri's eyes grow distant as she considers. "Perhaps he wanted a chance to know someone without them putting up a front because he is the prince."

"I wouldn't do that. You wouldn't do that."

"Who knows, maybe I would. I want him to think well of Froi, and if I need to put up a front to achieve that, then Froi comes first."

Uri's words hold the ring of truth, but my heart doesn't want to hear it. I stare at the hedges, willing the viridescent leaves to part so I can spy on Lars. Would he be looking for me? Or is he too busy making the other ladies swoon over him?

"He knew he would have to confess eventually," I mutter.

"True, but he has to marry one of us. Why not take every opportunity to learn about your potential bride?"

"It's not like we can do the same. Perhaps he was acting too."

"Did he appear false?"

"No, but—"

"Then he wasn't. Besides, you'll never know for sure unless you go back out there."

I blanch at the thought. "I made a scene, didn't I?"

"Some of the other ladies noticed, but I'm sure Tia has told them some story about a stomach-ache. You look pale enough to make it believable."

I wince. "Can't I wait out here until everyone leaves?"

"If you do, Olga will notice."

I grumble under my breath but get to my feet. Uri is right. Despite Tia's love of books and dedication to learning, Uri is usually the one who is right. I offer my arm to her, and she links elbows with me before we head back towards the party. Her warmth washes over me, dampening my nerves.

I lean into Uri as we walk. "Thank you."

"You'd do the same for me."

~

THE PARTY IS IN FULL SWING WHEN WE EMERGE FROM THE maze. Guests lounge on the rugs spread across the lawn, and merriment fills the air. A cluster of women vie for Lars's attention, blushing and tinkling prettily with laughter. Among them are Elisabelle and her loyal followers.

"What now?"

Uri joins me in scanning the tea party for a course of action. If I was Tia or Hazel-Mae, I might join the partygoers on the lawn in hopes of finding an eligible bachelor in case someone else ensnares Prince Antonio. But the High Priestess sent me as a diplomat – to encourage positive relationships with Arithenos, not to find my match.

"I doubt anyone here is of political importance," I mutter. "They all look so young."

Uri nods, following my line of sight to the young courtier glued to Quinn's side. His eyes gravitate to where the scalloped edge of her dress brushes against her collarbone as he feigns interest in their conversation.

"Let's get something to eat, then find Tia," Uri says. "Tutor Olga needs to see us making an effort."

My stomach rumbles in agreement. The spread looks

divine, from the decadent cheeses to the delicate pastries. My eyes widen at the honeycomb display and endless amounts of bite-size cakes. Caught up in the sights, I don't realise someone has joined Uri and me at the table.

"You should try the apple turnovers," Lars says.

I clasp a hand over my mouth to smother a squawk of surprise. Lars watches me closely, doubt clouding is usually bright-green eyes.

"They're best warm with a dollop of cream, but these miniature ones are an Academy specialty," Lars continues when I don't reply.

I select one of the pastries Lars gestured to but make no move to eat it. The tantalising scents that made my mouth water seconds ago now churn my stomach. I glance over at Uri. She makes a show of studying the honeycomb but still tilts her head towards us.

"Perhaps we should take a turn together?" Lars suggests.

I look from the pastry cradled in my hand to Lars.

"You want my apple turnover?"

Lars's dark brows furrow before a smile springs to life across his face.

"Turnover? No, Lady Nakoma, a *turn* means to walk together."

My face burns with embarrassment as I mentally add the phrase to the long list of Ellos terms Olga is determined will help create proper ladies. I glance at Uri, hoping her face will reveal that she also didn't know the phrase. Instead, Uri is staring daggers at me and making a slight shooing gesture.

"Fine," I finally concede.

Aside from the maze, there is not much space for walking left on the lawn. Lars's steps are slow and measured, filled with the natural grace I can now see is fit for royalty. Even though my head barely reaches his shoulder, I easily match his pace.

"Are you enjoying the weather this morning, Lady Nakoma?"

I check Lars's gelled hair for signs of horns. The man I met in the stables didn't talk to me like I was made of glass. Still, there are no bumps in sight.

"Please, just call me Nakoma."

Lars's smile widens to reveal shiny, straight teeth. "Only if you will keep calling me Lars."

We keep walking. I stare at the pastry resting in the cradle of my damp palm. A dusting of powdered sugar coats my fingers.

"Are you not hungry?" Lars asks.

I shift the turnover to my other hand and try to wipe away the sugar by stuffing my hand in my pocket. My stomach gurgles. I consider offering the treat to Lars, but shudder at the thought of him eating the sweat-moistened pastry.

Without further thought, I finish the turnover in two bites. My eyes grow wide as the flavours dance across my tongue. Saliva pools as my mouth begs for more. I fight the urge to lick my fingers clean.

"It's good," I say, once I've dusted my hands off.

"You should try what our cooks make. They create these tiny meringue swans and chocolate finches for every ball. They're so lifelike it feels like a crime to eat them."

Lars grows animated as he speaks. His arms lose their stiff formality as he paints images of the finest desserts in the air. My own shoulders loosen as I watch him, but the tight knot in my stomach doesn't fade. I have to ask.

"Lars, why didn't you tell me you are the prince?"

Lars pauses midstride. "I'm sorry. That should have been the first thing I said to you today, but I lost my nerve."

His eyes hold genuine remorse, but it's not enough. My lips tighten as I wait for him to finish.

"I suppose I got carried away. At first, it felt like a game to pretend to be someone else. Especially since everyone else I've met has recognised me."

I soft gasp of indignation escapes my lips. I turn towards Lars, my hands scrunched into tight fists.

"Please let me finish. That was only at first. You have no idea how guilty I felt when we went on our ride together. I wanted to tell you – I should've told you – but I was afraid you would leave before I could explain."

Every ounce of anger drains from my body as Lars's words hit me. They twist my gut, stirring the guilt deep within. At least Lars is being honest now. Meanwhile, I'm still lying through my teeth. He deserves to know the truth. Yet reason outweighs this little voice. I can't risk Arithenos.

"I'm so glad I met you," Lars says, rushing to fill my silence. "I've been dreading my marriage for years. It's the worst kind of torture knowing I'm bound by duty to marry a lady from the Academy, without a clue for what she will be like. Each province could send a shrew and I would still have to choose one to marry."

"I think I know how you feel," I whisper.

I stare at the grass beneath my feet and struggle to find the words to explain myself – something true. Lars deserves the closest thing to the truth that I can offer him.

"I didn't believe I would be the best woman to represent Arithenos, but the High Priestess asked, and I can never refuse her."

Lars offers me the crook of his elbow as he leads the way up the pavilion steps. The touch dances across my skin and sends shivers down my spine. Although open to the rest of the garden, the little domed roof above our heads makes the pavilion feel a million miles away from the rest of the party.

Lars clears his throat, and I drop his arm like a loaded beehive.

"So ... what are your thoughts on the other ladies so far?" Lars asks.

His question reverberates through my mind and fills what I had thought was amiable silence. I step away from Lars and scrutinise his open, smiling face. *Is this a test?* My mind jumps back to the initiation rite all rookies must pass to proceed with basic training. Our commanders would gain trust first before asking seemingly harmless questions.

"I'm undecided. How about yourself? Any immediate favourites?"

Lars snorts at my wariness but answers the question.

"It's difficult to have a favourite when each lady has nothing more to say than the usual court pleasantries."

I nod slowly and shove down the urge to continue to dodge the question. *Honesty*, I remind myself.

"I most enjoy the company of the ladies from Froi, the Mir Mountains, and Sebba."

"Froi is the closest neighbour to Arithenos, isn't it? Do you think you have the most in common with them?"

I smile at Lars, glad that he recognised the connection. Somehow, extolling the virtues of Uri, Tia, and Hazel-Mae sets me at ease, and I happily point out each girl to Lars. He listens patiently, probing for information at the right moments, until my tongue is loose.

"I wish I could say I've travelled to any of their provinces," Lars says. "I've been to Sebba, but it hardly counts. We barely crossed the border."

I frown. Sebba is in the north-west corner of Patel and doesn't afford easy passage to any territory except the Mir Mountains.

"Where were you headed?"

Lars blushes. "I was only a toddler. My father took me with him on a trip to visit the Rucans."

My mouth gapes as I mentally skim through my knowledge of the distant kingdoms that share our world.

Papa says generations of wizards form the Rucan dynasty, and magic is as common as birds in spring.

"You've been beyond Patel?"

"I wish I could say I remember it."

I drop the subject of the Rucans. If Papa is wrong, I don't want to look like a fool for believing in fairytales. "Visiting Ellos is the farthest I've travelled. I loved the changing landscapes, but the rivers and lakes..."

I shudder at the memory of my endless nausea on Lake Lynton. To my surprise, Lars doesn't react with his usual humour. His body stiffens, and his eyes lack mirth.

"It seems I have stayed too long," Lars says.

I follow his line of sight to the guests who are shaking hands with Tutor Olga before leaving. The Academy's maids collect discarded teacups and half-eaten treats from the rugs and clear the remaining dishes from the table. I step closer to the edge of the pavilion and gaze out at the sky. The sun has climbed to its peak, heating the once cool air. My stomach sinks. Lars cannot make it any clearer that my company is tedious.

"My apologies, Your Highness." I bow my head to cover my blush. "I've bored you with talk of the Academy when the ladies are here for you to form your own judgements."

Lars tuts and gently lifts my chin with his hand. His eyes swallow me, drowning out all thought.

"Call me Lars."

I blink and stumble away from him, creating as much distance as possible without diving into the bushes to escape. I squeeze my eyes shut until my thoughts return to order.

"The other ladies will be furious with me for keeping you from the party, Your Highness."

As I speak, I catch sight of Arabella whispering to Elisabelle and throwing looks over her shoulder towards us. The other ladies at least have the dignity to be subtle.

"They had their fair share when you disappeared."

I chew the inside of my lip and stare up at Lars. "It's not the same."

A glint of mischief lights up Lars's eyes. "Well, if they are determined to take offence anyway..."

Lars snatches my hand from my side and raises it until I can feel his breath dance upon my skin.

"May I?"

My heart leaps. I nod, enthralled by his simple touch. His eyes remain fixed on mine as his lips brush my knuckles.

"It has been a pleasure, as always, Nakoma."

Too stunned to speak, I watch in a daze as Lars joins a group of noblemen and exits the gardens.

CHAPTER
SIXTEEN

A week after the Academy tea party, I'm still thinking about Lars's kiss. The soft brush of his lips against my hand plays on an endless repeat through my mind. I sigh and force myself to focus on the book in front of me. A peal of laughter from the opposite end of the library pulls my attention from the page. I curse Elisabelle's name under my breath, even though only Quinn's laugh ever reaches that volume.

"Still moping?" Uri asks.

I scowl at Uri. "I'm not moping."

Uri rolls her eyes but doesn't argue the point. Unlike myself, Uri has no problems with reading. Her long legs stretch behind her as she lies on the floor of the library. Tia sits cross-legged beside her, book in hand.

"She's definitely moping," Tia says.

I turn my back to them both and scoot my chair closer under the only desk in this corner of the library. My leg bounces under the table. This morning's ride with Kato feels like a century ago. The golden sunlight warming our backs, and the wind rushing across my skin... I dawdled for as long as possible at the stalls to see if Lars would appear, but eventually, I had to return to the Academy.

It was stupid to wait. Nothing can come from us spending time together. Lars is looking for his future queen, and I do not want a husband. Besides, I promised myself I would finish our assigned reading this afternoon. Now, another ten pages feel like agony.

I slam the book shut. "That's enough. I'm going to visit my grandparents."

"Right now?" Tia asks. "Are they expecting you?"

I shrug. "Why not? Tutor Olga says we can spend our rest day however we please."

"At least send a messenger. It would be rude to show up unannounced."

I tuck my chair under the desk. "Fine. I'll send Wish first if it'll make you feel better."

"They're family, Tia," Uri says.

Tia huffs. "Go on, then. I'll tell you the key points if you don't finish the reading when you get back."

I smile my thanks to Tia and hurry out of the library, pausing to say goodbye to Hazel-Mae, who feigns interest in browsing the bookshelves.

I DRUM MY FINGERS ALONG THE SURFACE OF THE DINING TABLE as I wait for Wish to return with my grandparents' reply.

The sound echoes in the empty room, magnifying my boredom, but I can't return to the library. Tia would insist I keep reading until the message arrives. I stand, trailing my fingers along tabletops as I meander through the room and into the connecting kitchen.

The kitchen is twice the size of the dining hall, with rows of spotless marble countertops and gigantic cooking stations. I pause by a nearby oven and inhale the sweet aroma of fresh bread as it mixes with the rich wood smoke. In the corner of the room, a lonely pot of golden curry simmers over a contained flame. An array of spices lines the countertop beside it, each jar labelled with elaborate cursive, but I don't need a label to recognise turmeric. I grin and creep closer. Cook threatened to beat Jadera with her wooden spoon when she stole chocolate from the kitchen last week. Would she notice a missing spice? A voice of reason says she will, yet my hunger for revenge outweighs all logic.

I snatch the spice from the countertop and dart for the connecting door. Elisabelle's room isn't far, but who knows when she'll leave the library. With the turmeric concealed in the pocket of my dress, I slink down the hallways and slip into Embry and Elisabelle's shared room. I lean against the door until it shuts with a click behind me. The room is a mess of discarded shoes and trunks overflowing with accessories. Gowns hang from the bedframes, and the closet doors are flung open. I pad towards the bathroom, my eyes continually flicking back to the door.

A pile of dirty clothes waiting for collection sit by the

entry to the bathroom. I skirt around them, making a beeline for the array of sweet-smelling concoctions that line the bathtub. *Cleanser, toner, body scrub...* I mumble the labels of each bottle as I search for the right one. There. A brightening hair wash. I cast one last furtive glance about the room before twisting the cap free with trembling fingers. Palms slick with sweat, I pull the turmeric from my pocket and dump its contents into the bottle. Visions of Elisabelle rising from her bath with bright orange hair instead of her carefully curated blond fills me with manic delight. I shake the mixture for good measure and replace it along the bath ledge.

Distant footsteps send my heart racing as I retrace my steps back through the room. My legs twitch with the desire to run, but I force my limbs to be steady. I press my ear to the door and wait for the footsteps to pass before fleeing in the opposite direction.

"Lady Nakoma, there you are."

I freeze. My throat constricts as dread pools in my stomach. With the speed of a snail, I turn on my heel to face Perriwick.

"I've been looking everywhere for you," Perriwick continues, his thick, black moustache bobbing as he speaks.

"Sorry," I squeak. My fingers curl protectively around the spice jar, desperately hoping it will escape Perriwick's notice.

"Your grandparents have sent a messenger to lead you to their home."

I breathe a deep sigh of relief.

"He's waiting by the front door."

I smile my thanks to Perriwick, not trusting myself to form the words, before scampering off towards the messenger.

THE SUN'S RAYS CATCH ON THE MESSENGER BOY'S RINGLETS, highlighting the different shades from gold to red. His freckled face splits into a nervous smile that calms my own frayed nerves.

"Skip?" I ask. "Is that you?"

Skip hides his face with a deep bow. "Yes, milady."

Dressed in the plain street clothes that are common in Ellos, I almost don't recognise him.

"Please, just call me Nakoma."

Skip's voice trembles as he speaks, but this time he meets my eyes. "Yes, mi—I mean, Nakoma."

"I thought you worked for the king."

Skip shrugs. "If you want to dream big, work big."

I frown at him. "Doesn't the king pay you enough?"

Skip walks down the steps of the Academy and calls over his shoulder. "We'll be late, Miss Nakoma, if you stand there interrogating me all afternoon."

I grumble under my breath, dump the turmeric jar into a public wastebin, then hurry after Skip. Crowds do not fill the streets today, but Skip still sets an unforgiving pace.

"Apprentices in Arithenos never want for food," I say to Skip's back.

Even as the king's taxes keep rising, the High Priestess keeps watch over us and makes sure no one starves. Anyone can receive daily rations, even though there is barely enough to go around.

"I appreciate your concern, Miss Nakoma, but I'm not hungry. I've clean clothes and a safe place to call home. I'm just not rich like the ladies of the Pink Palace are."

Skip's voice has steadied since the first time I met him two weeks ago. The deep tone is a shock to listen to coming from such a round and boyish face, yet the words have the ring of an adult that I didn't see in Skip before.

Skip points at the houses lining the street as he speaks. "One day, I want a big house to call my own, not just a room at the palace."

Unlike the city centre, where each house presses against the next, these houses are tall and elegant. Courtyards overflowing with greenery welcome guests to each home. I crane my neck to get a better view of the top of the closest house. A man dressed in vibrant colours lounges from the balcony, enjoying the view of the ocean.

"That's a respectable dream," I finally say.

The streets are quiet on this side of town. Muted conversations only reach my ear when I strain for them. The coo of pigeons is the loudest sound other than our own footsteps and the whistle of the wind between buildings.

Skip stops with a flourish in front of a tall blue building that matches the sea more than the surrounding homes. I glance up and count at least four tiers of grand arched windows.

"The home of the Honourable Klaus and Yvette." Skip whistles. "You're lucky to be so well connected."

I press my lips shut and stare at the ornate wrought-iron gate and the lush courtyard beyond. The urge to argue spikes within me, demanding to give voice to the years of bullying I suffered because of my blue eyes.

I rein in my temper. "They're my grandparents."

Skip bows deeply from the waist. "Then perhaps it isn't luck but a blessing."

I blink at Skip, dumbfounded by his unwavering faith that my relationship with the owners of the house must be positive. My hand hovers above the gate. I try to picture my grandparents in Tutor Olga's office. Were they genuinely happy to meet me?

"You should go in," Skip says, his voice gentle and reassuring. "Master Klaus could hardly sit still when he summoned me."

I reach into the fold of my skirt and withdraw an Arithean coin.

"This is for you. Keep it for when you are rich and travelling across Patel to visit me in Arithenos, or trade it here in Ellos, at the marketplace."

Skip accepts the coin with a mischievous grin.

"Thank you, but we'll meet again before I'm rich enough to travel to Arithenos. You'll see."

A familiar pull tugs at my heart. For a moment, I swear I can see Jakob in the mischievous twinkle of Skip's eyes before he takes off down the street. I shove the thought aside for later and step through the front gate.

A sea of green welcomes me into the courtyard. Though each plant is neat and trimmed, the variety of shapes and sizes gives the illusion of a private wilderness. Ivy climbs the columns that stand tall and proud around a central mosaic. The glittering tiles depict a red bird with flaming tail feathers – one I've never seen before.

"Would you care to come inside? We don't bite," a voice calls.

I startle and press a hand to my chest. Klaus waves from the open front door. I step over the bird in the mosaic, not wanting to leave a trace of dirt on the beautiful design.

"How did you know I was here?" I ask.

"Thamsley, our family butler, saw you and thought we might want to know you had arrived."

I pause on the threshold, stunned by the portraits in golden frames lining the hall. Standing beside the door is a man dressed in a tailored black suit, who bows as we enter.

"Thank you, Thamsley. That will be all," Klaus says.

Without sparing Thamsley a glance, Klaus walks off down the hallway. I follow close behind him, trying to keep myself from gaping at the decor.

"It's a phoenix, by the way. They're not native to Patel, but before your mother was born and trade laws changed, you could find one at the markets every blood moon."

My eyes widen as images of a vibrant red bird strutting around Arithenos fill my mind. Father doesn't trade in live goods, but there are always farming animals at the markets in the centre of town. The smell of sheep, goats and cows is almost enough to smother the exotic spices also sold there.

"Why did the law change?"

Pausing under a chandelier, Klaus rubs his chin. Under its light, his face appears longer, like that of a prized hound.

"Well, most of the exotic creatures sold in Ellos were beautiful – a sight to behold. I would visit the markets as a boy to admire them. But others were heartbreaking. Animals kept in cages with a thick layer of excrement as a bed or with skin rubbed raw from shackles." Klaus speaks over his shoulder as he continues to walk. "Eventually, the complaints outnumbered the commendations. In Ellos, we treat animals with respect and kindness. It made little sense to encourage the traders to continue when their actions opposed our morals."

I trail my fingers over the bronze rail of the staircase as we ascend. Klaus takes slow, measured steps, his age apparent with each wheezing breath. I wait for him at the top and watch as he draws himself up, tall and proud once more.

"You can still purchase things like phoenix feathers, but the live trade has ended – at least officially. It's rumoured the marquess's son has a pet miniature dragon, but nobody has seen him in years."

I spy a white rug across the hall with black lightning strikes zigzagging across it. Even from a distance, I can see it is the fur of an animal, not an artist's design.

"Perhaps by the time my generation has children, there will be no trade of animal parts at all. Who says that they source ethically just because we do not see the live animal?"

Klaus looks at me for the first time since I entered the house. After a moment, he acknowledges me with a bow of his head.

"An intriguing thought."

Without further comment, Klaus turns on his heel. We enter a room with a roaring fireplace and an abundance of gold brocade lounges. Huddled close to the hearth is Yvette, dressed in a floral gown that makes the lines of age fade from her face. A low table with a full tea set sits before her.

"Please take a seat," Klaus says.

I step past Klaus and choose the lounge farthest from the heat of the fire without being rude. Already pearls of sweat collect on the backs of my legs, and I wish I'd worn Aunt Fifi's spring dress instead.

"Your home is beautiful," I say to fill the creeping silence. "Especially this room."

Yvette smiles cautiously at me. "Oh, this old parlour. It is a little outdated, but it's just for family."

Klaus takes a seat beside Yvette and pours the tea. Delicate pink flowers and gold details decorate each teacup. Steam floats over the cup, but the tea is the perfect temperature when it touches my lips. My eyes widen in shock. It's sweeter and more floral than the black tea we drink in Arithenos. My tastebuds sing, eager for more. Yvette studies my expression, her teacup frozen in its path to her lips.

"This tea – it's so unusual," I say.

"Unusual in a good way, I hope," Klaus says with an awkward chuckle.

"Oh yes. It's divine. I could drink this all day if I didn't think my stomach would protest."

Yvette sighs. "It was Elaine's favourite."

My cup clatters against its saucer in my haste to put it down. So, this is why they accepted my visit. My joy at escaping the Academy evaporates as a voice whispers *they're using you*. Embarrassment churns the tea in my stomach to acid, even as anger flickers to life beneath my skin. I clasp my hands together in my lap and squeeze until my stomach settles. Two can play at this game. Their influence in Ellos may be the advantage I need to gain an audience for Patel.

Yvette shares a look with her husband before speaking. "Could you... I mean, would it be ok if you told us a little about Elaine? What is she like? Is she happy?"

Klaus raises his eyebrows at me, the same face Mother makes when she wants me to speak. I take a deep breath to fight the impulse to lash out at his audacity. If I want them to like me, I can't tarnish their image of a darling daughter with all the ways Mother embodies my own insecurities. To me, she is my stumpy legs and bright eyes that don't match my Arithean face.

I shift on the lounge, angling my body towards the

portrait hanging at the far end of the room. The young woman is missing Mother's laugh lines, but I still recognise her. I force myself to remember the best parts about Mother. Slowly, the words come to me, and I tell my grandparents about the countless times Mother has tried to be the best parent an Ellos child could want. I weave a story of the love she has for Papa and the place in Arithenos she has carved for herself, despite the prejudice she's faced from others.

"Children still stare at her sometimes, but our neighbours all respect her and keep a close eye on our family when Papa is away trading."

Tears glisten in Yvette's eyes. She sniffles and hurries to snatch up a plate of biscuits.

"Butterscotch cookies, anyone? Cook made them fresh this morning."

Yvette takes a huge bite out of a cookie before I can respond. Klaus doesn't seem to notice, his eyes fixed on the portrait of Mother.

"Elaine is our only child. We tried for more. The infertility is probably my fault. My first wife passed away without conceiving."

Finished chewing her food, Yvette chimes in. "God only blesses a family with the children it needs."

Klaus rests his hand over Yvette's, and she leans into him, quiet once more. Without breaking his gaze from the painting, he tells me about Mother as a little girl. She was spoiled rotten and was quick to throw temper tantrums, but she knew how to charm everyone she met. She was a favourite at school and admired by many. I fidget as he speaks, his endless praise turning my own memories into a foreign land.

"We betrothed Elaine to a lord. Yvette and I arranged it when she was fifteen, after years of enquires to eligible families."

Klaus clears his throat as he speaks, but his voice doesn't lose the husky edge of emotion. His eyes flick back to me, and I sip my tea to smother any comments.

"The women in his family were all blessed with children, and we thought it would be a perfect match for her. Even if she inherited my own issues, the absence wouldn't be noticeable in such a large family."

I force myself to imagine a life where Papa let Mother pick out her ideal man for me. Arranged marriages are rare in Arithenos, but not unheard of. Instead, most women of marriageable age will visit the temple for guidance. It's their choice how they respond to the priestess's advice. This past summer, when I turned seventeen, I begged Papa to let me wait another year. My heart aches at the thought of being told to marry Omarion like Mother has hinted a thousand times.

Yvette is the first to break the silence this time, her voice gentle with concern.

"Arranged marriages might be a tradition for Ellos, but it is more than history that guides us. Our marriages last. Klaus and myself were an arranged match, and it's been fifty years of bliss."

Klaus squeezes Yvette's hand and reassures her with a look that amplifies her point. Even while speaking, Yvette and Klaus share a private bubble of joy. They gravitate to each other the same way I've seen my parents do in a crowded space.

"We feared Elaine didn't know your father well enough to marry him. What if he mistreated her?"

"It doesn't matter now," Klaus cuts in. "We drove away our only child. But now? Well, we're just so pleased to have you here, Nakoma. To have a little piece of Elaine back with us is more than we ever expected."

My chest grows tight as a rush of love surges through me. Is this another ploy to get their daughter back? I chew my bottom lip and stare out the window. As the setting sun turns the world to gold, my mind fills with questions that demand attention. *Have I judged Mother too harshly?* Maybe she is misguided, like Klaus and Yvette.

Yvette opens a narrow drawer well concealed in the table's wood. From it, she pulls a letter sealed with golden wax and the image of a phoenix.

"Would you deliver this to her? Please? More than anything, we want one more chance."

I accept the letter from Yvette as the toll of a grandfather clock resounds through the room. My eyes flick to its face.

"That's the time?" I ask.

The look on Yvette's face kills any hope they will tell me this clock is fast.

"Is anything the matter?" Klaus says.

I stand, my eyes already on the door. "The Academy introduced a curfew."

Klaus nods in understanding. "We will call for

another messenger to run ahead so that we can find an escort."

I shake my head. "Please don't. The road here was straight, and it's barely dusk. I will make it back without trouble."

"Well then, at least let me take you to the door."

Although it is agony to wait for Klaus to plod through the house, I agree. My legs are itching to run by the time we step into the courtyard.

"Today was too heavy," Klaus says.

My hasty farewell dies on my lips. Klaus grasps my arms, spreading warmth through me that makes my eyes water.

"We should not have burdened you with our woes when we want to know you, our granddaughter, better. Will you visit again soon? Our door is always open to you."

I blink rapidly, overwhelmed by the sudden urge to hug him. "That would be wonderful. Thank you."

I hold my head a little higher on the walk back to the Academy. The city streets and colourful buildings I have been admiring since arriving in Ellos also belong to me, in a small way. They are a part of my heritage – the side of me I had no reason to appreciate until now.

CHAPTER
SEVENTEEN

C lass is over for today, but I'm still cooped up inside the Academy library. I sprawl on the floor with Uri and Hazel-Mae, our heads pressed together as we stare at the arched ceiling. A thick rug keeps the autumn chill from creeping in through the hardwood floor, but Uri still has a shawl draped across her legs.

Outside, rain pelts against the windows and turns the world to grey. The drum of rain against the glass echoes through the Pink Palace and drowns out everything except for the people right beside me.

"Did you see the flowers that arrived for Quinn today?" Hazel-Mae asks, stretching each *r* like she stretches out her legs.

"Do you mean the purple irises or the pink roses?"

Tia's question is full of the mock sincerity that is so common in Ellos. I boost myself up so I can see her working at the nearby desk. Her quill dangles from her fingers, but a hint of a smile twists Tia's lips.

"Of course I meant the pink roses! They're divine."

Tia snorts and returns to her calligraphy. Since Tutor Olga compared Tia's penmanship to a barbarian's scrawl, she has been determined to prove Tutor Olga wrong.

"Everyone saw the roses, Hazel-Mae," Uri says.

I let my eyes drift shut and mumble my agreement. Uri's right. Perriwick delivered the roses to Quinn during breakfast. The bouquet was so enormous that he wheeled it in on a silver serving cart.

"I wish someone would send me dozens of roses," Hazel-Mae continues.

I roll onto my stomach and prop myself up on my elbows to get a better look at my friends. Hazel-Mae's waist-length hair fans out around her head and makes her look like a woodland nymph. She only needs a handful of daisies to weave into a crown to complete the look.

"A single rose would be good enough for me," Tia says, "but it depends on who it's from."

I sit up. There's an edge to Tia's voice that I don't recognise. I glance at Hazel-Mae. She's still lounging on her back; the slight wrinkle of her button nose is the only sign that she heard her roommate.

"Is there someone back home?" I ask Tia.

Tia shakes her head. "It's nothing."

"That's not nothing," Uri says.

Tia puts her quill back into the inkwell and twists

around in her seat. "Pa wants me to marry some *lord* if I can't secure the prince."

Hazel-Mae sits up. "It's not just that. He sounds like a male version of Tutor Olga."

Uri gags. "Do you have to marry the prince? Wouldn't any offer of marriage be good enough?"

"I don't know. Pa has this idea in his head that, as the second daughter, it's my job to extend their family's connections through marriage."

"Your pa and my mother would get along," I say. "Mother thinks I'm destined for a horrible, lonely life if I don't get married."

"But your pa? Does he think the same way?" Tia asks.

I swallow past the sudden lump that rises in my throat. "Papa has always encouraged me to chase my dreams. He even bought Kato for me."

Memories of Papa bubble to the surface and fill my heart with homesickness. The first steed the commander assigned me during basic training was unfit for service. The poor mare's joints creaked with arthritis, and her eyes wept with age. Riding her was the commander's ultimate test of my determination. I might have given up if Papa hadn't bought Kato from a travelling Arithean merchant.

"Did you hear that?" Uri asks, distracting me from the past.

I shake my head, but now that I'm listening, the sound becomes clear. Shrill voices trickle past the shelves that separate us from the rest of the library. Tucked away in our own little corner, I'd forgotten we weren't the only ones stuck indoors.

"It sounds like Elisabelle," Tia says.

I listen again, but the sounds don't sharpen. Uri doesn't waste time trying to listen from her spot on the floor and instead creeps along the bookshelves, following the sound.

"Where are you going?" Tia hisses.

Uri shrugs. "I'm bored. If Elisabelle is stirring trouble, I want to watch it unfold. Especially after I missed her tantrum in the dining hall the night her hair turned orange."

Tia grumbles, barely concealing her smile as she joins us to sneak towards the voices. We make our way past shelves Z to Q before finding Elisabelle. She's seated on a brocade lounge facing the central fireplace, the flickering light drawing out the remains of the orange stain in her blond hair. Embry and Arabella flank Elisabelle on the lounge. Across from them, Calypso stands, plucking at her pearl choker.

"Calypso, tell us about your father's pearl farm again," Elisabelle says.

Elisabelle's high-pitched Capital accent grates against my nerves and makes me wince. Still, I drop to a crouch. The leather-bound tombs that fill the shelves provide the perfect cover to watch Elisabelle with her minions.

"Uh, well ... the pearls are some of the best found in Lake Lynton."

"Some of the best," Elisabelle sneers. "Not *the* best? I thought that's what you told us when you first arrived."

Calypso's freckled face grows red as she looks from Embry to Arabella for support. Arabella shifts awkwardly under her gaze and stares at the dancing flames.

"He's the third-highest producer of pearls in all of Patel."

Elisabelle laughs, the sound cruel and mocking.

"Only third? Imagine coming from a province that cares so little about the prince that they send their third-best option."

"It's not like that. The other girls were all betrothed or married."

Elisabelle stands and stalks towards Calypso, who cowers before the fireplace. Embry and Arabella follow in Elisabelle's footsteps, their eyes glued to her for direction.

"So, you're the fishermen's leftovers. The unwanted daughter."

Calypso's bottom lip quivers as tears pool against her lower lashes. "My father..."

Elisabelle holds up a hand, silencing Calypso. "Save it for someone who cares. I've listened to enough of your dribble."

A single heart-wrenching sob rips free of Calypso before she runs from the library. Only Arabella has the decency to look sorry to see her go. I pull away from the shelves, my skin crawling with an invisible layer of grime.

"That was awful," Hazel-Mae says. "We should go find her. Calypso could use a friend right now."

My face scrunches up at the thought of talking to Calypso. "No. Let Quinn or Jadera deal with her."

Tia glares at me. "Nakoma! Don't be so heartless."

I glance at Uri. I can't be the only one thinking it. Uri rocks back on her heels and offers no input.

"Lake Lynton is still a central province, even if Elisabelle doesn't want her," I add. "Calypso would feel much better talking to someone like Quinn or Jadera."

"You don't know that," Hazel-Mae argues, but she's already backing away from the door.

I raise my eyebrows at Tia, daring her to go after Calypso. Nobody moves. Maybe I shouldn't have said it, but I'm certain the ladies from the central provinces think the same about us.

CHAPTER
EIGHTEEN

I let my fingers brush against the hedge that marks the start of the maze as we stroll the garden at lunch. The wilting plants help me breathe easier, after suffocating inside classroom walls every day. With our first exam looming, Tutor Olga expects everyone to spend their free afternoons studying.

"Did you know today is the first of winter?" Hazel-Mae says to no one in particular. She walks ahead of the group, her black hair swishing against her hips with each step.

When nobody replies, Hazel-Mae continues to speak. "That means we've been in Ellos for almost two moons now."

"Two moons and we've only seen the prince once," Tia grumbles.

My heart sinks at the thought. Two whole moons, and I feel as though I have achieved nothing for Arithenos. My body has grown soft without the constant drills and training to keep me in shape. Now, I look like the type of lady Mother wanted me to be. Even my grandparents don't know the real me, despite our constant letters. Olga's study regime includes no time for socialising, but Wish makes exchanging letters easy. I complain to them about our lessons, and in return, Yvette writes a memory of Mother's childhood, or Klaus jots a note about the past kings of Patel.

"I can't believe Tutor Olga can limit our opportunities with the prince from an exam that she writes and administers," Hazel-Mae says. "I thought everyone was supposed to spend time with him?"

"Quality assurance," Uri mutters. "Olga wouldn't want to embarrass the Crown by allowing a heathen into the palace for weekly tea and biscuits."

Hazel-Mae continues to complain as if Uri didn't speak. "We're all here so he can choose a bride. It's so unfair she can destroy our chances based on our knowledge of the king's birthday."

Although the king's birthday won't be on the exam, I can't help but agree with Hazel-Mae. Each night I fall asleep to memories of Lars. The tea party left me with a swirling pit of questions in my mind that I have no way of answering until I see him again. I pluck the last leaves off a low-hanging tree branch and watch as the golden edges crumble easily under my fingers. With each leaf, I try to shove my anxieties aside. They won't help me pass this exam.

"Is Lady Nakoma out here?"

My head shoots up at the sound of my name. Uri

replies before my mouth can form words. She waves over a maid and Skip. They scurry across the lawn, Skip's palace uniform catching the light.

Skip bows when he reaches my side.

"Lady Nakoma, you must come quick. Master Klaus has had a fall and is unwell. He has requested your presence at once."

Every protective instinct flares to life and sends my brain into overdrive. Without a thought for my friends, I rush across the lawn. Even Skip struggles to keep up with my pace. I am out the door and down the street before I have time to consider what I can do for my grandparents. Yet they're family. If they need me, I will be there.

"Wait! Lady Nakoma," Skip calls after me.

"There is no time to lose."

"Please, just a moment. Let me explain. Master Klaus is well."

I freeze midstep. "But you said he had a terrible fall."

"I lied. It was the only reason we could think of to get Tutor Olga to release you from your studies."

Skip rests his hands on his knees, panting. I walk back to his side and drop my voice to a whisper. We are not far enough from the Academy to forget caution.

"Why?"

Skip shrugs. "It's not my place to tell you."

My eyes narrow as I take in his uniform. Someone from the palace has sent him. My heart sings that this must be Lars's handiwork, but my head isn't eager to give in to false hope.

"You must know who sent you."

151

"I received a note detailing my message. It only said to take you to the dressmaker's once I had extracted you from the Academy."

My nose wrinkles at the thought of spending my afternoon of freedom in a dress shop. Recovered, Skip stands back up and leads the way.

"This way, Lady Nakoma, only a little further," Skip says before I can protest.

I follow close behind Skip, unable to keep the spring from my step. Dress shop or not, the fresh air is intoxicating. The ocean breeze leaves a trail of goosebumps across my arms that for once doesn't dampen my spirits. As we walk, the streets grow crowded with women herding their children and the boom of men talking beside storefronts. Their snippets of conversation wash over me without meaning while I search the crowd for a familiar face. Even with his back to us, I recognise Lars's broad shoulders and ink-black hair. He's dressed in the same ordinary clothes that led me to believe he was a commoner, but he still sticks out like a sore thumb. Tall and lean, his dark hair is like a beacon in a sea of blonds and soft browns.

A wild grin that matches the unkept waves of his hair lights up Lars's face when he sees us approach. Happiness bubbles through me until my chest feels light. My head buzzing with questions, I skip the Ellos formalities.

"How did you know to mention Klaus? Do they know as well? Are they here?" I ask.

"I have my ways," Lars says, with a wink at Skip.

Skip bows, his job now done. Without another word, he leaves us under the swaying dressmaker's sign. I'm half tempted to chase Skip down and weasel the answer out of him, but the fight leaves me when I glance back at Lars.

"At least tell me if Klaus knows about your ruse. I would hate for him to be caught in the lie by Tutor Olga."

"Skip is on his way there now to fill them in."

A small sound of surprise escapes my throat before I realise I have nothing to say. Since the tea party, I've dreamed of hundreds of conversations with Lars, yet none of them included awkward silence or the sudden feeling of butterflies filling my stomach.

"I understand you should be safe to stay out until dusk?" Lars asks.

"Yes. Can you?"

"Fredrick and Mikael have mastered the art of lying for me, but I'll still have to answer to Father. He won't be impressed when he realises I've skipped the Minister of Food and Agriculture's presentation on wheat production to the council."

I search my mind for a witty response about trading my manners lessons for his harvest meetings, but each quip seems more awkward and forced than the last. My eyes drift to the ground as I scuff my boot against the cobblestone street. *You are a guardian*, I chide myself, yet that piece of me feels stranded back home. Without my muscles earned through years of training, I'm back to being a lost little girl at her welcoming ceremony.

"I thought I could give you a tour of the city," Lars says.

My tongue grows heavy with doubt, but I force myself to speak. "I would love to see the marketplace."

Oblivious to the turmoil inside me, Lars leads the way down the street, pointing out interesting pieces of architecture. His words pass through one ear and out the other as my mind fixates on the angle of his jaw as he speaks. When Lars gestures to something new, my thoughts linger on admiring the graceful swoop and swing of his arms.

"So, why the marketplace?" Lars asks.

I blink stupidly at Lars for a moment before my brain can focus on his words. "My parents first met at this marketplace."

We stand by the corner of a booth to avoid the rush of the crowd. Merchants try to capture the attention of shoppers by extolling the virtues of their goods. I try to imagine Papa doing the same and luring Mother to his stall.

"For Papa, it was love at first sight."

"Do you believe in love at first sight?" Lars asks.

I tilt my head and meet his curious gaze. "No. It's a ridiculous notion."

Lars's shoulders droop, and my usual scepticism no longer feels like a protective armour. I consider Lars's question again.

"My parents' story is awfully romantic. I loved it growing up, but at some point, it stopped feeling true.

Maybe instead it was fate. I believe what Papa felt was the pull of destiny, not instantaneous love."

"I like that," Lars says, speaking with slow and deliberate words. "I haven't thought about it that way before, but I think you're right."

My heart swells. Although I cannot tell Lars I am a guardian, there is some relief in him understanding me as a person.

"Come on," Lars says. "There's something I want you to try."

As we weave through the crowd, I catch a whiff of garlic so strong it makes my mouth water. Lars leads the way to a stall with a large pot of boiling oil at its centre. We step closer and into the bubble of warmth that surrounds the stall. Sweat stains the man's apron, but his stall is spotless.

"You're in luck. Matheo only comes in winter. I understand your summer is warmer, but even in Ellos, it's too hot for this treat."

"What is it?"

"Golden potatoes. At least, that's what I've always called them." Lars ducks his head to hide the spot of red that colours his cheeks.

Matheo finishes with his last customer, and Lars places an order for us. With quick hands, Matheo fishes out a fresh batch of potatoes from the bubbling oil. The food is then dropped into a tray of powder and tossed until my stomach rumbles.

"What's it coated in?"

"Garlic and cheese." Lars smacks his lips together and kisses the air. "My parents accused me of being addicted to it when I was younger. I would pester them for weeks in autumn. I once begged them to force the cook back then, Mathis, to work at the palace just for me."

I laugh at the thought. With a wicked smile, Lars passes me one of the steaming hot potatoes. I cup my hands around the paper-wrapped treat, enjoying its warmth. To my horror, Lars finishes his golden potato in three giant bites.

"Careful not to burn your mouth," Lars says, even as he licks the grease from his fingers.

I blow on the potato and take a tentative bite. My eyes grow wide. I devour the rest of the potato faster than Lars did.

"That's not just garlic," I say with reverence. "Matheo has something else in that golden goodness that he's not telling you."

Lars grins. "If you think that's good, you had better try Manon's jerky chips."

~

THE AFTERNOON PASSES IN A BLINK. EVERYWHERE I TURN, there is something new to discover, or more culinary delights to enjoy. We eventually leave the market to stroll along the harbour. The setting sun sparkles against the ocean, transforming it into liquid gold. Boats dot the horizon and remind me of how vast the world is outside of Patel. Yet it's our kingdom that sits heavily on my mind.

"Do you know much about the conditions of trade and tax between provinces in Patel?"

Lars winces at my sudden change of conversation, but I don't back down. Hope of speaking to the king or his advisors directly is as distant as the ships on the horizon. Lars is my best chance.

"Perceptions of Ellos are very negative in Arithenos, and while I've grown to love parts of Ellos, I still understand the concerns of my home."

The words tumble out of me, formal and strange. I have repeated them a hundred times to myself, but they feel unnatural with Lars. I square my shoulders as Lars studies my face. A blush creeps into my cheeks.

"I'm not sure if I'm the best person to make such inquires to," Lars finally says.

It's my turn to flinch. His words leave no room for discussion. Lars's lips press together, and his eyes grow clouded. For a moment, he is the kind of prince I imagined meeting – cold and distant in his arrogance.

Defeated, I offer a feeble apology. "I didn't mean to offend you."

Lars softens and becomes the man I know once more. "No, I must apologise. Please tell me why Aritheans are angry with Ellos."

I twist my hands together, pinching and squeezing the skin in thought. Tutor Olga's diplomacy class was all about acknowledging the feelings of others to create empathy for your own case. Lars reaches down and covers my hands with his. Warmth seeps into me, easing my frayed thoughts.

"Arithenos has been taxed heavier each season for the last two decades. We're struggling to afford many of the goods offered from other provinces because our exports no longer cover those expenses. At first, our High Priestess took on this burden so that our farmers would not feel it, but now everyone can feel the pressure."

Lars rubs his chin, drawing my eye to a faint line of stubble. "The economy is an ever-changing beast. All the provinces have experienced an increase in tax since the flood of Lake Lynton."

"And I could understand that if this tax increase lasted for a year until Unke and Petra's crops recovered. Instead, the council has announced a tax increase for Arithenos every year for the last two decades."

Lars runs a hand through his hair. "Well ... that's because there were bush fires devastating Eyre before the floods."

I shake my head, rejecting Lars's deflections. "All provinces experience hardship, but instead of sharing the load, Arithenos has become a target. We've always protected the southern borders. Our guardians patrol all of Patel, and even now you have called upon us for guardians to defend the Capital while we're at the Academy. I believe your father has forgotten that we already pay our tax in service to the Crown. To ask for more is to deplete the strength of our guardians."

When I finish speaking, the only sound left is the

splash of waves lapping against the docks. Lars stands with his hands clasped behind his back. I follow his line of sight out to sea. I gulp as doubt sets in. *Did I say too much about guardians?*

"If I have overstepped the bounds of our ... friendship, then I apologise, but I cannot apologise for expressing the truth for Arithenos."

"Our friendship," Lars repeats. "Tell me, is there a guardian that waits for you back home? Is that where these feelings stem from?"

Frustration makes me curl my hands into fists. Did he not hear a word I said? I almost yell in protest.

"No!"

Light returns to Lars's face, and his body grows animated once more.

"Then it's settled. I'll speak to Father, but I think it would be best if you explain the situation yourself."

My jaw drops in stunned silence. The fire in me cools to a mere ember, doused by Lars's quick change of heart.

"Perhaps some of the other provinces should like to join the hearing," Lars says. "It's clear that it has been too long since we have listened to our own people."

"Thank you," I mumble, when my brain can finally process his words.

Lars walks with a spring in his step, as if propelled by his speech. "I can't promise it will be soon, but I'll be clear that we should hold the hearing before the end of winter. That way we can hope for better relations before the Academy closes in spring."

I hurry to keep up with Lars. My short legs are used

to working hard to keep up with the men in my platoon, but never while also trying to process such news. Wish is fast, and the winter frost is yet to arrive, but I'll have to act quick for the High Priestess to advise me in time.

Lost in my own thoughts, I don't recognise the change in the streets until the pink walls of the Academy are visible over the townhouses. The sun's last rays wash the already vibrant buildings in rose gold. I turn to Lars, and his eyes flick away from me.

"Thank you again for this afternoon, but more for listening."

"The pleasure is mine, Nakoma."

More words climb up my throat, but I forget how to speak. The fading light urges me to hurry back. Yet, at the same time, the golden glow encourages me to stay. I stare at Lars, willing him to look at me and understand. Then he does, and it's like his green gaze has swallowed me whole. Lars closes the short distance between us, and my breath escapes in a silent prayer. My body sways towards him. Every nerve begs to pull him closer. Lars leans in, and I turn my cheek in time to catch his lips.

I stumble away from Lars.

"I'm sorry," I mumble. "I have to go."

I run before I can see the hurt on Lars's face. He doesn't bother to call after me. Tears pool in the corners of my eyes. I swipe them away with the palm of my hand before they can fall. Lars doesn't know me. The real Nakoma spends every day in the saddle with a sword on her hip, not trapped in pretty frocks. Lars doesn't want to kiss the real me. He *shouldn't* want to kiss the real me. Lars deserves to choose someone who won't run off to work as a guardian, but the thought of him kissing someone else doesn't make me feel any better.

~

URI IS CURLED UP WITH A BOOK WHEN I RETURN TO OUR ROOM. She perks up at the sight of me and flicks her night braid over a shoulder.

"How is..."

I silence Uri with a look. My heart hammers to the same tempo as the march of my feet as I cross the room. I slump into the desk chair and whip out fresh sheets of paper. The blank space calls to the hurricane of thought in my mind. Perhaps writing things down will help quell the storm.

"Tutor Olga was almost hysterical when you left without permission this afternoon," Uri says.

I put down my quill and watch Uri. She fluffs her white nightdress and tucks her feet under it.

"Once we explained the situation, she calmed immediately. She even suggested sending a basket of baked goods to Klaus to aid his recovery."

Uri's words are delicate, but there is still a hook buried in them, waiting for me to bite. I sigh and turn in my seat.

"Klaus is unharmed. It was a rouse created by Prince Antonio to help me escape for an afternoon."

Uri's black eyes bulge, and her jaw drops. I hold up a

hand before she can ask a single question.

"That's all I want to say about it tonight. I have a lot to think about."

Uri bites her lip. I count in my head, hoping my silence will encourage her to do the same. At ten, she nods and turns back to her book. As I pick the quill back up, my fingers tremble until the moment it hits the paper. Words bloom across the page, explaining every moment with the prince. I try to describe how I feel, only to write the questions that have plagued me since the High Priestess gave me my assignment. *What if I love him?* I blot out the word love and replace it with *care for*.

At the end of the note, I write a last request. *Tell me what to do, Mother.* Before I can second-guess myself, I go back to the top of the page and address it to her. There's no room left to go back and apologise for every time I criticised Ellos. I can only hope that Mother will understand how much I wish she was here now to guide me.

I fold the letter carefully and seal it with wax. As it dries, thoughts of Mother and Papa cloud my head. Papa singing Mother's praises even when she is sick and snotty. Mother planting a kiss on Papa's cheek moments after an argument. *But that's not what I want, is it?* I can't throw away my life as a guardian for a chance to be admired. To be loved.

There are still five moons until the Academy will deem any of us a suitable bride for the heir of Patel. Wish could deliver my letter within a week if she travelled without rest. I stroke the soft feathers of her chest and know I won't ask her to do it. As much as my heart screams this is an urgent matter, I know better. I tuck the letter from my grandparents and my own letter to Mother in the pouch that Wish will carry, then sit down with a fresh sheet of paper.

Within the hour, I write my final letter, seeking advice from the High Priestess, and send Wish off into the night. My hand aches from writing, but my chest feels lighter with someone else to share the burden. I can only hope it will be enough to allow me to sleep tonight.

CHAPTER
NINETEEN

The narrow hallway outside the classroom is alive with the hum of whispers and the heat of our bodies. All ten of us gather in the cramped space, waiting for the exam to begin. My stomach rumbles, complaining that it didn't receive breakfast this morning, yet the idea of food causes the sting of bile to rise in my throat. Beside me, Hazel-Mae and Tia take turns repeating the past kings of Ellos to Uri.

"I just want it to be over," I say.

Tia frowns. "I would rather it be next week."

"Or next moon," Hazel-Mae says.

I chew on the inside of my cheek until the pain chases away my fear. "I hate the pressure. If it was already over, I could eat without throwing up."

Uri's eyes linger on the door to the classroom as she nods. "It's a lot to pin our hopes on just one exam."

"It's ridiculous," I grumble.

Hazel-Mae sighs and cups her hands over her chest.

"Maybe. But the prince is worth it. He's so dreamy. Better than I thought any Ellos man could be."

Tia hums and smiles to herself. "If only. I would sell my left leg to pass this exam so I can meet more of the courtiers. Expand my options."

"Your leg?" Uri asks, her eyebrows raised in shock.

Tia laughs. "Another expression, Uri. I've heard the maids say it about Cook's chocolate cake."

I bite my lip. The words to argue with Tia rest on the tip of my tongue. Without my left leg, I wouldn't be able to ride Kato. Life would be misery. But maybe it's different for her. At least if I fail here, I still have my life as a guardian to return to.

"Prince or no prince, this exam is the only way I'm going to get close enough to the members of the king's council. Froi could use a friend in the palace," Uri says.

I try not to wince at the reminder I never told Uri that Lars has already promised to arrange a hearing for Arithenos.

A hush falls over us as the distant click of Tutor Olga's heels echoes down the hallway. She swings the classroom door open without ceremony, and we file in silently under her watchful gaze. My stomach sinks, weighed down with endless what-ifs. I drop into my seat and stare at the page in front of me. The bell chimes to start the test. I flip over the paper and lift my quill. My racing heart slows with each question. Every answer comes easily. A rush of air escapes my lips as I smile. I can do this.

AS THE DAY STRETCHES TO NIGHT, MY CONFIDENCE WANES. Nobody has seen Tutor Olga since the exam except for Quinn, who was brave enough to peek into her office. Word spread quickly through the dining hall that Olga was still at her desk, deep in thought.

"Perhaps our answers were so far from expected that the papers are difficult to mark?" I say.

I twist the fabric of my skirt in my hands, creating deep wrinkles that will make the maids curse. Hazel-Mae shakes her head at me and takes a delicate sip of her soup.

"Just two hours ago, you were discussing with Uri the answers to questions that Hazel-Mae and I can't even remember," Tia says. "Try to stop thinking about it. You need to eat. Tutor Olga might not finish until tomorrow."

Hazel-Mae nods in agreement but doesn't speak. She takes another white bun from the centre of the table and breaks it into bite-size pieces to dunk in her soup. I stare at the bowl in front of me and wish I could have half of Hazel-Mae's appetite. My nerves have turned my stomach to lead. Not even the heavenly smell of fresh bread is enough to make it rumble.

Before I can force myself to finish a single spoonful, my ear catches the telltale clicks of Olga's heels. I bolt upright in my seat and glance around the room.

"What is it?" Tia asks.

"She's coming," I whisper.

The clatter of spoons against bowls quickly dies as

ladies at nearby tables hear her approach as well. Olga stands in front of the serving station and faces the scattered tables of the dining hall. Her eyes flick between faces and rest on no one.

"Good evening, ladies," Tutor Olga says.

Olga pauses, waiting for us to chorus our reply. "Good evening, Tutor Olga."

"There are few students who deserve my congratulations tonight, though I must thank you all for participating in the exam."

My fingernails cut crescent moons into my palms. The pain does little to distract me from Olga's choice of words. *Few* students.

"The following students have demonstrated their aptitude for court life and may attend the first weekly visit to the palace tomorrow. Congratulations Lady Elisabelle, Lady Quinn, Lady Arabella and Lady Uri."

I join the others as we clap politely for our peers. As soon as Tutor Olga exits, the dining room erupts into hushed conversation. Hazel-Mae pushes the remains of her meal away. Her chin wobbles as tears pool in her eyes.

"Oh, Hazel." Tia wraps her arms around Hazel-Mae's shoulders, even as her own eyes glisten with tears. "We'll be ok. You'll see. In a few weeks, we'll retake the test and ace it."

I stare at the cold soup in front of me. A tear drops into the bowl, and I watch as the ripples spread. Tutor Olga's words echo through my mind, a constant reminder that this is happening. I squeeze my eyes shut and slump in my seat. I failed. *How can I be so stupid?*

Uri squeezes my shoulder, breaking my train of thought. "Let's get out of here. Nobody has an appetite, so we might as well go."

Hazel-Mae makes a choking sound behind her hand as she struggles to contain herself. Tia pulls Hazel-Mae to her feet and guides her from the room. I trail after them, blinking hard to squash my tears as Uri leads us back to our bedroom.

"Something is very wrong," Uri says, as soon as the door clicks shut behind her. "Those results can't be true."

Tia helps Hazel-Mae onto my bed before flopping down beside her. I sit at their feet and pull my legs to my chest.

"Easy for you to say," I grumble. "You've passed. Tutor Olga's marks are final."

Uri paces the floor as she tries to explain herself. "Aside from Elisabelle, all the chosen ladies are not a target for the prince, not by Ellos standards. Think about it. I'm not conventionally attractive. I'm too tall, and my nose looks like a beak."

Tia crosses her arms and frowns. "Don't say that, Uri. You're beautiful the way you are."

Uri acknowledges her with a tilt of her head before continuing. "Regardless, I make no secret of my heart belonging to diplomacy. Then there is Arabella. She has been making moon eyes at Calypso since we first arrived."

I dry my eyes against the hem of my dress and frown

at the mark they leave behind. The puzzle pieces of Uri's argument slowly blend in my mind until a clear image of injustice forms.

"Quinn already has a suitor," I say. "She's received flowers every week since the tea party."

Hazel-Mae sniffles, drawing my attention back to her. Her eyes are puffy and red but lit with fire.

"Enough of this," Hazel-Mae interrupts. "I've had enough. We can talk about it tomorrow, but tonight I need to rest. I don't want to hear another word about that test."

Shocked into silence, I stand as Hazel-Mae storms out of the room. Tia glances at Uri briefly before following, calling out Hazel-Mae's name.

"You're on to something."

Uri's intelligent eyes light up with the thrill of a good riddle, but I shake my head, stopping Uri before she can launch another theory. Uri might be right, but tonight, my heart can't handle the glimmer of hope she is offering.

"I have to agree with Hazel-Mae. I just need tonight to process all this."

I leave to change into my nightclothes in the adjoining bathroom before Uri can argue. Somehow, it is easier to wallow in my self-pity than to take the chance of believing in Uri's theory. At least for tonight.

TWENTY

The next morning, Tia and Hazel-Mae arrive at our dorm room before breakfast, carrying an emerald-green gown.

"I thought you might like something special to mark the occasion," Tia says.

With Hazel-Mae's help, Tia drapes the gown over Uri's bed. Uri twists the end of her sleeping braid in her hands and stares at the dress. Like all of Tia's clothes, it's the finest silk and shimmers in the morning light.

"You might as well try it on." Tia nudges Uri with her elbow. "We're not going anywhere special today."

Uri grimaces at the comment but gathers the dress into her arms and disappears into the adjoining bathroom. A few moments later, she re-emerges with a barely concealed smile. Unlike her dress from the tea party, this gown brings out the best in Uri and transforms her into a unique beauty.

"Give us a twirl," I say.

Uri beams as the gown flutters around her, its bell sleeves gracefully trailing her every move. It's a perfect fit, thanks to Uri's and Tia's similar tall and slender frames.

Hazel-Mae ushers Uri over to the desk chair. "Let me do your hair."

I give Tia's hand a gentle squeeze as we watch Hazel-Mae work her magic. Her hands deftly pin Uri's hair into artful loops that give the illusion of curls while Uri speaks.

"I can't stop thinking about those test results. If anyone should have passed, it would be Nakoma, not me."

Hazel-Mae freezes momentarily before carefully saying, "There were an awful lot of questions on court culture and etiquette on the paper."

"Exactly! Ouch—"

Hazel-Mae tugs Uri's hair until her head is straight once more. "Hold still."

"Sorry. We all know my strengths lie in political history, not present day."

Tia plonks herself down onto the nearest bed and stares at the ceiling. "We know that, but the other ladies think you're the smartest person here."

"That's beside the point. The thing is, Nakoma should have done better than me on that type of exam question."

Uri's words reopen last night's wounds, making them ache anew. I glance to Wish for comfort, but her head still droops in sleep. With each steady rise and fall of her chest, I slowly push aside my pain until I can focus on the truth. Uri's right. I shouldn't have failed. But I can't dwell on it right now. Uri deserves to enjoy her day at the palace, regardless of who's with her.

"We better hurry," I finally say. "You still need to eat breakfast before you leave."

Hazel-Mae steps away from Uri and curtsies. "My lady."

The combination of Hazel-Mae's and Tia's touch has left Uri glowing. Without her hair slicked back, her usually sharp features soften into those of a lady worthy of any prince.

I grin. "If someone picked you for being 'less' pretty, then they are going to be very disappointed."

"Thank you," Uri says, blushing as she quickly hugs Hazel-Mae and Tia.

URI EATS HER FOOD IN A RUSH BEFORE TUTOR OLGA CALLS HER to leave. I look up from the muffin I have been tearing into bite-size pieces and watch as she joins Quinn, Arabella, and Elisabelle. Quinn's short hair has been curled into waves that soften her boyish features. She talks animatedly to Arabella, who looks less than pleased in a dress that must weigh a tonne, yet it is Elisabelle who holds my attention. The bodice of her dress sparkles with gemstones worthy of a ball. She holds her head high as she saunters out of the room, slowly enough for everyone to see her smirk.

As the group departs, the air shifts in the dining hall. Smiles are few and far between at each table, and the conversations lack the joy of laughter. I push my plate towards Hazel-Mae, offering her the dissected remains of my muffin.

Tia sighs. "I wish I knew where I went wrong."

Her words spark a light within me. My eyes flick between Hazel-Mae and Tia, both of whom stare at the table with sad, distant eyes.

"What if we have a look at the tests?" I whisper. "We need to know our mistakes if we want any hope of passing the next exam."

Hazel-Mae says, "I suppose Olga might show us them in class next week..."

I shake my head, but Tia speaks first. "Tutor Olga isn't that sort of teacher. Next lesson will just be her chance to criticise us for being so stupid."

"And she isn't here now. It would only be a peek," I say.

Tia lifts her head from her hands and gapes at me.

"You want us to sneak into her office?"

I shrug. "Why not? It's our exams. We deserve to know."

Hazel-Mae stops eating and pushes the food around on the plate. "What if we get caught?" she asks, her voice small and afraid.

"It's a Sunday," I reason. "Most of the staff have the day off, and none of them are going to care that much about what we are doing when Olga isn't here to rouse on them."

Tia stands. Her eyes skim the room. "We should go now, while the others are still eating."

I smile for the first time since leaving the dorm room this morning. With soft footsteps, we abandon our breakfast and leave the dining hall. Tutor Olga's office is on the other side of the Academy, but we don't cross paths with any of the maids on our way. The dorms are already clean, and the remaining staff are all busy in the kitchen.

We pause before the oak door of Olga's office. I reach for the handle, my breath caught in my throat. If it's locked, then the next moon of study will be agony with no guidance. With a soft groan from its hinges, the door gives way to us. I smile and slip inside, Hazel-Mae and Tia close behind me.

Everything is exactly the way it was when I first met my grandparents. The room is immaculate, from the leather couch to the polished serving table, except for the pile of papers stacked on Olga's desk. Drawn to them, I skirt around the wooden chairs and lift the first page. Handwritten answers to the exam questions fill the sheet, but I can't find a single mark against them.

"Here." I pass a bundle off the pile to Tia and Hazel-Mae. "See if you can find your paper."

A frown creases my brow as I search through the rest of the pile. I find Uri's exam first and scour it for any sign of Olga's looping handwriting. Nothing. Uri's scratched responses fill the page without a single tick or mark from Olga. My mind races.

"Do those papers have any results on them?" I ask, even as my gut tells me the answer.

"Nothing," Tia says.

Hazel-Mae's hands shake as she flips a paper over again and again. "It's exactly the same as when I handed it in yesterday."

"Maybe she marked them on a separate page?" Tia suggests.

Tia steps behind the desk and rummages through each drawer. I stare at Uri's paper in my hands. Anger makes my fingers itch to tear it in two. I grit my teeth and drop it back onto the pile.

"She never marked them," I growl.

Hazel-Mae winces and glances at the closed door. "Maybe we should go..."

"No," Tia and I say in unison.

The pounding of blood in my ears replaces the sounds of the Academy. Trusting that Hazel-Mae is watching the door, I help Tia search the last few drawers. Old ink pots and extra quills fill the first drawer. I open another to find spare sheets of paper. I flick through the pages, my eyes skimming for any sign of a marking scheme. *There...* Something different is wedged between the sheets. I sigh, realising it is just an open envelope.

"What's that?" Tia asks. She abandons her own drawer and pulls out the envelope.

"Nothing—"

The words die on my lips. A single banknote with the Ellos crest drifts to the floor.

"Money?"

"Holy heavens," Tia whispers. "This is a small fortune."

Hazel-Mae joins us at the desk as Tia counts the notes. "That's enough to feed an entire village for at least a moon."

"It's certainly more than an Academy tutor would earn in a season, right?" Tia asks.

I nod as my mind quickly calculates how long it would take to earn that money as a guardian. Tutor Olga's role is important to the future of the kingdom, but surely not that priceless.

"Someone bribed Olga to not mark those exams," I say.

"You don't know that," Hazel-Mae says.

"No, I don't, but it makes an awful lot of sense. We can't find a single shred of evidence that Olga marked these exams, and we already have doubts about those who passed."

"Maybe she's really good at saving money?" Hazel-Mae suggests, but her voice lacks conviction.

I stare at the envelope, but it's Elisabelle's opulent dress that fills my mind. This morning, she looked as if she had won a game that only she knew we were playing. Hazel-Mae is right. There is no proof to tie anyone to the unmarked exams. I throw my hands up in defeat and storm away from the desk in a huff. Something has to be done. We can't let Olga hold us hostage under the pretence of a failed exam.

"You must see it the same way I do?" I plead with Tia.

"Elisabelle is ruthlessly competitive, and wealthy enough to bribe half the kingdom."

"Even if I did, we have just as much evidence that Uri bribed Olga to fake the exam results," Tia says.

I start to protest, but Tia holds up a hand to stop me.

"Think of our diplomacy class. Your arguments are all based on personal experience. If you try to accuse Elisabelle of anything, she'll use it against you."

"Then we take the blank exam papers with us and show the others before Olga comes back. They deserve to know they didn't stand a chance."

"It's not just Tutor Olga we need to watch out for," Tia replies. "It would only take one maid for us to get caught."

Tia and Hazel-Mae don't meet my eye, and their silence is suffocating. A wave of homesickness washes over me. Arithenos has systems of power, and guardians are trained to follow orders, but we would never allow corruption to take root in our land. Justice, peace and security should always be our priority.

"There has to be a way to make this right," I say.

Tia chews her bottom lip and flicks absentmindedly through the pile of exams. If Omarion was here, he would know the exact words to bolster their courage. All I've ever done is follow him with bow, sword, and dagger. But he's not here, and it's up to me to make this right.

"What if we tell the others without showing them the exams?" I suggest. "We can spread the word without jeopardising our own position at the Academy."

Tia's head bobs slowly as she thinks. "We'll do it like Quinn when she peeked at Olga while she was busy. We can tell them we checked the papers but found no exam marks. Leave it up to them to draw their own conclusions."

Tia quickly returns the desk to order and straightens the pile of exams. Excited to have her on board, I try to join her, but she stops me with a gentle hand on my shoulder.

"You should probably sit this one out, Nakoma."

My eyes flick from Tia to Hazel-Mae, who can barely look at me. I try not to let it sting. Without further discussion, we finish tidying the room and leave after checking the hallway for servants.

Most of the other ladies are still in the dining hall when we arrive. I stand back and watch as Hazel-Mae and Tia approach each lady. Despite their differences to the ladies of the central provinces of Patel, Hazel-Mae and Tia are welcome at their table. From the looks on their faces, the others believe them too. I bite my lip and know that it wouldn't be the same for me. Hazel-Mae's and Tia's sweet dispositions are easier to love than Uri's and my harsh honesty. But it's not about me. Pushing aside my bruised ego, I watch my friends with pride. Today won't earn me a promotion, but I know today I acted like a true guardian.

CHAPTER
TWENTY-ONE

Winter in Ellos brings endless days of clouds thick and heavy with the promise of rain. As the trees outside bend with the wind, I watch from my bed and ache for Arithenos's warmer winter. At least for now, the rain is only a threat.

Uri and the others left for the palace over an hour ago, and all I have done since then is lie in my bed, hiding from the cold. Spread across the quilt in front of me are the letters from Mother and the High Priestess that arrived last moon. I smooth out the lines in Mother's crumpled letter and reread it for the hundredth time.

"It is clear there will be no solution without heartache."

My voice echoes in the empty room. The hollow sound is as frustrating as I imagine hearing the words firsthand would be. But the last few lines of the letter are enough to cool my temper.

"Yet, in the quiet moments before dawn, when the

world is still, your heart is speaking. Listen to it and learn to trust it. Your heart will be a better guide than I can ever be."

I blink back the sudden rush of emotion that comes from knowing Mother trusts me to make the right choice. If only my heart would start speaking. I fold Mother's letter and slip my hand between the mattress and bedframe. Cold metal greets me as my fingers brush against the engraved length of my dagger. The touch alone is enough to chase away the ache of homesickness and replace it with certainty. The High Priestess chose me for the Academy for a reason. I just have to see Lars again. But according to Tutor Olga, I'm still a backwater barbarian who hasn't earned her place at the Sunday luncheons.

I bolt upright. There is someone with enough connections to pull strings within the Academy. I scoot out of bed and pull out a fresh scrap of paper from the desk. Within minutes, I'm blowing the ink dry on a brief note to my grandparents, informing them of my intention to visit. I fold the scrap of paper and attach it to Wish. She blinks her wide, sleepy eyes at me as I scratch the feathers beneath her beak. As soon as she's alert, Wish dives out of the window and disappears from sight. I don't waste time before following her, only stopping to collect my cloak and to tell Perriwick where I will be.

Few people brave the weather today. As I hurry towards my grandparents' house, I can't help but count the little white flags hanging from the windows. Lars explained in a letter they are to draw in good luck for his sister, Tulia, who is unwell. In this weather, I can believe it too. The fabric squares are the only points of light in all the winter gloom. I hope they work. While the princess is sick, the king will only meet for matters of extreme urgency.

When I arrive at my grandparent's home, Thamsley is waiting in the doorway with a silver box in his hands. Wish perches on the coatrack behind him and watches him intently. As I step into the courtyard, Thamsley bows with a stiff back.

"Welcome, Lady Nakoma," Thamsley says. "Master Klaus is away from home today, but Yvette would be delighted to greet you in the upper drawing room."

Wish squawks at Thamsley, her eyes never leaving the box. The faintest glimmer of a smile flicks across his lips as he carefully hands Wish a slice of raw meat from it. The treat disappears in an instant. Satisfied, Wish launches off the coatrack and back towards the Academy. Thamsley changes his gloves and gestures for me to follow him to the family drawing room.

"Nakoma," Yvette exclaims as I enter the room. "It's so lovely to see you in person again."

I cross the room to join Yvette near the fireplace. She clasps my hands in hers and kisses the air on either side of my face. I blush at her warm greeting but do not pull away.

"Sorry. I should've come sooner."

I stare at the floor as I speak, guilt turning my cheeks pink. Part of me wants to explain that Kato needs me when I can spare the time, but even that isn't the full truth. I need a favour.

"How have you been?" I ask instead. "Thamsley said Klaus is out today. Has he been busy?"

Yvette is happy to brush aside my apology and gently tugs me onto the couch with her. She pours us both tea before speaking. The drink's floral aroma mixes with the deep undertones of a wood fire.

"Oh, he's visiting some old friends of ours today. I would usually go with, but this weather is stirring a terrible headache."

"Why didn't you say? I should leave you to your peace and solitude." I try to stand, but Yvette's hand is firm upon my wrist.

"Pish posh. You're family. I'm only unfit to visit those who would likely make the sting of pain worse."

I nod and chew the inside of my cheek to avoid saying something rude. Words clatter about my brain as I try to remember how much small talk is polite in Ellos. *Is it too soon to mention my own complaints?*

"Do you have a remedy for your headaches, or is rest enough to cure them?"

Yvette rolls her eyes in a very unladylike fashion. "Oh, come now, Nakoma, why did you truly come for a visit?"

My jaw drops for a moment before I recover and reply sheepishly. "The weather is too unpredictable to take Kato out beyond the palace fields."

"And?"

"I was hoping you might have some advice for me."

Yvette places her teacup onto the serving table and leans towards me. "What's the matter, dear?"

"I'm sick of being stuck at the Academy while the other ladies get to spend the day with Prince Antonio, all because of that cursed exam."

"When was the last time you saw him at an Academy function? Not the tea party, surely."

I make a noise of confirmation and enjoy the outrage that plays across Yvette's face.

"You know the exam I keep studying for? Our tutor uses it to determine who's ready to attend the weekly visits to the palace. But it's rigged."

"Are you certain?"

"No matter how hard I try, I can't pass it. We don't get feedback either. Tutor Olga refuses to return past exams and simply announces the results instead."

Yvette huffs, but otherwise remains silent. The clear horror on her face is enough encouragement to speak my mind.

"That's not the worst of it. After our last exam, only one new student passed."

I don't add that this student was Embry, another friend of Elisabelle's. To Uri, this was just another reason for suspicion, but I don't want to spread rumours of a potential bribe to Yvette. Not yet.

Yvette clicks her tongue against the roof of her mouth three times as she delicately clasps and unclasps her hands in her lap. My stomach does a nervous flip as my mind whispers that she's mad at me for not trying hard enough. Eventually, she rests her hand over my knee, stilling my jittering legs.

"Let me look into it."

My chest deflates with a rush of relief. "Thank you."

For a few moments, I enjoy the crackle and snap of wood burning in the fireplace. Although it's raining, the sky seems brighter now there is someone to check the legitimacy of our results. I take a long sip of my tea and enjoy its warmth.

"It may sound odd, but I think I am one of the luckier ones at the Academy."

"Oh?" Yvette raises an eyebrow and peers at me over her teacup.

"The prince asked Uri to deliver letters to me each week after their visit, so I haven't missed out entirely."

I blush, though there are no embarrassing details in our correspondence. Most of the time Lars writes about the appeals he's read or his latest meeting with a stuffy official. Uri is happy to help, but I can't imagine going from lady to simple messenger girl.

Yvette stirs her tea with a tiny silver spoon. I've mentioned in our correspondence that I met Lars before our introduction at the tea party, but I'm sure Yvette has questions she isn't asking.

"I suppose that is something. Wouldn't you prefer to speak face to face?"

"Of course."

My answer is immediate. If Uri or I are caught, who knows what Tutor Olga would do. To her, these letters are an unjust reward for a pupil who continues to fail. However, it is easy to convince myself that I am not betraying Lars's trust when it's only letters. I can be honest about myself while steering clear of my life as a guardian.

Yvette takes my growing silence as a signal to redirect the conversation. "So, which ladies have permission to visit the palace?"

I count out the five women on my fingers as I speak.

"Lady Uri of Froi, Lady Arabella of Twynton, Lady Elisabelle of Unke, Lady Embry of Petra, and Lady Quinn of Inja."

Yvette frowns and rests her teacup back in its saucer.

"Lady Elisabelle? How odd that I haven't heard that name before. Who are her parents?"

"Some viscount or baron with too much money." I scrunch my nose, thinking of Elisabelle's ridiculous dress on the first visit to the palace.

"Strange... One would think that the duke's daughter, Lillianna, would be at the Academy. She is the correct age, after all."

Yvette quickly brushes aside the thought and continues to chat about the other eligible women of Unke, yet my mind lingers on her words. They sit heavily in my stomach and cast a shadow over me. I try to keep up with her conversation, but it's no use. As soon as I drink the cold dregs of my untouched tea, I excuse myself for the afternoon. Whatever peace Yvette's assurance of checking the exams had brought ended with the simple mention of a name. Lillianna.

CHAPTER

TWENTY-TWO

The first rays of sunlight are seeping through the curtains when I wake from another nightmare. My heart races, but the dream had no blood or horrors of a battlefield. Rather, a lingering sense of dread crept through each thought. I stare at the ceiling and try to blink away the image of the faceless girl – the duke's daughter – that is keeping me awake. Lillianna.

Unable to stand it anymore, I climb out of bed and make myself comfortable at the desk. The quill calls to me. I write quickly, before I can change my mind. With each word, I try to channel Tia's perfect manners to introduce myself, and Hazel-Mae's gentle touch to ask about Lillianna. As the wax cools on the sealed letter, my head already feels clearer. It's worth it, even if he doesn't reply.

Wish dives out the window as Tia bursts into the

room. Hazel-Mae is hot on her heels, still dressed in her nightgown. I freeze by the windowsill and stare at both of them.

"You'll never believe the news!" Tia exclaims.

Uri throws her arm over her face and mumbles from beneath it. "I don't want to know."

"Yes, you do," Tia argues. Her hair cascades down her back, free from its usual braids. The loose waves make me run a hand through my bed-hair to tame the morning frizz.

"The results of both exams are on the board outside the classroom. Everyone has passed."

"What?!" I screech.

"Quinn was there when the results went up. She said a royal tutor came to cross mark the exams and found an error in the marking scheme."

Uri scoffs. "That's got to be a load of horse manure. The palace just doesn't want to throw blame yet before investigating further."

"Who cares?" Hazel-Mae says, her eyes shining. "I passed! And Nakoma had a perfect score for the second exam."

My hands drop from my hair to cover my grin. "You're serious?"

Uri climbs out of bed with a smile to match my own. Pride floods me as I take in the happiness in the room. My chest puffs up with the image of Yvette storming into the palace and demanding answers. I should've thought to speak to her sooner.

"That's not all," Tia says, interrupting my train of thought. "A dance tutor has arrived. Calypso saw her last night. She says they're here to help us prepare for the Spring Ball."

Uri rolls her eyes. "More likely they're here to watch Olga."

"She'll be lucky to have a job come summer if the parents catch wind of this," Hazel-Mae agrees.

"Imagine the uproar," Uri says, "if the provinces believe their daughters didn't have a fair chance at the crown. It could lead to civil war."

The blood drains from my face. It's the opportunity I keep asking for – the chance to prove myself and climb the ranks – but the thought of war no longer fills me with excitement. My stomach turns sour at the thought of earning my promotion at the cost of someone's life.

"Surely the king has plans to make amends before it can come to that," I say, dread turning my voice to a trembling whisper.

Hazel-Mae freezes, and Tia's smile falters.

"He will," Uri says. "It won't come to that."

Uri's assurance falls flat on me, and after a moment of awkward silence, we get dressed for the day ahead. I force the thought from my mind. Lars is a gentleman and will do everything in his power to prevent conflict in Patel. Somehow, it is easier to place my faith in him – a man only one year older than me – than the king.

~

AFTER BREAKFAST WE FILE INTO THE BALLROOM, EACH LADY craning her neck to catch a glimpse of the new dance tutor waiting for us with a straw hat in her hands. She is everything you would expect from a dancer and more, with long limbs that move with the grace of a swan. She reminds me of a finch as she flits between us, examining each lady while we enter.

"Welcome, ladies. You may address me as Tutor Lenora," she says, with a deep curtsey.

Tutor Lenora holds the straw hat high enough for us to see it from all angles of the room. Even this display seems as artful as a step in a well-rehearsed dance.

"Over the next two moons, you'll get to know me and my hat quite well. Each lesson, I will draw your names from the hat to select your dance partners."

I flick my eyes to the ceiling and suppress the urge to groan. As if dance lessons aren't torture enough. I count the exposed beams of the high ceiling before I dare to look at the hat again. It stares back at me, its brim a deadly smirk.

Tutor Lenora's lips twist into a knowing smile. "To be an exceptional dancer, you must be comfortable and capable of dancing with any partner. His Highness has the grace of a lion, but at the ball, there will also be many less-qualified suitors for you to dance with."

Elisabelle raises her hand, and Tutor Lenora acknowledges her with a swift nod.

"What about those of us who have already mastered the art of court dance?" Elisabelle asks.

Tutor Lenora raises her chin ever so slightly and paces closer to Elisabelle. "I will be the judge of that."

Lenora does not look away from Elisabelle, even as murmurs fill the room. After a long moment, she turns away and calls us to attention with a few clicks of her fingers.

"Right. Since this is the first lesson, you can choose your dance partner for today only. Then, after your day off, we'll start the real work."

A soft mumble of voices slips across the wooden dance floor as each of us echoes the same two words. *Day off.*

"Sorry, Tutor Lenora," Quinn says, her voice silencing the whispers. "Did you say we have a day off tomorrow?"

"Yes. The Academy felt that a visit to the palace midweek would help make up for the time you have lost already."

I turn to Uri with my eyebrows raised. Hazel-Mae bounces on her toes as she whispers to Tia. The room fills with the hum of excitement that builds steadily. A shrill whistle splits the conversations before we can reach a crescendo. The sound ricochets off the walls and forces me to return my focus to Lenora.

"That's enough gossip for now, ladies. You will have plenty of time to discuss your dresses during your midday meal."

I close my mouth and step closer to Uri so it's obvious we're dancing partners. Around the room, other ladies do the same. Lenora starts us in two neat rows, with half of us acting as the male dance partner. Uri puffs up her chest and bows, offering to take the lead. Together, we fumble through the steps as Tutor Lenora teaches us a cotillion. Prickles of sweat line my back within minutes.

"Now, take hands with the lady on your right diagonal and turn once."

I reach for Tia's hands but stumble into Calypso's back. The rest of the line has ground to a halt as Elisabelle turns her back on Embry.

"Tutor Lenora, why are you teaching us a country dance?" Elisabelle wrinkles her nose. "It is unfashionable by court standards."

"A good line dance is the building block of all great dances. You must master this before you even dream of waltzing with the prince," Lenora says.

Elisabelle opens her mouth and appears ready to argue this sentiment, but Lenora turns away from her and encourages us to keep moving. I can almost see the steam coming from Elisabelle's ears. I press my lips together to fight back a giggle. Across from me, Uri has gone bright pink from suppressing her own laughter. Elisabelle is at the other end of our line, but even from here, I can hear Embry trying to calm her down.

As the lesson continues, my body recognises parts of the dance as ones I practiced as a child, yet my movements lack grace, and I keep stepping on Uri's toes. I mouth "sorry" and wonder if Lars will brush off my apologies like Uri does. My stomach dips. Lars's letters are easy to reply to, but tomorrow, I won't be able to hide behind my quill. I swallow and try to erase the feeling of slime slipping down my throat. Somehow, ignoring my life as a guardian feels like a bigger lie in person than when I'm avoiding the subject on paper.

TWENTY-THREE

It's strange to think that it has been almost two full seasons since I left home and today is the first time I have stepped inside the palace. The brilliant, yellow, tiered roofs and pristine white walls of the palace are breathtaking up close. I salute the orange gargoyles that peer from the main entryway, embarrassed I once thought they were demons.

Tutor Olga leads the way inside the palace under the watchful gaze of several purple-clad servants. Elisabelle follows close behind her, keeping a firm distance from Tutor Lenora, who brings up our rear. Despite Olga's admonishing looks, I can hear the muffled gasps of my peers. The ceiling is so high that I couldn't touch it even if I stood on top of Kato. As I tilt my head back, I have to stifle my own sounds of awe. Every inch of the ceiling is a vivid painting of the history of Patel that continues into the main throne room.

After several twists with even more grand sights, we

finally reach a parlour with vast windows that span the length of the far wall. A gentle breeze slips through the open glass door and fills the room with the scent of fresh-cut grass. I turn my nose towards the lush garden beyond and take a deep breath.

Hazel-Mae tugs on my elbow. "Look."

I follow her line of sight to the raven-haired queen who seems to glow from within, as if lit by moonlight. Her simple elegance outshines the ladies-in-waiting that cluster around her. Among them is a woman wearing layers upon layers of lace. My skin crawls at the thought of being trapped beneath so many ruffles. I scrunch up my nose at Hazel-Mae, but my stomach sinks. Maybe I'm underdressed.

I brush aside my thoughts and plaster on a smile as I follow Uri further into the room. She curtsies towards the queen before making a beeline for a table filled with dozens of delicate teacups. Each cup has a unique floral design that matches its saucer. A servant in royal purple selects and pours tea for each of us into cups that match our gowns. Uri thanks him by name, but I don't register it. I'm too busy scanning the room for Lars.

The moment I catch sight of Lars, I wish I hadn't looked. Elisabelle flutters her eyelashes at him and taps his arm playfully every time she throws her head back to laugh. My fingers tighten around my teacup as the sunlight glistens off her neck. I pretend to drink my tea and look away from her, only to realise Lars has caught me staring. He bows his head to Elisabelle and her friends before weaving through the room to me.

"Lady Nakoma, Lady Uri," Lars greets us, bowing his head towards me, then Uri. "I hope you're both well this morning."

We curtsy in reply, Tia and Hazel-Mae echoing our movements.

"Would you do me the honour of introducing your friends?" Lars asks.

"This is Lady Tia and Lady Hazel-Mae, good friends of mine from the Academy," I reply, gesturing at each girl.

Lars nods but doesn't spare a glance for either of them.

"Ah, yes, I remember now. Of the Mir Mountains and Sebba, correct? I apologise for my poor memory for names. The Academy garden party seems so long ago."

"Of course," I mumble.

"Why don't I fetch you some tea, Your Highness?" Tia suggests.

"And I'll get some biscuits to go with it," Hazel-Mae adds.

"You'll need my help," Uri says. "I can point out which treats to avoid if you don't want to be covered in crumbs."

Before either of us can thank them, all three girls have left. A blush creeps into my cheeks, and I pray Lars is oblivious to their ploy to give us privacy. I stare down at the drink in my hands.

"It is so good to see you again, Nakoma. I was beginning to fear they would never let you back out of the Pink Palace."

I blink up at Lars, surprised by his honesty. The flutter of my heart makes my voice waver as I speak.

"I'm glad to see you too, Lars."

"Your friend, Lady Uri, has been the only thing to look forward to about these visits, until now. Her wit was a welcome distraction from some of the other ladies of the Academy."

I swallow down a sharp spike of jealousy and try to find something to say. When I remain silent for too long, Lars hurries to explain himself.

"Of course, it was Uri's discreet delivery of our letters that made me like her the most. Without them, I probably would've demanded that the Academy change their blasted rules so I could speak to you again."

I stare at Lars. His green eyes are serious and piercing, without their usual twinkle of humour. My breath catches in my throat. I almost tell him how I spent countless hours re-reading each of his letters and dreaming of what the next might say. Before my heart can speak for me, I drain the rest of my tea and shove the cup into his hands. Confusion clouds Lars's face as he stares at the dirty dish.

"If you'll excuse me, I think I need to use the ladies' room."

Fleeing before Lars can protest, I hope Tia or Hazel-Mae will be back soon to distract him. He deserves someone like them. Hazel-Mae is charming and honest, unlike me, and Tia is the perfect dance partner – graceful, and a great conversationalist. I blink back the urge to cry as I peer down the hallway. Nobody is in sight, and I'm hopelessly lost. Each doorway looks the same and I don't know how far I travelled before I finally slowed down. I slip through an open door into a small library.

Dark wooden shelves line the walls, each one full of thick volumes. I let my fingers trail across their spines as I breathe in the musty air. The smell brings me back to the temple and the hundreds of scrolls kept there. I used to visit frequently while in reserve, as the commander thought I made a useful messenger. Another reminder I'm not the lady Lars thinks I am.

"Nakoma?"

I freeze at the sound of Lars's voice and press my back up against the bookshelf, but it's too late. Lars sticks his head in the room and spots me immediately.

"What are you doing here?"

"I got lost," I mumble to my feet.

Lars steps closer. The bookshelf holds me in place. My eyes flick towards the doorway as I calculate how to escape without explaining myself to him.

"You can tell me the truth." Lars's voice is gentle, but I still catch the twinge of hurt in it.

I shake my head. "They'll be looking for you."

"I'd wager I have at least ten minutes before anyone follows me."

Lars's mischievous tone is enough to make me look at him. Did Uri cause a distraction? Or maybe Lars loudly announced he was off to the bathroom. I open my mouth to speak, but no sound comes out. Defeated, Lars steps away and lets the air cool between us. Without him near, I slump against the bookshelf.

"I'm not the best choice," I finally say. "You'd be better off with one of the other ladies."

Lars raises his eyebrows, but I cut him off before he can speak.

"I'm not elegant, or gracious, and I always offend people when I speak."

I'm not a lady, I think. Instead, I tell him the next truest thing.

"I'm not fit to be a princess."

Lars smiles and pulls my hands away from the folds of my skirt.

"That's where you're wrong. You're selfless and loyal beyond all measure. When you speak, people listen. All great qualities for a princess."

I shake my head. "You hardly know me."

"I would wait a thousand days to know you well enough."

My heart crawls into my throat and leaves me speechless. The soft sounds of our mingling breaths fill the silence. Lars wets his lips, and my eyes track the movement. The slight curve of his mouth consumes my thoughts.

"Is that what you want?" he asks.

What do I want? Lars's breathless words are so much more than an innocent question. I brush a lock of his unruly hair away from his face. Lars catches my hand and kisses the palm. The touch sends a jolt of electricity through me.

"Nakoma?"

I answer him with a kiss. Lars cradles me against him, each touch of his lips tender. I cling to him and let the spark that he's lit burn into a blaze.

When my head feels light from lack of air, I force myself to pull away from him.

"Is everything ok? Was that too much?"

I smile at his concern and rest my hand against his chest. The quick thump of his heart matches my own unsteady tempo.

"More than ok."

Lars grins and sweeps me back into his arms. Before I can protest, he covers my neck in a flurry of hungry kisses. I try to warn him we're still in public, but his name comes out as a delighted sigh. When Lars releases me, my legs are jelly, and my brain is a puddle of sensations I've never felt before.

"I want to introduce you to my parents. You'll meet them eventually, of course, but it would mean the world for them to know you before the Spring Ball."

"The king and queen," I squeak.

"They are my parents."

I crane my neck towards the exit. As my sense return to me, my body longs to escape into the garden and never step foot in a library again. Lars's thumb rubs against the back of my hand and draws my attention back to him.

"Is that too sudden?"

I gulp. "I need time."

"That's ok. Come for a ride with me this weekend instead?"

My shoulders relax a fraction. "Day one of a thousand?"

"If that's what it takes, then yes."

"Tutor Lenora, I insist you pair me with someone of an appropriate skill level," Elisabelle says, loudly enough for the entire class to hear.

Tia stands beside Tutor Lenora, her frown growing deeper with each passing minute. Lenora announced our pairs at the start of the lesson, and the only person who has dared to demand a change is Elisabelle. I doubt I hid my own disappointment well when Tutor Lenora said I was dancing with Quinn instead of one of my friends. Still, Quinn is nice enough for someone from a central province. She's loud and isn't afraid to laugh like she means it.

"It is unethical to force me to practice with someone who thinks stomping about counts as dancing," Elisabelle continues.

My fists curl at my side at her comment. Papa has recounted stories from trading in Sebba, and I believe him when he says the people of Sebba dance with fluid grace. The barb about stomping would be more accurately directed at me, not that I would ever call it that. In Arithean ceremonies, our guardians dance to the beat of pounding drums. I'm no master at it, but when I watch others like Omarion, I'm always impressed by the ferocity and beauty of each dancer.

"That's enough, Lady Elisabelle," Tutor Lenora snaps. "I've tolerated your complete lack of respect for my teaching methods, but I'll not stand here while you insult the other ladies of this Academy."

When it is obvious Elisabelle doesn't intend to apologise, Lenora continues to speak.

"You have a choice now, Lady Elisabelle. You may forfeit the opportunity to be taught the court's dances and risk making a fool of yourself at the Spring Ball, or you may follow my instructions without further complaint."

Elisabelle's reply is quiet enough that I'm spared from hearing it. Satisfied, Tutor Lenora leaves Tia's side and resumes her position at the head of the hall. Despite my distaste for dance class, my fingers uncurl as the tension leaves my body. There is something about Elisabelle's sullen face that is worth every second of embarrassment I might endure with Quinn.

Tutor Lenora teaches us the first dozen steps to a new waltz before allowing us to practice with our partner.

"I can lead today if you would like?" Quinn offers.

"Mother always complains that I look like a boy with my short hair, so I might as well."

I laugh awkwardly and accept, grateful that Quinn does not mention my clumsy feet as the reason for her to lead. Sweat slips down my spine from exertion before I finally complete a full circle without stepping on her toes.

"I never thought that a court dance would take so much effort," I admit after some time. "You make it look as easy as walking."

Quinn grins and pushes back a clump of damp hair. Her hazel eyes glow as the sunlight filtering into the room catches specs of gold within them.

"It's like the dances my governess taught me growing up. I used to have a bath after every lesson. My brothers would torment me for being so girlish, but I can't stand the feeling of sweaty skin."

Somehow, the news that Quinn has siblings is more shocking to me than the thought of a full bath being drawn after every lesson. It's strange to think of her as a person with a childhood rather than a figurehead for Inja. I glance around the room. If Quinn has siblings, how many others from the central provinces have I misjudged?

"*You* have brothers?"

Quinn's thick brows crease into a frown, casting her eyes in shadow. I wince at my stupid question. Of course Quinn does. Tia would scold me for being rude again. I hurry to explain myself.

"I have a brother too. He's two years younger than me, but still teases me without shame."

"You should count yourself lucky. I have five older brothers. They are a nuisance." Quinn twirls me under her arm and adds, "I wouldn't trade them for the world."

Quinn and I share stories of our brothers until Quinn's donkey's-bray of a laugh sends me into a fit of giggles. I clasp her arm, doubling over as I fight for air.

"Lady Nakoma, how are you going to dance with the prince if you can't manage half an hour with Lady Quinn?"

"It's my fault, Tutor Lenora," Quinn says before I can catch my breath. "I told her about the time I put a frog in my brother's shoe and convinced him it was our younger brother's fault."

I stare at Quinn, surprised by her honesty. Tutor Lenora's face pales.

"Very well then... Just try to focus on the waltz."

Tutor Lenora hurries off across the hall, her satin gown flowing behind her like the tail of a butterfly koi.

"Thank you. You didn't have to do that."

Quinn brushes off the comment and instructs me on where to place my hands so we can keep dancing. As we fumble through the steps, I chastise myself for not trying to know Quinn before now.

"Do you have a lot of dances in Inja?"

"Yes and no. When I was little, people rarely danced. Father couldn't afford the festivities with the proposed levies. Now he hosts a feast at the city hall every full moon."

Quinn's hand guides me through a turn, and I try to imagine life in Inja – a city so overflowing with wealth they can afford to feast every moon. I grit my teeth and fight the urge to stomp through the next steps.

"Is it similar in Arithenos?" Quinn asks.

"No. Most Aritheans can't afford to eat three times a day, let alone an entire feast."

For once, Quinn is speechless. Her lips form a delicate O as she glides through a half turn, but the effect doesn't last long.

"You should create a petition. That's how things changed in Inja. We were struggling after the floods, so Father asked all the merchants to sign a petition for fairer trade exchanges."

I stop midstride. "And that worked?"

Quinn shrugs. "Why not? It's like a class debate. If you have more people to support your argument, you're more likely to win."

I let Quinn lead me back into the dance as my mind whirls in time to the music. Quinn's analogy is a little naive, but it's worth a try.

"Would you sign a petition to lower taxes in Arithenos?"

Quinn falters, catching herself on my shoulder. "Why me?"

"Imagine how powerful it would be if representatives from outside of Inja had joined your petition."

"In that case, let me be your trial run. Explain to me why I should sign a petition. We'll make you so convincing that all the ladies will sign."

For the rest of the lesson, Quinn guides me around the wooden dance floor as I explain the situation in Arithenos. Together, we turn my plea for help into a pitch anyone would listen to.

Tutor Lenora keeps us dancing until our stomachs grumble so loudly they drown out her voice. She gives us strict instructions to stretch in the garden before settling in for lunch, but half the ladies ignore her. Uri and I link our arms through Hazel-Mae's, keeping her from following her stomach to the dining hall. She pouts a little at first, but quickly forgets her stomach as she shares her news.

"Calypso has a cousin who works for the king as the Minister of Food and Agriculture," Hazel-Mae relates.

I share a confused frown with Uri. "Is she married? I didn't think the king would have women in his council."

Hazel-Mae rolls her eyes. "No, silly. The cousin is a he, and *he's* not married."

Tia shoulders Uri out of the way so she can squeeze in next to Hazel-Mae. "What's he like?"

Hazel-Mae practically melts against me. Her grin turns her already round face into a ball of joy.

"Calypso says he is her favourite cousin. He's been taking her to lunches every fortnight since we arrived because he was afraid she would miss home too much."

Tia makes the same sound Mother made when she

saw me in Aunt Fifi's finished dress – half squeal, half sigh.

"Did she offer to introduce you?" Tia asks.

"She said I should join them for lunch this weekend!"

If it was ladylike to do so, I'm sure Tia and Hazel-Mae would have jumped for joy in the middle of the hallway. Instead, their pace quickens until they leave Uri and me in their wake, wondering what just happened. My eyes flick from their retreating figures to Uri's puzzled face.

"That was..."

"Odd," Uri finishes for me.

We continue towards the garden in comfortable quiet but only make it a few steps before Perriwick calls out to us.

"Pardon me, ladies. The pixie dove post just arrived for Lady Nakoma."

Perriwick offers me a letter on a silver platter. I can't help but smile at the ridiculous formality of it. Still, I curtsy before taking it.

Uri peers over my shoulder. "Who's it from? That's an impressive wax seal."

She's right. The wax doesn't contain the phoenix my grandparents use to sign their correspondence with, nor is it the king's purple. I break it open and almost drop the locket that falls out. My brows lift as I scan the bottom of the page.

I angle the letter towards Uri. "It's the Duke of Unke. It feels like an age since I wrote to him. I wasn't sure I would get a reply."

Uri's eyebrows shoot up into her hairline. "You wrote a letter to the Duke of Unke?"

I glance around the hallway. "Maybe I should explain somewhere quieter. Let's go find Tia and Hazel-Mae."

We find them quickly, and Uri leads us to the pavilion in the far corner of the garden. I stare up at the elegant arch of its roof and try not to blush at the memory of Lars.

Uri plonks herself down on a bench and crosses her arms. "Spill. Why is the Duke of Unke writing to you?"

"Is he handsome?" Hazel-Mae asks.

Uri shakes her head. "He's old."

"I sent him a letter first," I admit. "My grandmother mentioned his daughter Lillianna one time, and I couldn't get the thought of her out of my head."

"Perhaps she is already married, or unsuitable for the prince," Tia suggests.

Hazel-Mae frowns, not following our line of thought. I skim the letter before the girls can ask any more questions. It takes a moment to read the large flourishes, but once I see past them, my stomach churns with dread.

"The duke writes his daughter has been missing for ten years. No one ever demanded a ransom. His advisors all suggest he give up searching for her."

I open the locket that fell out of the letter. Inside is a miniature of what must be Lillianna, along with a lock of golden hair. The girl has a sweet face, with wide eyes and rosy cheeks that makes my heart ache for her father. I pass the portrait to the others.

"She's beautiful," Tia murmurs.

As they pass the locket between them, I reread the last line of his letter. *If you have hope for her too, please keep these mementos close to your heart. I will be forever grateful for any news you can share.*

"He'll find her someday. Surely a father can't love his child so much and lose them forever," Hazel-Mae says.

My eyes flick to Uri. The set of her lips speaks volumes. The duke's advisors are probably right. Ten years is a long time for a child to survive unharmed in the hands of kidnappers. Instead of crushing Hazel-Mae's spirit, Uri deftly changes the subject, and Tia joins in and chatters away about our next class with Tutor Olga. While they speak, I tuck the letter into the folds of my dress and push aside any lingering thoughts of Lillianna.

CHAPTER
TWENTY-FIVE

As we exit the Pink Palace, Wish launches off my shoulder, enjoying her freedom. The brisk morning air helps to wake my muscles and cools the blush that rises to my cheeks the moment I see Lars. He's waiting for me outside the stables, holding both Blossom's and Kato's reins in a white-knuckled fist. But it's not the horses I'm looking at. Lars is wearing a white cotton shirt that is somehow loose enough to look casual while still hugging his shoulders. My cheeks turn to twin flames as my imagination runs wild with the thought of running my fingers along his chest.

Afraid my face will betray my thoughts, I rush to Kato's side. Lars relinquishes Kato's reins to me, but I still scold him.

"I thought I warned you to leave Kato alone."

Lars shrugs. "You did, but I could hardly leave Kato in his stall while the sun is putting on such a display."

I frown at Lars, but my heart isn't in it. Kato is no

pony; he will only stand politely when he chooses. For him to be saddled already speaks volumes in Lars's favour. Still, I carefully check every strap of Kato's gear before mounting him.

Lars leads the way through the morning crowds and out of the city. As we pass through the gates of Ellos, two familiar faces join us without a word. I raise an eyebrow at Lars, but it doesn't come as a surprise that Fredrick and Mikael must follow him now that I know I'm riding with the prince. They keep a respectable distance from us, and as the scenery shifts from city to farmlands, it becomes easier to forget about them.

"It's been too long since I last rode past open fields," I say.

The land is more brown than green this time of year, but I'm still comforted by the shimmer of blue that is visible where land meets sky.

"Does it make you homesick for Arithenos?"

I open my mouth to say yes, but the word freezes on my tongue. I've had brief moments of homesickness since arriving in Ellos, but they are fewer than I expected. The sight of workers tilling the earth has only drawn it to the surface once more.

"Yes and no. I think I miss the days spent outside more than I miss Arithenos."

I don't look at Lars as I speak so that I can drink in the skyline. It's easier to breathe out here, without the city walls and clusters of buildings to fill up the horizon. Days like this make the solitary weeks of sentry duty seem almost as divine as a priestess's hours of meditation.

"Would you ever leave Arithenos to live in another part of Patel?" Lars asks.

"Permanently?"

"Yes. Well, that is ... you could still visit."

I glance at Lars, surprised by the nervous catch in his voice. The question used to have an easy answer. I love Arithenos, but now my heart tugs towards Ellos too.

"I've never given it much thought. Would you?"

Lars laughs at my deflection. "I could never. I have a duty to the Crown."

I clamp my mouth shut and stare at the road ahead to stuff down the urge to protest that I also have duties. I've never heard of a guardian leaving their station while in their prime. We may get posted across Patel, but rotations don't last for more than a few moons. The idea of sacrificing all my training is enough to dampen my mood. I kick Kato into a trot to break free of my thoughts. Lars matches my pace without question.

We cover miles in silence. Open fields slowly become more populated with livestock grazing the pastures. Birds squawk to alert each other of a nearby predator, and I look up to see Wish is no longer a distant speck on the horizon. I click my tongue to Kato, and he slows to a walk once more. Kato flicks his ears back at me, but I ignore his annoyance. Blossom's fur is slick with sweat, and I know she can't endure this pace for much longer.

"Should we visit the village?" Lars asks.

I look up from scratching Kato's ears and finally

notice the houses scattered amongst the distant trees. Wish swoops in to land on my shoulder and squawks her agreement. The sound surprises a laugh from me, dispersing my bleak mood.

"It seems Wish is eager for a break."

We pause beneath a barren tree and wait for Fredrick and Mikael to catch up with us. Like Blossom, their cream horses shine with a thin coat of sweat.

"There are markets held here each Saturday. I've heard the food is worth the ride."

I wriggle my eyebrows at Lars. "His true motives are revealed."

"If only that was the reason. I admit, I'm not made for the saddle like you, Nakoma. Blossom and I could both use the break."

"In that case, I'll race you there. Whoever loses will pay for lunch."

Lars leans back in his saddle and rolls his eyes at me. "You've already won. Today is my treat, and I would not ask you to spend your coin."

"Fine. Winner buys lunch ... *and* I'll give you a head start." I extend my hand to Lars. "Deal?"

Lars glances from Kato to Blossom, then finally shakes. "This had better be a good head start."

"Ten!" I start the count.

Lars yelps and kicks Blossom into motion.

Eight.

I shift above Kato until I am almost flat against his body. Wish springs off my shoulder, but her flapping wings don't distract either of us.

Five.

I fix my sights on Lars's retreating form. Dust kicks up around Blossom's hooves as she gathers speed. This race might be close.

One.

I squeeze Kato's flanks with my thighs, and he bursts forwards. The wind whips my face, but I don't lose sight of my goal. The earth rumbles beneath us as Kato thunders towards Blossom. Lars's eyes flick towards me, and I revel in the moment his jaw drops with shock. With the day's ride to warm him up, Kato easily outpaces Blossom. Villagers scatter out of the way of Kato's hooves, even as we slow and the dust settles.

"Next time I want a thirty second head start," Lars huffs when he eventually catches up.

I dismount and grin like a wild thing. Wish returns to my shoulder. Her feathers puff up in what I imagine is pride. Or perhaps it is a priestess warning me to be careful.

Lars dismounts Blossom and flips her reins over her head to lead her. "Come on, the food is this way."

I lift my nose to the air as we walk and enjoy the mixed aroma of sizzling fat and toasted sugar. The markets are as colourful and lively as the ones in Ellos, but thankfully less crowded. Lars and I walk shoulder to shoulder with ease, our horses trailing behind us.

"So, what will it be, Your Highness?" I sweep my arm towards a line of food vendors. "Herb sausages, or perhaps some fried cheese?"

"Not so fast, my lady. It seems you have forgotten lunch is your choice."

I frown at Lars's smug smile and twinkling eyes.

"I had my fingers crossed," Lars explains, "so the deal never counted."

I stop in the middle of the street. "You what?"

Lars's smile broadens into a grin that is both childish and infectious.

"It's a rule in Ellos," Lars says, and I can't help but laugh at him.

Before Lars can explain himself further, Wish dives off my shoulder with a piercing cry. I flinch away from the sound and curse. Keeping my eyes fixed on Wish, I leap back into the saddle and urge Kato to follow her. Lars does the same, but this time, the villagers part for us like honey. Kato tosses his head in frustration, but Wish is still in sight. At the farthest end of the markets, a farmer cries out as Wish swoops his produce again and again. I whistle at Wish to summon her, but the only one who seems to hear is a young girl who has abandoned her shopping basket to help. The sun glints of her white-blond hair as she looks up at me.

"What has gotten into your bird?" Lars asks.

I shake my head and search the inner seams of my gown for the locket I had stashed away. It can't be her. She is plain and covered with freckles. Yet she looks like the correct age, and Wish is determined.

I lean across Kato and hand Lars the locket. "This is a miniature of Lady Lillianna, the missing daughter of the Duke of Unke."

Lars's eyes flick between the portrait and the girl, who now swats the air to shoo Wish away.

"I've heard of her. Are you sure it's her? Most courtiers are of the opinion that she has passed."

I chew my lip and urge Kato to walk faster. At this distance, the similarities are uncanny. Her limbs have the thinness of a hard life, but her face is still soft and genteel.

"I have no idea," I admit, "but Wish thinks she is."

Lars nods, dismounts, and strides towards her with an air of importance that somehow transforms him. I trail behind Lars with wide eyes, shocked by the sudden return of his court persona. Wish disappears into the nearby treetops as soon as we are in range to speak. Her dark eyes follow me as I dismount, and my nerves hum with the thought that a priestess may be watching.

"Can I be of any assistance?"

The farmer bows. "Thank you, Your Highness, but the damned bird is gone now."

The girl's eyes widen, and everything clicks into place. It has to be her. My entire body sings with the truth of it. My eyes flick back to Wish. Did the High Priestess know this was how I would serve Patel? Or did destiny guide her hand until all the pieces fell into place?

"Can I offer you a sample of my fresh apples? I guarantee they are crisp and sweet. The perfect refreshment for a long ride."

"No, thank you. However, I will purchase some carrots from you for our mounts."

The farmer bows again and takes Lars's request as a

hint to make himself busy. He disappears into the back of the stall, and the girl turns to leave as well. Lars stops her with a gentle hand on her basket.

"Are you alright, miss? I'm sure that bird gave you quite a shock."

The girl's long lashes flutter as she gapes at Lars. "Yes... I mean, yes, Your Highness."

"You may call me Antonio, and this is my good friend, Lady Nakoma."

My curtsy is enough to make Tutor Olga proud, but I don't trust my voice to speak. A blush spreads across the girl's cheeks. It's the same shade all my classmates turned on the day of the tea party.

"My name is Harlow," she murmurs.

Lars's mask of manners slips, and he flicks me a look as if to say *this isn't her*. I shake my head at him. It's just a name, and Wish is still watching.

Worried that Lars won't push the subject, I swallow my pride. "Could we impose on your family for a moment? The change in weather has left me feeling faint."

Harlow nods so fast I fear her head will fall off. "Of course, Lady Nakoma. Right this way. Our home is a short walk from the town centre."

With a fake smile plastered on my face, I let Lars take Kato's reins from me and follow Harlow. One of Lars's guards lingers at the farmer's stall to pay for the carrots while the other watches me like a hawk. I wish I could explain to them both that I'm fine, but it's not the time nor the place. Instead, I accept Fredrick's arm to climb the tiny step that leads into Harlow's garden.

The house is a modest brick structure surrounded by freshly sown gardens, but Frederick approaches it like a tavern swarming with criminals. He scans the perimeter for potential danger, while Mikael takes the horses to wait under a nearby tree. After a subtle nod from Fredrick, we follow Harlow inside to a cosy drawing room.

"So sorry about the mess," Harlow says, tucking away any exposed clutter. "We rarely have guests."

Lars leads me to a two-seater couch. "It's not a problem at all."

Lars's words fall on deaf ears, but I don't blame Harlow. She flits about the room, her hands trembling as she quickly folds blankets and straightens cushions. Lars sits on the edge of the couch and watches each nervous movement with interest. I elbow Lars, but his sharp gaze doesn't falter.

When Harlow returns to each item for a third time, I finally speak. "I think some tea would really help me recover."

Colour rushes to Harlow's cheeks as she realises people usually offer tea to their guests.

"Of course. Just a moment, please. I'll ask my aunt to put some on."

I turn to Lars the moment Harlow leaves the room.

"Cut it out. The poor girl is so nervous around you I'm surprised she hasn't collapsed."

Lars leans back into the couch. "Sorry."

"And try to act like your normal self," I add. "Not the polite prince face you use in court. Harlow is probably scared out of her mind to have royalty in her house."

Lars holds his hands up in mock defeat before turning back towards the doorway. A rattling tea set announces the return of Harlow, and with her, an older woman, who I assume is her aunt. The woman wears her salt-and-pepper hair in a loose bun. Her brow knots with concern. She has the same chocolate-brown eyes as Harlow, but the resemblance ends there. Her nose is straight and broad, while Harlow's nose ends in a sweet little point. I suppose the uncle could carry more of a family resemblance, but my gut says he won't.

"Welcome to our little home, Your Highness," Harlow's aunt says.

"Prince Antonio and Lady Nakoma, this is my aunt, Maggie. My uncle, Aldwin, will be with us in a moment."

"It is lovely to meet you," I say, and Lars echoes the sentiment.

Harlow spills equal measures of milk and tea as she pours for us, leaving Maggie to mop up the mess with a corner of her apron. Once we are all settled with our teacups, Maggie is still in motion. Her eyes dart about the room, and her foot taps out a continuous rhythm.

"Have you been enjoying the fine weather this morning, Your Highness?" Harlow asks.

"We have, thank you. However, I fear I have pushed my friend too far this morning after a long winter indoors."

I nod in agreement, but keep my mouth shut. Lars

easily fills my silence with the meaningless small talk that is so popular in court. A master of manners, I'm sure he could maintain a droll conversation all afternoon. Outside, Kato neighs, and Maggie jumps from her seat.

"Perhaps you should check on the horses, *Prince Antonio*?" I gesture towards the door.

Lars stiffens at the emphasis on his name before he nods in understanding. The door clicks behind him, and the sound of Maggie's tapping foot slows. Harlow lowers her teacup without a clatter against the saucer.

"Your home is lovely, Maggie. Have you always lived in Ellos?"

Maggie's eyes dart towards the doorway before she replies hesitantly. "Not always. Why do you ask, Lady Nakoma?"

I pitch my voice to match Hazel-Mae's light, innocent tone. "Only because I am from Arithenos, and the people of Ellos continue to fascinate me."

The hard lines around Maggie's mouth soften at my reply. I take a sip of my tea, unsure how far I can push my luck.

"Have you been enjoying your visit to Ellos, Lady Nakoma?"

I smile at Harlow's attempt to avoid an awkward silence.

"Yes. Although, I've felt cooped up by the city walls. The only people I have met are those in the court's inner circle. I would love to know more about the rest of Ellos. What it is like outside of the Capital?"

"Of course. What would you like to know?"

I tap my finger against my chin and pretend to think. "Is it usual for children to live with their extended family?"

Harlow hesitates and looks at her aunt for guidance.

"What an unusual question, Lady Nakoma," Maggie says.

"I hope I did not cause offence."

"No, my lady. I suppose our family situation differs from others."

"I see."

I switch my attention back to Harlow, hoping she might reveal more than her aunt will. "Are your mother and father well, Harlow?"

Harlow blinks in rapid succession, but tears still puddle on her lower lashes. Maggie's chair scrapes against the floor as she stands. My heart quickens, but I don't lower my teacup.

"The hour grows late, Lady Nakoma. It would be best if you were on your way."

I don't budge from my seat. Maggie's glare burns into me. With no other cards left to play, I pull the locket from my dress and hold the portrait out to Harlow.

"Does this little girl look familiar to you? Her name is Lillianna."

Harlow's hands clench into fists, but she leans forwards to get a closer look. The tears she had held at bay now drip down her cheeks. Maggie drops back down into her chair and hangs her head in her hands.

Harlow sniffles but holds her chin up as she speaks. "I know her, but her name is Harlow now."

TWENTY-SIX

efore Harlow can go into further detail, Maggie suggests Harlow's uncle should be present. Uncle Aldwin appears younger than Maggie and has a wild beard, shot through with grey. His thick brows almost hide his sunken eyes, which are quick to assess the room before he slides into the seat beside Maggie.

"Sorry for my delay in joining you," Aldwin says.

I brush aside his apology, disinterested in any false excuses Aldwin might make.

"Could somebody please explain why Lillianna – I mean, Harlow – is here and not in Unke with her father?"

Maggie's eyes flick to Aldwin. "Harlow lives with us to remain safe."

"Safe? How is it safer for Harlow to be here than with her loving father?"

"It was Father's plan," Harlow explains. "For years, he protected me from attacks. Hired killers would attempt to assassinate me or steal me away. One night,

Father broke down and decided the safest place for me was far from home."

Harlow rubs her thumb tenderly across the top of the locket as she speaks. Her tears have already dried, and her voice is steady, as if repeating a well-rehearsed story.

"He hired Aunt Maggie and Uncle Aldwin to protect me by starting a new life together. We don't use my old name so that my enemies can't find me."

I peer at Maggie and watch as she chews her bottom lip. Aldwin rests his hand on her leg and stills her jitters. His eyes are distant and haunted.

"Why do you think people wanted to hurt you, Harlow? Wouldn't it be safe to go back now?" I ask.

Harlow frowns at her hands. "There will always be people who wish to hurt me."

Harlow's answer is vague and exactly the sort of reply I would expect from someone who has heard hollow lies their whole life. My mind whirrs as I study Maggie and Aldwin. They might not be the mercenaries who kidnapped Harlow, but they certainly know more than she does. I stand, unsure of what I will say until the words tumble from my mouth.

"I wish to see your kitchen, Maggie. Is it the same as those in Arithenos?"

Maggie stands, and I follow her out of the room. The kitchen walls are a cheery yellow at odds with Maggie's stooped shoulders. I lean against the cabinets across from her with my back to the glistening knife rack. Maggie leaves the only door to the kitchen wide open, so I pitch my voice low enough for only Maggie's ears.

"Did you kidnap her?"

Maggie has the gall to look offended before her jaw snaps shut. I cross my arms over my chest and drop the mask of a lady that I've adopted for use at the Academy.

"You can either tell me or Prince Antonio. I would suggest, however, that it's in your best interests His Highness does not force you to speak."

Maggie's eyes linger on the doorway, but I clear my throat to draw her attention back to me. I cock an eyebrow with the same arrogance I've watched dozens of guardians use to get their way.

"What will it be?"

Maggie finally meets my cool stare with eyes round and pleading.

"You must understand. We did everything we could to protect Harlow."

"Answer the question. Did you kidnap her?"

"They hired us to kill her. She was just a girl. Sweet. Innocent. Harlow wouldn't dream of harming a fly."

"Who hired you?"

Maggie stares out the window above the kitchen sink, her jaw ticking as she clenches the muscle.

"We're not sure. It's not my job to ask questions. But I know it was a woman, and it's not too difficult to connect the dots. With Harlow practically in line for the throne, I've always assumed it was a jealous mama who dreamed of securing the crown for her own daughter."

I flinch at Maggie's words. Nobody is ever in line for the throne outside of the royal family. As far as I know, Harlow isn't a cousin. Unless she is referring to the fact

224

that the last three generations of brides were all from Unke. The only other woman I know that believes Unke's success is certain is Elisabelle.

"We faked her death by sending a pig's heart to our benefactor and used the funds to purchase a home here. Aldwin took up a new trade as a carpenter, and I stayed home to raise Harlow. We both knew we had to abandon our own lives to keep her safe."

My eyes fall on a framed charcoal sketch pinned to a hanging board. The edges of the drawing are brittle with age, but the image of a family is still clear. Beside it is a watercolour replica of the drawing. Both leave no room for doubt that Harlow loves Maggie and Aldwin.

"Do you love her?"

Maggie nods helplessly as tears drip down her face.

"What will happen to us?" Maggie's voice hitches, and she gulps to keep it steady. "I know... I know in the eyes of the law, what we did was wrong, but we love Harlow. We can't abandon her now, even if that means we have to answer for our crimes."

Maggie's words tug at my heart, but I keep my face cool and emotionless – the face of a guardian. I wish Lars was with me to answer her question. The Academy's lessons on diplomacy feel like a child's game compared to the enormity of real life. The only thing I know for certain is that I must protect Harlow. She deserves the truth and a life with her father.

"Only the king can determine your fate, Maggie," I say as gently as possible. "For now, Harlow needs to return to the Capital."

I LEAVE MAGGIE TO BREAK THE NEWS AND SLIP OUT THE FRONT door. The wind plays with the loose hairs that have escaped my braid and tickle my neck, leaving behind a trail of goosebumps. Still, Lars waits for me in the shade, unaffected by the cold.

"Is it her?" Lars asks.

I nod and rub my hands over my arms. Lars looks back to the house and frowns at the closed front door.

"Where is she, then? We should return to the palace at once."

My lips twist into something between a frown and a smile. "I would agree, expect she doesn't know."

"What do you mean?"

I rest my hand on Lars's bicep to stop him from charging back into the house. The muscle flexes under my touch and sends heat sizzling through my fingers, despite the circumstances. I drop my hand before I forget why I came outside.

"She knows she is the duke's daughter but believes he sent her away to protect her. I need time to help her understand they kidnapped her and that her father misses her dearly."

Lars paces between me and the horses. "That could take a lifetime."

"I'll make do with an afternoon."

"Then what do you propose I do?"

I watch the muscle that ticks in Lars's clenched jaw

and know my plan won't soothe him. To him, I'm still a lady in need of protection.

"You'll go back without me to prepare King Alessandro and the Academy for Harlow's arrival. Wish will also travel with you. She can deliver a letter to the Duke of Unke."

"And leave you alone with these people! Nakoma, do you think I'm insane? For all we know, this aunt and uncle are her kidnappers."

I try to keep my face neutral, but my silence speaks volumes. Lars grips my shoulders and crouches until we are at eye level. This close, I can smell the intoxicating mix of sun and sweat on his skin. My mind reels with all the things I want to tell him.

"They're her kidnappers! Nakoma, this isn't safe."

"I'll be fine. Besides, Harlow will feel safer with me. We're both strangers to her, but you represent the world she has been hiding from."

Lars presses his forehead against mine and breathes deeply. "I don't like it."

"If I'm not home by nightfall, then you can send a search party after me."

"What if one of them runs off?"

Lars's question catches me off guard. I jerk away from him. What would I do if Maggie or Aldwin try to escape before we reach the palace? I shake my head and dismiss the question. It doesn't matter, in the grand scheme of things, as long as they don't take Harlow with them.

"Fredrick or Mikael can stay with me. I'll watch Harlow, and they can deal with the aunt and uncle."

Lars sighs but finally lets go of my arms. "Be safe. I won't forgive myself if they hurt you."

Without Lars holding me, I deflate, my whole body becoming limp and hollow. But now's not the time to pine for Lars. I can't tell him the truth either.

"I'll be back before you know it," I promise.

"I'm counting on it."

I watch Lars and Mikael ride away, my shoulders becoming heavier as the distance grows between us. With a deep breath, I straighten my spine and march back into the house. Right now, Harlow needs a guardian, even if she doesn't know it.

CHAPTER
TWENTY-SEVEN

The Pink Palace is crawling with officials when we arrive. Shouts echo through the night as both guards and guardians run in and out of the front rooms. Lanterns cast a flickering glow over the pink facade, turning the Academy blood red. Staff and ladies alike crowd the front steps, some shivering in their nightclothes. I squeeze Harlow's hand and pull her closer to me.

"It's not normally like this," I whisper.

Harlow's eyes are red, puffy and wide as saucers as she takes in the chaos around us. Her cheeks have only just dried after a tearful departure from the throne room. My ears still ring with her cries for Maggie and Aldwin as a guard led them away.

"Come, let's find someone who knows what is happening," I say.

Harlow nods weakly, her teeth chattering in the evening chill. Even with the extra lanterns, shadows consume most of the crowd. If only Wish were here – her eyes could guide me through this mess with ease – but I can't rely on her for everything. I take a deep breath and march up to the first guardian I see. Thin chain mail covers his red tunic, but I can still make out the sergeant's embroidery on his collar.

"What's happening?" I ask. "What are your orders?"

A flicker of disgust crosses the guardian's face before he conceals it with bored indifference.

"Sorry, ma'am, that's confidential information. Please wait with the other ladies until further notice."

I glower at him and pull myself up to my full height, though my head barely reaches his chest. He strokes his long, black beard as he peers down at me.

"There must be some misunderstanding. I am Lady Nakoma of Arithenos. You can tell me your orders."

The sergeant folds his arms with slow menace so that the sabre at his hip catches the light. When I don't flinch, he raises a single arrogant eyebrow.

"I do not repeat my captain's orders to ladies."

My teeth grind together as my blood simmers. Can't he see who I am? Aunt Fifi's tartan riding gown may look like an ordinary dress, but I'm still wearing Wish's leather shoulder pad over it. My nails bite into the palm of my hand as it curls into a fist. The urge to scream my true rank and commanding officer rages through me, but Harlow still cowers behind me.

"Please join the other ladies so I can continue to keep your Academy safe."

My eyes narrow to slits as the guardian gestures

towards the cluster of ladies gathered along the curb of the cobblestone street. I lift my chin and press my lips together as a new emptiness sets in. To him, I am just Lady Nakoma, not a guardian worthy of his time.

I spin on my heel, dragging Harlow with me before he can see my lower lip tremble. Harlow remains a silent ghost, trailing behind me as I steel my heart and carve a path for us towards the other ladies. As we draw closer, Arabella's gentle singsong voice becomes clear. Her arms hug Calypso as she rocks them both back and forth on the curb. Calypso's head is buried in Arabella's shoulder, but I can still hear her muffled sobs. She's not the only lady with tears in her eyes. Quinn and Tia are doing their best to comfort Hazel-Mae, who's as pale as a ghost. I weave past them with Harlow until we finally reach Uri.

"What's happening?" I ask.

Uri presses a finger to her lips and inclines her head towards Embry, who has fallen asleep with her head on Jadera's shoulder. Jadera watches us from the floor with one arm around Embry to keep her upright, while she chews the nails on her other hand to a bloody pulp.

I lower my voice. "Why is everyone outside? The guardians won't tell me anything."

"Elisabelle got away," Uri says. "They've kicked everyone outside to search for her, but we all know she isn't inside the Academy. I guess they're just looking for any evidence she left behind."

"Got away? What do you mean 'got away'?"

With only the lanterns to illuminate her face, Uri's eyes are seething pits of rage. "As soon as the messenger mentioned Lillianna, Elisabelle became frantic. She started screaming about destinies and the queen of Patel. Next thing we knew she had a kitchen knife to Embry's throat."

I stare at Uri as horror reopens the gaping chasm in me. My fingers curl tighter around Harlow's hand as my protective instincts flare to life. I squint at Embry, but under the flickering lights she appears unharmed.

"Is Embry ok?"

Uri nods slowly. "Elisabelle only used her to escape the Academy. She made us swear we wouldn't sound the alarm after she'd fled."

"And you listened?"

Uri turns away from me and stares at the Pink Palace. My heart sinks. Of course they did. Why else would the Academy be teeming with guardians hours after the first messenger?

"At first we did. Everyone was so terrified for Embry that we just didn't think... Tutor Lenora snapped out of it first."

The rest of my questions fade at the solemn tone of Uri's voice. I frown at the street. With Elisabelle's outburst, there can be no doubt her family is guilty.

"Is that her? Lillianna?" Jadera asks, startling me from my thoughts.

I step aside to introduce Harlow, but she huddles behind my back.

"Yes, but she prefers to be called Harlow now."

"Harlow," Uri echoes.

Harlow remains mute behind me. I force a smile and introduce her anyway.

"Harlow, this is Lady Uri of Froi, Lady Jadera of Eyre and Lady Embry of Petra."

At the sound of her name, Embry yawns and blinks us slowly into focus. She rubs at her eyes and squints at Harlow. Recognition flashes behind Embry's eyes. She opens her mouth to speak, but then, like Uri and Jadera, thinks better of it.

"It looks like they're giving up," Uri says.

I follow Uri's line of sight to a guard talking to Tutor Lenora and Tutor Olga. As they speak, guardians trickle out of the Pink Palace and remove the lanterns from around the building.

"Good," Uri mutters. "Elisabelle is surely smart enough to have taken any condemning evidence with her."

Jadera gasps. "Don't say that."

"Uri's right," Embry says. "They might as well let us sleep."

Jadera turns to me for support, but with Harlow shivering behind me, I can only echo Embry's sentiment. I can't scare her by raging about Elisabelle. Besides, Elisabelle is more likely to be hidden somewhere in the depths of the Capital than in the Academy. I can only hope they won't wait until morning to search the general populace for her.

❦

"ARE YOU READY TO GO INSIDE YET?" I ASK.

Harlow shakes her head for the hundredth time. The steps to the Pink Palace are empty now and the lights inside a dim glow. Only Harlow refuses the call of sleep. She hugs her arms to her chest and shivers against the night air.

"The bedrooms are lovely here. Warm and soft."

Harlow chews on the inside of her cheek. Her blond lashes clump together with dried tears that turn my chest into an abyss. I've failed her. It's written all over Harlow's face. Elisabelle is missing, and the guardians wouldn't listen to me. I force myself to smile through the feeling of emptiness.

"And the baths – hot water pours straight from the tap. You'll feel like a new person."

"Ok." Her voice is small and fragile, like a bird with a clipped wing.

I lead Harlow towards the grand oak door and enjoy her shock as it swings open before I knock. Perriwick bows towards Harlow in greeting. My heart twinges with guilt for keeping Perriwick up so late.

"Your room is this way, Lady Harlow." Perriwick gestures towards the depths of the Academy with a gloved hand.

The Academy is quiet as we follow Perriwick, but my skin prickles with the sensation of being watched. I glance at Harlow to see if she feels it too, but her face is impossible to read. We stop outside a room at the end of the hall. The lamps are lit, and the smell of fresh linen fills the room, yet despite the warm glow, it is devoid of life.

As soon as Perriwick leaves us, Harlow dumps her bag by the dresser and stands stiffly beside her bed. She clasps her hands in front of her and looks right through me.

"I think I would like to sleep now," Harlow says.

"If you're sure. I could stay with you and help you get settled."

Harlow silences me with a shake of her head. "No, thank you. I'll be ok."

I flinch at her rejection. "Well ... I'm down the hall if you need me. Uri and I share the fourth room."

Harlow doesn't answer, but I take a long moment to get the hint and leave. My ears strain for the slightest sound as I walk back to my bedroom, but only my footsteps echo back to me. With each stride, my eyelids grow heavier, and more of my adrenaline fades, but I can't sleep yet. Light seeps from under my bedroom door, and Uri is bound to have questions. I nudge the door open with my foot and poke my head inside. Uri sits in the middle of my bed with her legs crossed.

"Can't sleep?" I ask.

At the sound of my voice, she jumps up from her meditative position.

"How is Harlow? Did she go to bed?"

My lips press upwards into a smile that doesn't reach my eyes. The door clicks shut behind me, and I settle into the spot Uri vacated.

"I think she's in shock. Today has been a lot for her to take in."

Uri tucks the long strands of her black hair behind her ears and watches the door as if she expects Harlow to appear at any moment. Thoughts cloud her usually sharp gaze.

"The Pink Palace is daunting enough in the light of day. I can only imagine what it looked like to Harlow, with all of its occupants crowded on the steps," Uri says.

My head drops into my hands at the memory of Harlow's red-ringed eyes. Should I have taken her to the palace instead? We'd have traded the chaos for an immeasurable castle that would swallow her whole.

Lost in thought, we both jump when a knock sounds at the door. Tia sticks her head in and smiles sheepishly before either of us can answer.

"We thought you might be up," Tia says softly. She slips inside the room with Hazel-Mae at her heels.

"Will you tell us what happened today?" Hazel-Mae asks. "Prince Antonio's note was so brief, and Tutor Olga was beastly about the privacy of the matter."

I glance at the perch where Wish usually rests, and beyond it to the twinkling night sky. It will be days before the palace releases an official statement, but the Academy is not the general public. The ladies here deserve to know the full truth. I pat the bed beside me and wait while Tia and Hazel-Mae make themselves comfortable.

"The prince and I left on a ride this morning that took us to a small village."

236

I do my best to tell the full story of today's adventure without dwelling on the details of Wish's involvement or my own mixed emotions for Lars. As I speak, more of the Academy's ladies appear, until our bedroom is full of the representative from almost every region. Calypso's blue eyes glisten with tears when I share Harlow's initial reaction, and Jadera clutches at her chest as I explain the sacrifice Maggie and Aldwin made. All the ladies do their best to hold their questions in, but I can tell Uri and Quinn are both biting their tongues to stay quiet.

The moment I finish speaking, Quinn declares, "We have to make this right for Harlow."

"But how?" Embry asks. "We can't change her past."

Embry is dressed in only her nightgown. Her usually soft brown hair hangs limp and unruly around her shoulders. Her eyes are gloomy blue thunderclouds that reflect the turmoil of tonight.

"She deserves justice and a fair chance to meet Prince Antonio as a lady, not a commoner," Uri says.

The room erupts into murmurs that grow in volume as each lady struggles to be heard, yet no one is arguing. Jadera, who has surpassed us all on the dance floor, suggests that she will be Harlow's dance partner for all future lessons. Uri insists she will be the one to tutor Harlow in history and diplomacy. Embry offers to share a bedroom with Harlow so that neither of them will be lonely. Meanwhile, Hazel-Mae and Calypso debate who would be best at teaching Harlow the correct manners for a palace meal.

Despite these conversations, my stomach sinks with

the weight of reality. Harlow has been through enough already. I wouldn't blame her if she didn't want to stick around to meet Tutor Olga's dubious standards for a lady just to attend a ball. One by one, the other ladies notice my silence, and their eyes fall on me.

Tia's voice is gentle, but I can still hear the accusation in it. "You don't think it will work?"

My mouth opens to deny Tia's claim, but I force it shut again. I don't want to lie to Tia or any of the other ladies. At a loss for words, I look at Uri.

"We have to try, Nakoma," Uri says.

Try. The word lifts my spirits. It's the sentiment that kept me going throughout the trials of my training. Maybe I can't protect Harlow like a guardian, by tracking down Elisabelle, but I can still protect her like a lady. I can offer her a chance at the place in society she lost. A chance at justice.

I feel myself nodding even before the words pass my lips. "If Harlow wishes to stay, we will start her training before the week is over."

CHAPTER
TWENTY-EIGHT

After a week spent in bed, Tutor Lenora declares dance is the perfect distraction for Harlow's broken heart. To our surprise, Harlow agrees. Her doe eyes soften as we stretch, colour returning to her hollow cheeks. Lenora has us repeat the steps of a court dance we've been practicing all week, but nobody can keep their eyes off Harlow for long. Under Lenora's instructions, Harlow transforms into a breath of spring air, filling the entire room with her warmth. She floats across the wooden floor, spinning and twirling like a petal caught on a breeze.

"See how her feet glide, ladies? This is what we are aiming for. This is dancing," Tutor Lenora proclaims at the end of the lesson.

Jadera copies the movement again, exactly how Tutor Lenora showed us. Under the flickering chandelier, her scarlet hair burns brighter than a flame. Still, Jadera lacks the natural elegance Harlow adds to the dance.

"Tutor Lenora, I don't understand what you want me to change," Jadera says.

"It's not something I can tell you. You have to feel it in your heart."

Jadera shares a blank look with Embry, who's wearing a training skirt clipped over her day dress. The ridiculous contraption sticks out an arm's width from her body and is full of overstarched lace.

Lenora brushes Jadera off with a wave of her hand. "We'll try again tomorrow."

With a sigh so heavy I expect the maids at the opposite end of the Academy can hear her, Tutor Lenora dismisses us for lunch. The sound makes my cheeks sting with jealousy. I search the room for another red face, but it's impossible to tell if the others are just flushed from the exertion. At the start of the lesson, Lenora's praise for Harlow made my chest swell with pride. Now each compliment is like a kick to the gut. I'm happy for her, but it's tinged with nausea. Harlow is the classic Ellos beauty, and unlike Elisabelle, she is lovely inside *and* out. The perfect fit for Patel's future queen and to be Lars's bride.

I bend to stretch out my sore legs and try to focus on the ache that releases from my muscles. When my thoughts still linger on Harlow, I squeeze my eyes shut as well. If Lars chooses Harlow, I will remain a guardian. It's what I always wanted. A life worth sacrificing love and a future with a family for. Yet, before I met Harlow, riding through the fields with Lars felt like a life worth living too.

The sound of footsteps approaching saves me from my disastrous train of thought. I straighten and watch the doorway. Perriwick enters with a bow, another gentleman in lavish clothes at his side. Streaks of silver shine in his fair hair, and deep wrinkles ring his eyes.

"Tutor Lenora, may we interrupt to request the presence of Lady Harlow?" Perriwick asks.

I look at the man again, and my hand jumps to my mouth to stifle a gasp. Harlow steps forwards on shaky legs. The family resemblance is obvious, even as her eyes pool with tears.

"It is my honour to introduce Lord Augustus, the fifth Duke of Unke."

Tutor Lenora curtsies, but Harlow's cry drowns out her reply. Harlow runs at the duke and leaps into his waiting arms. He stumbles under her weight, and the two fall to their knees. Perriwick steps aside and shares a meaningful look with Lenora.

"Come, ladies," Tutor Lenora says. "We will resume our cool down in the garden."

I spare one last glance for Harlow and her father before I follow Lenora out the opposite door. We spread out across the lawn in a wide circle that rings Tutor Lenora as she leads us through stretches. When we are done, she has us sit cross-legged like children, and her face turns grave.

"I've had news," Tutor Lenora says. "I believe it is only right to share it with you all."

I watch Lenora's hands twist as she struggles with her thoughts. The only sounds in the garden are the whistle of the wind and the chirps of birds. No one else dares to speak.

"You may have guessed that King Alessandro employed me to be more than just your dance tutor. There was also an expectation that I would observe Tutor Olga's interactions with you all."

Tutor Lenora takes a deep breath and forces her hands to be still by her sides.

"Yesterday, His Majesty stripped Olga of her title of royal tutor after she confessed to accepting bribes from Elisabelle. Elisabelle paid her to exclude certain women from the palace and all interactions with the prince."

A murmur ripples through us. I glance at Uri and raise my eyebrows at her. She does the same and mouths *Your grandparents?* I shake my head. Elisabelle's disappearance must've finally prompted King Alessandro to act.

Tutor Lenora waits for silence before she continues. "Harlow's kidnappers have also claimed that they acted under the employment of Elisabelle's parents."

While this isn't news to me, it's still strange to hear the truth from Lenora's mouth. Tutor Lenora pulls a letter from her pocket and reads directly from the parchment.

"Lord Fitzwhilhem, Lady Lilith, and Lady Elisabelle are guilty of petty treason and conspiracy against the Crown's law."

My stomach rolls, and my ears ring with the words *petty treason*. Angry whispers fill the air, but I can't keep my voice to those hushed tones.

"That's ridiculous!" I yell. "Lord Fitzwhilhem and Lady Lilith ordered for Harlow to be murdered, not kidnapped."

The price for violating the authority of a social superior is surely far less than they deserve as attempted murderers.

Tutor Lenora turns the parchment so we can all see it. "I'm only the messenger, Lady Nakoma."

I slump back down and make myself small. "Sorry."

Lenora turns the parchment back around to finish reading.

"As punishment for their crimes, all members of the family will lose their current title and land. King Alessandro has also exiled them from both Unke and Ellos. Lord Fitzwhilhem and Lady Lilith were escorted from their home only yesterday, but Elisabelle still hasn't surfaced."

I stare at Lenora, gobsmacked. My heart wants to scream that their punishment isn't enough, but I hold my tongue and scan the faces of my peers. It's not the only one that wears a mask of outrage.

"This is wrong," Quinn mutters, daring to break the silence.

"It's likely the best King Alessandro could do without backlash from the other landed gentry," Uri says.

Lenora smiles weakly at Uri but doesn't add her own opinion.

"It's fitting punishment if you think about it from an Ellos perspective," Uri continues. "Without their title, land, or the support of the Crown, Elisabelle and her family will live in poverty compared to what they're accustomed to."

I can feel myself frowning, but I can't ignore Uri. She has a point. Yet my stomach is still uneasy.

"Try not to worry about it, ladies. King Alessandro is a wise man. Trust in his decision so we may enjoy the rest of our afternoon."

Tutor Lenora's advice is easier said than done, and she knows it. She folds back up the letter of proclamation and disappears into the Academy before any of us can comment.

TWENTY-NINE

Early the next morning, a summons arrives requesting the attendance of all ladies in the market square at midday. Tutor Lenora says to dress plainly but adds nothing more on the subject. When the sun is almost at its peak, Harlow and her father arrive from the palace to join us. Harlow clings to his arm, her face ridged with determination as we follow Lenora in a single line down the busy cobblestone streets.

When we arrive at the heart of the city, it's obvious we're not here to peruse market stalls. The air is devoid of the usual jovial chatter. People speak in hushed tones that set my nerves on edge and goosebumps racing down my arms. We walk past an unattended cart with fruit flies buzzing around it. Tutor Lenora grimaces as others help themselves to the overripe fruit before continuing on their way. My stomach drops. In Arithenos, we only waste food like this for one reason: punishment.

I scan the market square for confirmation and shudder when I see it. In front of a masonry workshop, someone has erected a rough wooden stand. Two ropes hang from the top of the structure, each tied in an unmistakable noose.

"All kneel for His Majesty, King Alessandro."

The call comes from a stout man in a purple uniform whose voice is bigger than his body. As we remain kneeling, I watch King Alessandro, stunned by his similarity to Lars. A purple cloak trimmed with artic fox fur drapes from his shoulders and gives him the appearance of a man twice his width. His green-eyes survey the crowd with the same arrogant indifference as Lars's court persona as he makes his way over to a wooden throne. Once he is seated, we rise, and a servant artfully arranges the cloak around his feet.

The stout man climbs onto a podium and bows to King Alessandro before he speaks. "We are here today to witness the trial of Aldwin and Margaret, the mercenaries that kidnapped Lady Harlow, formerly known as Lady Lillianna of Unke."

Chills crawl down my spine at the stout man's choice of words. Mercenaries. Kidnappers. He sounds as if they are already convicted. My eyes land on Aldwin and Maggie as he speaks, and I wonder how I could have missed them before. They both appear a century older, with shackles binding their wrists together and a guard at each of their shoulders. The nooses swing in the wind, casting a menacing shadow over their heads.

To the right of King Alessandro stands a jury wearing

black ceremonial robes. While most of them watch the stout man with a stern expression, one faces Maggie and Aldwin. His face is younger than the rest, and oddly familiar.

The stout man begins the proceedings without delay. He calls on Aldwin and Maggie to describe their assignment in all its horrid detail. Harlow trembles as they speak, and before long, she buries her head in the duke's shoulder.

As soon as Aldwin finishes their version of events, the stout man asks pointed questions with a clear bias. When he is through with them, he turns to King Alessandro for an immediate verdict, announcing, "Aldwin and Margaret, it is the recommendation of the council that we sentence you to death by hanging, unless opposed by those of our esteemed jury."

My jaw drops. A wail of despair resounds across the square. I follow the sound and watch with my heart in my throat as Harlow struggles in her father's arms. Uri's hand finds my clenched fist and squeezes. The touch is all the encouragement I need.

"Wait!"

My voice rings in my ears as every eye turns to me. I straighten my spine and face the crowd, but my eyes are on Harlow. She stares at me with tears dripping down her cheeks.

I swallow, but my throat is dry and scratchy. "I apologise, Your Majesty. I understand this is not my place, yet as the one to find Harlow and her kidnappers, I feel I must speak."

I pause. The only sound is my heart thumping a frantic rhythm. The gathered crowd watches me with bated breath. Each person waits for my next words, but now that the floor is mine, my tongue is thick and useless.

King Alessandro's brows press into a deep frown. Still, he gestures for me to continue.

"I acknowledge the hurt Aldwin and Mag—Margaret have caused for Duke Augustus and his family. Still, their actions after Harlow's kidnapping are enough to reconsider their sentencing, in my humble opinion."

The words tumble out of my mouth faster than I can think. I scan the market square, scared I make no sense. My eyes land on the jury. Most of them look furious, except for one. Dressed in his black cloak, I almost didn't recognise him, but Lars's proud smile is unmistakable.

"They were instructed to kill Harlow," I continue. "Instead, they sacrificed their own lives to keep her safe."

I turn to Maggie and watch as she sniffles back tears. For a moment, I'm struck by how similar the worry lines of her face are to my grandmother's.

"They loved her and became a family," I say, my voice now firm. "This, Your Majesty, is not a case of heartless slave traders who would deserve the suggested punishment."

With nothing left to say, I curtsy towards King Alessandro. The crowd erupts into a sea of noise as commoners state their opinions. The stout man shouts for attention, but the people drown him out. Duke Augustus pushes his way through the chaos until I can just see the top of his blond head as he bows to King Alessandro. A curious hush falls over the crowd in time to hear him speak.

"With all due respect, Your Majesty, I would like to offer my heartfelt thanks to Aldwin and Margaret. I have spent the last decade suffering through the worst agony a parent can know. My only comfort is that my little girl was safe and loved all those years. To Lili- Harlow these people are her family. I would hate to take them from her as well, when she has already lost so much."

The king's mouth twists, and I imagine he is as stunned as the rest of the crowd. He finally nods to Harlow's father, then faces the jury.

"While Lord Augustus is not a member of our jury, he is perhaps one of the most important voices in this case. However, I feel it is time for the jury to determine Aldwin and Margaret's fate."

The market square fills once more with the sound of urgent chatter and hushed conversation. I chew the inside of my cheek and watch the faces of the jury for any sign of compassion. From this distance, it's impossible to read if their frowns and sweeping gestures are anger towards my input or arguments in favour of a lighter sentence. When my patience is near its end, a spokesperson from the jury comes forwards and bows before the king.

"We, the jury, recommend Aldwin and Margaret are cleared of all prior charges for their act of service to Unke. We propose that the staff of the palace retrains them so they may re-enter society as model citizens."

The king's voice is solemn when he speaks, but his eyes are smiling. "Let it be thus."

With those four words, my body floods with relief. Harlow is crying again, her face red and puffy as she pushes through the crowd towards me. As soon as she is close enough, she flings her arms around me. I stagger at the impact but hug her back with everything I have. Over her shoulder, I watch as Aldwin and Maggie have their shackles removed and hug each other just as tightly.

CHAPTER
THIRTY

Under Quinn's direction, we drag all the tables in the dining hall together to celebrate Maggie and Aldwin's pardon with Harlow, while her father is busy at the palace. Without him near, Harlow clings to me for support, her almost invisible brows pressed into a permanent frown.

"Do you really think they're safe now?" Harlow whispers in my ear.

I pat her arm and watch as the other ladies add vases of fresh flowers to the awkward collection of tables.

"The king is a man of his word. He'll treat Maggie and Aldwin well."

Harlow nods, but her eyes say she doesn't truly believe me.

"Father is requesting a private residence in the Capital for us from the king. It's only until the Spring Ball, but I can't bear to leave Aunt Maggie and Uncle Aldwin yet."

I pull Harlow onto the seat beside me as dishes emerge from the kitchen. Wafts of garlic butter and fresh bread erase the memory of rotting fruit and leave my mouth salivating. Chatter fills the room, even as knives and forks clink against porcelain plates.

"Will you visit them?" I ask, serving us both from a central platter.

"Father's asking for permission now. You don't think... Would he refuse?"

My thoughts drift to King Alessandro's quick acceptance and Lars's presence in the jury. Something tells me Lars had already persuaded his father to reconsider the council's initial sentence. I squeeze Harlow's hand under the table.

"I'm sure King Alessandro wants to help you. He probably feels partially to blame for this whole mess, especially after Elisabelle weaselled her way into the Academy."

Reassured, Harlow picks up her fork and digs into her meal. We eat until my stomach feels ready to burst and we've reduced the platters to crumbs. I lean back in my seat and listen to Jadera argue with Arabella about their favourite jousters. Calypso interrupts them, arguing that the sport is outdated. Jadera turns to her with a fire in her eyes that matches the flame of her hair.

"So, Jadera ... if you don't marry the prince, what will you do?" Quinn asks before the table can become a war zone.

Jadera blinks at Quinn in stunned silence. Quinn

pretends to flick her short hair over her shoulder and puts on a haughty tone.

"I'll be living in style with Baron Ernold, of course."

Her answer quickly eases the competitive edge from the room as others hurry to add equally dramatic replies.

"If Papa has his way, then my husband will be far wealthier than yours, Quinn," Tia declares.

"Your husbands might be rich, but I'll have my own money," Uri claims.

Quinn snorts with laughter. "When pigs fly! Diplomats don't make half as much as nobles."

Calypso rests her chin on her hands, and her blue eyes fill with a dreamy look. "If the prince doesn't want me, I will gladly continue my father's legacy. He doesn't care that a boy won't inherit his business."

Hazel-Mae glances at Calypso with a sheepish expression. "It would be lovely to become the wife of the Minister of Food and Agriculture."

I wish I could be as honest with these girls as Hazel-Mae and Calypso are. When we leave the Academy, I'll miss this moment, surrounded by friends and the comforts of palace life. I stare at my hands, now soft and without calluses; soon they'll pull my bowstring tight as I spend endless days patrolling Arithenos's border. My heart aches, even though the thought of serving as a guardian used to bring me pride.

I chew the inside of my cheek, opening a sore I created during Maggie and Aldwin's trial. The metallic tang of blood and sting of pain clears my mind long enough to realise Tia is watching me. Before I can smile and reassure her, Tia is on her feet.

"If I am lucky and don't marry my pa's choice, I'll become a tutor and teach Hazel-Mae's many children to dance."

Embry scoffs and stands as well. "The only person fit to tutor dance in this room is Harlow."

Tia cocks an eyebrow and shoots me a mischievous grin. "Then let her prove it. Come on, Harlow. Dance with me."

Harlow stares at Tia with wide eyes and an even bigger smile. "Now? There's no music!"

"I'll count the tempo to one of the country dances. They're simple enough," Uri offers.

"I know the tune," Arabella adds.

Quinn pulls Harlow to her feet. "There's plenty of room for it with all the tables together."

Coerced into the dance, Harlow joins Tia in the middle of the cleared space. Jadera and Embry jump up as well to form the second pair in the tight circle. Together, we clap out the rhythm, and Arabella sings so sweetly I'm sure she has missed her calling as a soloist. The girls giggle with each twist and twirl until their faces are bright red. When Tia trips over Embry's feet, I forget to clap, swept up by the wave of laughter that fills the room.

Once I calm down, I rub my face to soothe my aching cheeks and glance at the grandfather clock. I promised Grandmother I would be over by now.

"Oh shoot, I've got to go."

Still consumed by occasional fits of laughter, most of the others don't hear me. Uri glances up from her perch on the tabletop and waves goodbye.

"Have fun with your grandparents."

GRANDMOTHER GREETS ME AT THE FRONT DOOR BEFORE I HAVE the chance to knock. Thamsley stands behind her, dressed in his usual suit and white gloves.

"Shall I look for another post, ma'am?" Thamsley asks. "You seem to have little use for me these days."

I raise my eyebrows at Thamsley and pause on the threshold. Perriwick would never be so bold. Grandmother simply titters and waves off his remark with a flick of her wrist.

"You know we could never do without you, Thamsley," she says.

Grandmother loops her arm through mine and whisks me away down a corridor, leaving Thamsley to close the door behind us. Even though her legs are as short as my own, I struggle to keep pace with her on the winding staircase. There's a secretive smile on her face by the time we stop in front of one of the many closed doors.

"This was your mother's bedroom," she says.

I take in the cream door and its brass handle with fresh eyes. There's nothing special about the door except for how it makes my heart yearn for home.

"You're her size, you know ... plus a few extra curves."

I laugh in shock and hide my body under my crossed arms. My face burns with embarrassment.

"Thank you ... I think."

Grandmother winks, and I might die on the spot.

"Why—Why are you showing me this?"

Grandmother answers by opening the door and striding across the room. The air is stale and frigid inside, but the bedroom is free from dust. An enormous four-poster bed takes centre stage, wispy curtains concealing the mattress. While the rest of the house is full of gilded glamour, this room is bright white and pastel pinks. Even the plush carpet is a pale pink. I run my hand along the top of a shelf and study the knick-knacks that used to hold a special place in my mother's heart. The glass swan figurine and collection of exotic coins are meaningless to me, but I make a mental note to ask Mother about them one day.

"Over here, Nakoma."

I spin at the sound of Grandmother's voice and finally notice the closet bursting with colourful gowns. My feet take me closer without conscious thought, but I resist the urge to grab them.

"I thought you could use something new for the ball."

I open my mouth to speak, but Grandmother hushes me before I can utter a sound.

"I know your mother would've prepared a dress for the occasion; she isn't thoughtless. Still, the finery available in Arithenos on short notice is nothing compared to what others will be wearing."

I close my mouth and step closer to the gowns. My fingers trail the sparkling beads of a dress that are no match for the simpler ballgown I'm planning on wearing. Grandmother joins me by the closet and tucks a strand of hair behind my ear. I flinch away from her touch, but she doesn't let my reaction deter her.

"You deserve to shine like the blessing you are. I saw how you spoke for up for Harlow today."

I nod, too overwhelmed by Grandmother's generosity to speak. There's a lump in my throat as I browse through Mother's collection. The finery is so different from the plain cotton dress she wears while working dough in our kitchen. To leave all this behind for a merchant should be preposterous, but it's not that hard to imagine when I think of Lars.

Grandmother searches through the gowns for a moment before pulling one off the racks. The gown is lavender with pink pearls sewn into the bodice. Layers of pink and purple chiffon, that float like clouds at sunset, form a full skirt that swishes as she fans it out before me.

"This is the gown that Elaine was supposed to wear for her betrothal ceremony. In the end, she never wore it outside of the dressmakers."

I take the offered dress from Grandmother and frown. From the back, I can see a built-in corset and unforgiving boning. I run a hand over my own comfortable dress, which is flattering without restricting my movements.

"I don't know, Grandmother. It doesn't look like my type of dress..."

"You might surprise yourself. Please, try it."

When I don't argue, Grandmother pushes me behind the privacy screen in the bedroom. I hold the dress up again. It's gorgeous. The dress Mother prepared is nothing in comparison. It won't hurt to at least try it on.

"I'll need help with the laces," I call out to Grandmother after I've slipped on the gown.

Grandmother is by my side in an instant. As she pulls the corset tight around my body, I can't help but admire the gown. She keeps the laces loose enough that the boning only hugs and refines my waist without stealing my breath.

"There, now let me see you."

I spin around to face Grandmother and marvel at the way the skirt shimmers when I move. She inspects every inch of the dress, pinching various sections as she tuts and mutters to herself.

"If we lengthened the train, it would add a modern touch."

The thought of altering the gown curdles my stomach. In this dress, I'm closer to Mother than I've been for moons. I blink back the threat of tears.

"No train. I like it the way it is."

"At the very least, it needs to be taken out in the shoulders to accommodate your muscular frame. I'll have it dropped off as soon as it's done."

I gently push away Grandmother's hand and repeat myself. "I like it the way it is."

"You haven't even seen yourself in the mirror," Grandmother protests.

"I don't need to. If it was right for Mother, it will be right for me."

Grandmother wraps her arms around my waist and holds me close. "Oh, Nakoma, you'll do your mother proud. I just know it."

This time, I don't flinch away from her touch.

CHAPTER
THIRTY-ONE

I peek at the lavender gown hanging in my closet
for the third time since Skip delivered it this
morning with minor alterations. With each stolen
glance, butterflies fill my stomach and my palms grow
sweaty. Tomorrow I will get to wear the most beautiful
dress I've ever seen, but it comes with a price. I have to
tell Lars the truth. He deserves it.

"Why don't you go for a walk? Visit Kato perhaps?"

I jump at the sound of Uri's voice. She leans against
the doorframe with a knowing smile. How long has she
been watching?

I glance back at the closet once more. "Will Tutor
Lenora mind? What are the other girls doing this
afternoon?"

Uri shrugs. "Becoming glamorous, I suppose."

I step past Uri and shoot her a teasing smile. "In that
case, you better go join them."

Uri wrinkles her nose and sticks out her tongue

before retorting. "Says you. Try not to fall in any dung while you're there. You already smell like a horse."

I laugh and shake my head as I walk away. Somehow, Uri always knows exactly what to say. I wish I could read people as easily as she does.

ALL THE HORSES ARE OUT IN THE FIELDS WHEN I ARRIVE AT THE palace, but I still head for the stable to collect Kato's gear. Stablehands clear the stalls of muck and hose the floor clean. I avoid the puddles and make my way towards Kato's stall. One worker leans against the wall and watches my approach. I squint at the figure. There's something familiar about him.

"Omarion?" I call out. "What are you doing here?"

Omarion smiles, but his eyes look distant. "It's good to see you in one piece, Nakoma."

There's something about his tone that sets my nerves on edge. I step in front of him and plant my hands on my hips.

Omarion rubs his hand over his face. "The High Priestess sent me."

"Why? She could have sent a message via the eagles, or Wish."

Omarion watches the stablehands work. His hesitation makes me lower my defensive stance and try to see things the way a guardian should. We are in a public space with dozens of ears to listen to our conversation. I motion for Omarion to follow me

261

towards the back of the stables. We don't have clear access to an exit here, but at least we are far from prying eyes.

"The High Priestess was worried about the recent developments with the child of Unke. She thought you could use some backup in case the situation turns sour."

My brows press into a frown as I try to picture what the High Priestess would've seen through Wish. Harlow is certainly unexpected, but nothing beyond my capabilities as a guardian.

"Harlow is no danger to Arithenos or myself."

"She might not be, but what of the other lady of Unke?"

I catch myself midshrug. Omarion is my superior; he deserves a better response than what I might say to Uri.

"I appreciate the concern," I say carefully, "but I still don't understand why she selected you for the task. There are Arithean guardians in Ellos already who are prepared to offer assistance."

"That's not all, Nakoma. Your ride with the prince has caused the chiefs to question your professionalism." I flinch at Omarion's voice. I've heard him admonish my peers, but I've never taken the brunt of his anger. "You've been reckless. Have you forgotten your commands?"

I step away from Omarion. My hands curl into fists by my sides. A protest rests on the tip of my tongue, but I swallow it. This isn't the Academy. Omarion is my commanding officer, not a tutor who has stepped out of line.

"The prince doesn't even know the real you. Or have you disobeyed a direct order?"

"I've done my duty," I growl through clenched teeth. "I've not breathed a word to anyone."

"Then where is the Nakoma I know? The reports describe you as a lovesick admirer, not one of Arithenos's finest guardians."

Omarion's words rub salt in a wound I haven't felt before. Heat rises as my chest fills with anger.

"Is that not the job of the lady of Arithenos?"

"Perhaps if you were a true lady."

Omarion glances over my shoulder before continuing in a low voice. "Your task was to improve the relationship between Arithenos and the Crown."

"And I have!" I yell. "The king will listen when Arithenos next speaks of unfair tax burdens. The other ladies of the Academy are even willing to sign a petition on Arithenos's behalf."

Omarion holds his hands up in surrender. The gesture reminds me of him calming a startled horse. I glower at the comparison.

"Nakoma, I am your friend."

"Friend?" I spit out a cruel laugh.

The word stings my ears. But if Omarion wants to be treated like a friend, then I will speak to him like one.

"Friends trust each other. Friends don't accuse you of failing your people."

Omarion's face remains cool and impassive. "I left the rest of our platoon behind to be here for you. I didn't want it to be a chief that came to question you."

Omarion keeps his voice soft, but its soothing tone falls on deaf ears.

"So, am I a burden, or your friend? I can't be both, and it's apparently such a sacrifice for you to be here."

"You could never be a burden to me, Nakoma..."

I pace, fury forcing my legs to control my temper. Omarion reaches for me, but I swat him away. My mind plays his words on repeat, telling me again and again that I'm a lovesick fool.

"Please calm down. Let's talk about this. We can create a plan of attack for the Spring Ball."

I shake my head. "Why do you even care? It's not like the ball matters anyway, right? You've made it pretty clear no man should love a guardian like me."

My words strike their mark. Omarion's mouth twists with pain, but I'm not interested in hearing his excuses. I turn my back on Omarion and flee. Tears pool against my lower lashes and blur my vision as I run. My shoulder knocks against someone, but I don't stop to check if they're ok. I mutter an apology and pick up my pace until I am safe within the walls of the Academy once more.

CHAPTER
THIRTY-TWO

Although it's dusk when the first carriage arrives, the Academy has been a whirlwind of activity all day. Grandmother warned me it would take time to prepare for the Spring Ball, but I still didn't expect the full day of beauty treatments. Now my skin is raw from sugar scrubs and my neck aches from hours waiting for the hot rollers in my hair. But it's worth it to see my hair shimmer with Grandmother's pearls and my natural waves transformed into tight curls.

A single ringlet tickles my collarbone. According to the maid who designed my coiffure, the curl is seductive and extends my neckline. I flick the lock aside, earning me a scowl from Uri.

"The curl will fall out if you keep playing with it."

I poke my tongue out at Uri but replace the ringlet onto my shoulder.

"Easy for you to say," I grumble.

Uri's hair sweeps up into a knot of braids that is

both practical and elegant. Twin rubies dangle from her ears and extend her neck into a swanlike arch. The jewels are the only ornamentation her attire needs, with hundreds of intricate lace roses decorating the bodice of her burgundy gown and exposing her delicate collarbone.

"Lady Nakoma and Lady Uri, you'll both go with Lady Harlow, since you should all fit in the same carriage," Tutor Lenora calls from the doorway.

I eye Harlow's dress with suspicion. It will be a miracle if she can even sit in the contraption. The ivory gown has a full skirt that makes her narrow frame appear twice its size. Maids protect the skirt from trailing against the ground as we follow Harlow to the carriage. She catches my eye, and I know she's caught me staring at her. She beckons me closer with a tilt of her chin and lifts the front of the gown.

"Look, it's just this hoop frame that makes the cloth stick out."

My mouth opens into a silent *oh*.

"Sorry, I didn't mean to be rude," I murmur.

"It's ok. I wouldn't have picked it, but this was supposed to be my debutante dress."

Once Harlow arranges the hoop so that she can sit comfortably, Uri and I scoot onto the opposite seat. I glance at Uri, but her face mirrors my confusion.

"What is a debutante?" I ask, once the carriage is in motion.

Harlow's fingers linger on the pearls that circle her throat.

"It's when a young woman reaches maturity and she's presented to society as an adult."

"Oh, we have something like that in Froi," Uri says. "We call it *'the welcome'*."

I shudder at the memory of my coming-of-age ceremony. Mother insisted that I wear a new bright-blue dress, when all the other girls wore creamy linen. I stuck out like a sore thumb. Yet the memory no longer holds the weight of embarrassment over me. Not when I think of the finery Mother had as a child, or when I remember it was also the day that the High Priestess declared I would join the ranks of the guardians.

"Nakoma? Are you okay?" Uri asks.

I nod and try to keep my thoughts in the present. "I'm fine."

Harlow reaches for my gloved hand and squeezes it. "Your eyes went all distant and cloudy." Her gloved fingers are cool to the touch. I slip out of their hold easily, afraid the touch might give away my thoughts.

"I was just thinking of my coming-of-age ceremony," I say. "We call it a 'welcoming to Arithenos'."

Harlow accepts my explanation and shifts her attention to the window. I watch as the glow of the streetlights illuminates her. She's always reminded me of a porcelain doll, with her smooth skin and button nose, but now she appears more delicate than ever. Her face echoes the uncertainty that twists my stomach and leaves me hollow. I reach across the carriage for Harlow's hand, and this time, I don't let go until we reach the palace.

EVERY INCH OF THE PALACE GLITTERS WITH OPULENCE. MY heels click against the sparkling marble floor as we follow a purple-clad footman to the ballroom, but I can't smell the fresh wax over the abundance of flowers circling the banisters and columns.

"Oh look, there's Arabella," Uri says.

I follow Uri's line of sight to the front of the queue, where Arabella glows in her golden dress. The herald beside her stamps his cane and announces her full title before she descends the winding staircase into the ballroom.

The footman bows and instructs us to wait in the queue before disappearing back down the hallway. As soon as he's out of sight, I rush to the edge of the landing and gaze out at the ballroom beneath us. Guests cluster around the edges of the dancefloor, their jewel-toned gowns shimmering under the light of the chandeliers. My hands drop from the railing as their faces swim before me. Who knew Patel had so many noble families?

"Lady Harlow of Unke, representative of the Pink Palace," the herald calls.

My head snaps up in time to see Harlow descend the staircase. Her iron grip on the banister is the only sign of her nerves as she moves towards the dancefloor. Murmurs trail her as she rushes to her father's side, but I can't watch her for long. The herald's white glove beckons us forwards.

I link my arm through Uri's and press myself to her side. "Don't leave me."

"Lady Uri of Froi, representative of the Pink Palace."

Uri offers me a gentle smile and extracts her arm. Without her, the air grows thin, and my chest aches. I breathe deeply, but the sickeningly sweet perfume of roses does nothing to loosen the tightness restricting my lungs.

"Lady Nakoma of Arithenos, representative of the Pink Palace."

My gloves stick to my sweaty palms as I tug them higher on my forearms. Still, too much of my skin shows. Heat burns my skin at the thought of my platoon seeing the low cut of my corset. Their distant laughter echoes in my ears, but I force myself to take the first step. *The laughter is not real.* I scan the crowd for a familiar face to anchor my thoughts. *There.* A gleam of raven hair catches my eye, and I can breathe once more. The last few steps melt away until all I see is Lars grinning like a wild thing, even with his hair slicked to perfection.

Even with my heels, Lars towers over me. His royal purple jacket hugs his broad shoulders and leaves my heart in my throat. I dip into a curtsy, my eyes fixating on the marble between us.

"Your Highness," I say, the words soft and breathy.

Lars pulls me closer with the slightest touch, his lips lingering over my gloved fingers long enough to set my body aflame.

"Everybody is watching," I whisper.

He tilts my chin up so I can see the hungry look in his eyes. "Let them."

The first notes of a flute float across the dancefloor and wrap around us in a delicate embrace. As the strings of a quintet join the melody, Lars bows with a grand flourish.

"Lady Nakoma, may I have this dance?"

Afraid my voice will betray me, I let my actions speak for me. I step into the circle of his arms, my body soft and pliable under his touch. Together, we glide across the dancefloor, the world a whirl of rich colours. In his arms, I'm graceful and delicate, all the things a princess should be.

"I've dreamt of this moment since I first saw you in the stables," Lars says, his voice pitched for my ears alone.

I scoff to cover the fizz of happiness that bubbles through me. "But I was so rude to you."

"It was nothing I didn't deserve. The stablehands warned me against entering Kato's stall, but I was desperate to prove to myself that I could do more than sit in meetings all day."

Lars twirls me under his arm and my breath escapes in a rush. The music swells around us blurring the nameless faces of the court into pinpricks of light.

"I like you best when you're just Lars," I murmur as I curl my fingers around his neck. "Not Lars the stablehand ... or Prince Antonio Lawrence."

I pinch the gelled ends of Lars's hair and fight the urge to muss it back to the unkept mess that I love.

270

Lars dips his head towards mine until our noses touch. "So who's *just Lars*?"

"He's the boy who introduced me to golden potatoes and dared to race me down a narrow valley path."

We break apart as the song fades, and with it, our illusion of privacy.

"Come with me?" Lars asks.

I nod, too embarrassed by the gaze of courtiers to form a sensible thought. Grand glass doors lead us to one of the palace's many courtyards. Night-blooming jasmine greets us as the air sends goosebumps dancing across my skin.

"Have I told you yet how beautiful you are?" Lars whispers in my ear.

His breath caresses my cheek and chases away the chill. I bite my lip, afraid of what I might say.

"There's something I've been meaning to ask you," he says. "I thought it would be better to hear it from me first, though my announcement tonight shouldn't come as a surprise."

My heart stops.

"No." I say the word before I have time to think.

Hurt is written all over Lars's face. "What do you mean, no?"

I struggle to swallow past the lump in my throat. "I mean there is something I need to tell you first."

Lars steps away from me, but he keeps hold of my hands. I rub my tongue against the roof of my mouth, searching for the words I need. My eyes flick to the stars.

"I—"

I stop myself. Something isn't right. Goosebumps race across my skin. I spin to face the night, but hands drag me away from Lars before I can see our attackers.

Instinct takes over, and I break free of their hold. With my back to Lars, I take in the scene. Three palace guards form a half ring between me and the door. Distant shouts tell me more are coming.

"What on earth is going on?" Lars asks, his voice deep and commanding.

The guards ignore Lars and edge closer. I widen my stance. Although the men wear the purple uniform of the palace guard, I don't trust that they mean Lars no harm.

"Don't come any closer!" I growl.

They creep further forwards, and I spring into action. Years of training take over. I aim a punch at the closest guard. My dress resists the movement and weakens the blow. I dodge under his next swing and kick hard at his legs. A grunt tells me I've hit home. I focus on the next target. His nose breaks with a satisfying crunch and spurt of blood. He stumbles back, clutching at his face.

Behind me, Lars continues to yell orders. Nobody listens. More guards join the fray, charging forwards from their posts around the palace. I keep moving, slipping under arms and always keeping Lars behind me. Hands lunge for my dress, and I stumble as the fabric tears. The moment of weakness is all it takes. I writhe in their grasp, but it is no use. The guards twist my arms behind my back and force my hands into cuffs.

"As the Crown Prince of Patel, I demand you release her."

The leader of the group steps forwards, clutching at his ribs, his breathing laboured.

"My apologies, Your Highness, but I cannot. We act on the king's orders."

"What orders?" Lars spits out. A vein in his jaw ticks as he glowers at the men who hold me.

The guard turns to face me. With some effort, he pulls a scroll from the belt in his tunic. "Nakoma of Arithenos, you are hereby charged with false impersonation, and deception of the Crown."

I freeze. The fight drains from my limbs. With little effort, the guards shove me until I am kneeling in the dirt. Even in the dark of night, Lars's confusion is obvious. His eyes implore me to speak.

"Tell them it isn't true, Nakoma."

A tear slips down my cheek as Lars's voice cracks. I want to curl into a ball, but he deserves the truth.

"I wanted to tell you, but the High Priestess insisted nobody could know."

Lars crouches in front of me. He wipes the tear from my face with such tenderness that more well forth. His voice is soft and measured, meant only for my ears.

"What do you mean?"

"I am a guardian, Lars. I have sworn to protect Arithenos with my life."

His hand drops to his side. He backs away from me, his face contorting into something unrecognisable. His eyes are a dagger that carves my heart in two.

"You lied."

I struggle to stand and go to Lars, even as the guards shove me back into the dirt. "I wanted to tell you, Lars."

"Don't call me that."

"Please believe me. I wanted to tell you the truth. You know how much I care for Arithenos. It wasn't my choice."

Lars shakes his head, unable to look at me. "I don't know you anymore."

His words hit as hard as any physical blow. I slump forwards in the guard's hold. My head hangs, and I let my tears drip to the earth.

"Take her away."

I don't struggle as the guards lift me back to my feet and drag me away from Lars.

THIRTY-THREE

Water drips from the ceiling and seeps from the walls. My teeth chatter from the cold spray that hits me with each splatter, but I don't move. I can't move. A deep ache spreads through every inch of my body with each beat of my broken heart. I squeeze my knees to my chest to seal away the pain, but I can't hide from it. My mind keeps forcing me to relive the disgust on Lars's face. His final words torture me. *Take her away*.

My eyes sting, but tears no longer blur my vision. There's nothing left in me to give. Each moment stretches into an eternity in the silence of my cell. How long have I crouched like this?

Gradually, I pull myself upright and rub the dried snot from my face. The air is stale, but I force myself to take deep, steady breaths. I cough on the stench of human waste and mould. The trickle of light from the narrow window is enough to know this cell has not been cleaned since its last prisoner. I scoot along the rough hessian sacks that form my bed to escape the dripping ceiling but end up pressed against the damp wall instead.

I glance at the rusted window, but there's no point in inspecting the walls for a weak point. Even if I escape, I've still failed. Nobody will trust Arithenos now that I've made palace guards bleed.

The sound of footsteps draws my attention away from the pit of despair inside me. I crawl back onto the bed and feign disinterest. The other prisoners have already shown me that begging or screaming doesn't help. As I pick at my nails, the voices of my new neighbours are different to prior guard visits. They whistle and shout like they're calling for a stray dog.

"Hey, pretty lady, why don't you bring your *fine self* over here?"

"I could use a piece of that ass."

"If you're looking for meat, I've got some that would love your attention."

Curiosity melts my resolve, and I crane my neck to see the visitor through the gloom. As she draws closer to my cell, I realise calling for a dog might be right. With her blond hair and pale pink dress, Elisabelle brings light to the gloom of the dungeon, yet I know she is no beacon of hope. She stops in front of my cell, and I scoot further into the darkness.

"What do you want?" I mumble, my voice fragile after crying so hard.

"Is that any way to greet a visitor?"

Elisabelle's voice is no louder than a whisper, but there is nothing soft about it. Her words crawl across my skin like roaches with razor-sharp teeth. I remain silent. If I wasn't wearing the tattered remains of Mother's dress, I would spit at her.

"Someone in your position can hardly afford to cause offence."

"Until my trial, my position within society is still miles beyond yours. I'm not exiled."

Elisabelle stiffens, the only sign that my insult has hit its mark. Still, I wonder how much truth it holds when she is the one standing free within the dungeon. Even if she bribed the guards to be here, there must be others who support her. Her dress is too clean for her to be spending the nights sleeping outside the comfort of a home.

"What do you want?" I sigh.

She stares at her cuticles as she speaks. "I came to confirm that His Highness has not forgotten himself and stooped below his station to visit a commoner."

"I am no commoner."

Elisabelle turns to me with the wicked smile of a cat that has found a mouse trapped beneath its paw.

"Would you prefer I call you a guardian?"

I frown. Has the news really travelled that fast? Realisation hits me like a punch to the gut. My vision turns red, and rage boils my blood. I clench my fists, imagining my fingers squeezing the life from Elisabelle's swanlike neck. This time, I do spit.

"You." The word seethes with all the venom I can muster.

Elisabelle acts as if she hasn't a care in the world, but I can see her eyes dart towards the stairway. She slips back a step, just out of reach of the bars.

"You really should be more careful about who might overhear you at the stables."

I grind my teeth. My body trembles with the desire to make her pay. I breathe through my nose and force myself to think like a lady. The guardian in me wants to channel my anger into pain, but the outburst would only condemn Arithenos to a lifetime of poverty. Afraid that I will explode if I stay still, I turn my back on Elisabelle and press my forehead to the damp wall. The cool stone seeps into my skin and helps to calm the fire within me.

"What do you want?" I finally ask once I can trust myself to speak.

"I wanted the prince, but you couldn't just let me have him."

"He was never a prize to be won," I mutter.

"Of course he is! That's the whole bloody point of the Academy."

I push away from the wall and slowly shake my head. "Lar—Prince Antonio made his own choices. I didn't chase after him."

"Maybe not, but you're the one who snuck into Tutor Olga's office after the exam. It was your grandmother who forced the Academy to check Tutor Olga's marks. And it was you who found Harlow!"

Arguments rise, but I keep my mouth shut. It wasn't

just me. Hazel-Mae and Tia are the ones who spread the news about the exams. Wish discovered Harlow in the marketplace. Even Grandmother acted on her own.

"Why do you hate me so much?" The question slips out before I can reconsider it.

"Because you are nothing. People like you shouldn't even be at the Academy. You're just here as a token, and still, everyone likes you. You didn't even have to force them."

Elisabelle frowns, and her chin quivers. Without her composure, she looks like a teenager, not a monster who deserves to be behind bars. I try to imagine Elisabelle's world – a world where every relationship is bought, not earned. A childhood where love meant new toys, not time and fond memories.

"I pity you, Elisabelle."

"You can't pity me. You're locked in a stinking cell. You smell like you've slept on a bed of manure. You have nothing!"

I don't flinch. Her shrill voice echoes through the dungeon and stirs mutters from the other cells, yet her rising temper only keeps my own at bay.

"I do pity you. You might have escaped your exile for now, but eventually, you will run out of money. Real friends don't ask for favours when they help each other. Without friends or money, the world will be cruel to you."

"Shut up."

Her voice is small, and her gaze lost. Perhaps honesty is not what she deserves, but it's what she needs.

Learning to live without her wealth and influence could be the only thing that saves Elisabelle from being a wretch for the rest of her life.

"I wish you the best."

With nothing left to say, I turn my back on her. My mind and heart are too heavy with my own emotions to watch Elisabelle process her own. I hear her sniffle before the slap of her slippers against the floor announces her exit. When I'm sure she won't come back, I slump against the wall and hang my head in my hands.

CHAPTER
THIRTY-FOUR

The clatter of keys against the cell door wakes me. I bolt upright, only to see two guards at the door. I slump back against the cold wall. Everything aches after a night of fitful sleep on the hessian pallet.

"Don't bother trying anything," the first guard calls out.

"You won't make it anywhere within the castle without a pair of cuffs around your wrists," the second guard adds.

I nod mutely. If I'm going to trial, another escape attempt won't help my case. If they lead me to the noose, then I need to know what I'm up against first.

Once my wrists are secure, the guards push me out the door and through the dungeon. The corridor that connects the various cells is only marginally drier, thanks to the constant warmth of the mounted torches. They illuminate parts of the dungeon that I would rather not see. Rats scurry from one room to the next, and dried blood stains one of the cell doors.

The bright sunshine hurts my eyes as we exit the dungeon. I squint against it, but the walk between the dungeon and our destination remains a blur of light. From the gasps and murmurs that reach my ears, I guess we've entered a more populated area of the palace. With each step, the abandoned Spring Ball decorations slowly come into focus. The sweet floral fragrance is still overwhelming, but now with it comes a hint of decay.

We pause in front of a pair of familiar oak doors for the guards to confer with their comrades. I take the opportunity to count my exits. The hall branches off in three directions, but there are guards stationed at every turn. The odds are not in my favour. Before I can count the guards, we are on the move again, and this time, through darker corridors. There is no decor here, and the servants we meet keep their eyes on the floor.

When I'm sure we're lost, the guards open a side door, and we enter the throne room. I suck air in through my teeth and try to keep my head held high. The entire court is here, but I can't see a jury. My heart thumps out a wild rhythm as I step up to the stand.

The moment I find Lars, I can't look away. He's dressed in a fresh white doublet that almost brightens the dark circles beneath his eyes. Beside him, the queen appears glacial, her raven hair swept up beneath a golden crown. She rests a hand on Lars's shoulder as I stare at him and I soak in the shape of his lips as he whispers to her. My mind begs him to just look at me. Let him see the soiled remains of my ballgown. Maybe then my heart won't ache as much. But he won't even do this one thing for me.

The Minister for Justice announces himself and starts the proceedings. I don't bother to glance at him. Instead, I watch as Lars stares at a distant spot at the back of the room. The only sign of life is a slight nod of his head when his mother murmurs in his ear. The movement pierces my heart and deepens the already gaping hole in my chest.

"State your full name and occupation for the court."

I look at the Minister for Justice blankly for a beat until my brain catches up with the trial that I'm ignoring.

"My name is Nakoma Elainedaughter. I am a guardian of Arithenos."

"Nakoma, we have brought you before King Alessandro for your crimes of false impersonation, and deception of the Crown. How do you plead?"

My throat constricts. No answer comes to mind. With each passing second, my tongue grows fat and heavy. My eyes flick back to Lars. This time, he meets my gaze. His lips twitch with the slightest movement. A few seconds more and I realise what he is mouthing. I repeat the phrase and hope I understood Lars correctly.

"Not guilty."

The minister nods, and I get the sense that he expected this response. He turns to King Alessandro and reads my charges.

"Nakoma has declared herself to the court as a

guardian of Arithenos. Yet her entry visa omitted this occupation. Arithenos claimed she was the most appropriate candidate for a lady of Arithenos. She has masqueraded and lied to her peers at the Academy. This, Your Majesty, is false impersonation."

A shiver runs down my spine as the minister speaks. His frigid voice is enough to turn any heart to ice. I grip the wooden stand, even as the cuffs bite into my wrists, to keep myself from panicking.

"Not only did she lie to the ladies of the Pink Palace, but she has also lied to Prince Antonio. We must ask ourselves why Arithenos would allow such deception of the Crown. A skilled guardian would be fatal if they gained the trust of our prince."

"Arithenos wished no harm—"

A sword presses against my neck and ends my protests. I clamp my mouth shut and stare daggers at the guard that holds it.

"Tell me, Nakoma, do you recognise this weapon?"

My stomach drops. The minister holds my dagger aloft with a knowing glint in his eye. Light from the chandeliers dance along the engraved edge of the blade and shatter into tiny rainbows against the quartz hilt. My knuckles turn to white against the wooden stand as I imagine wrenching my weapon free.

"Yes, but—"

"It was found beneath your mattress shortly after your arrest," the minister continues, handing the dagger back to an assistant. "Nakoma has proven her capabilities during her arrest. One broken nose and three broken ribs. She inflicted these injuries with deadly accuracy and against impossible odds. Imagine what she could have done to Prince Antonio if she had brought her dagger with her to the Spring Ball."

I shrink away from the sword at my neck. Any argument I might have made seems pointless now.

"We must send a message to Arithenos that the Crown will not tolerate any attempts at treason. It is for these reasons that the recommended punishment is death by hanging."

Dread pierces me and sends my thoughts spiralling into despair. I stumble backwards and slump against the stand. The raised sword echos my movement. This can't be happening.

"This is an outrage!"

My head snaps up. Omarion storms up the aisle, guards chasing after him. The gathered court scrambles out of their seats, distancing themselves from the commotion. A high-pitched scream punctures the air. Terrified, the Minister for Justice dives behind a potted plant. His retreat brings the life back to my limbs. I twist my wrists against the cuffs and let my hope dull the pain of the metal cutting into my skin.

Omarion stops at the foot of the king. He's close enough that I can see the vein throbbing above his left brow. King Alessandro returns his stare without flinching.

"This trail is a sham! Where is the jury?"

The guards press swords to Omarion's chest and

shout for him to stand down. Omarion barely glances their way, but he does lower his voice.

"You've provided Nakoma with no opportunity to defend her actions. Arithenos did not send her as a threat to your prince; we sent her because our people do not trust Ellos to be a safe place for an ordinary lady."

Omarion shoots a look of disgust at the sword still raised to my throat, and I stand a little straighter. The guard wavers under his stare, but the sword remains.

"Arithenos has no interest in a marriage with the Crown. The only thing we hoped for was a chance to be heard."

"That is enough," King Alessandro declares. "Hold your tongue, Arithean, or I will have you removed from today's proceedings."

A man I don't recognise rushes up the aisle, calling for Omarion. He's tall and muscular like Omarion, but he's not dressed in a guardian's uniform. The man bows before King Alessandro, his black beard almost sweeping the floor.

"Please excuse him, Your Majesty. Omarion is not well versed in the manners of court." The man's thick Arithean accent is softened by his eloquent address. I glance at the embroidery on his tunic. Perhaps he is our ambassador for Arithenos.

I clear my throat, causing the blade to press deeper. "Your Majesty, Omarion speaks the truth. The High Priestess trusted me to improve Arithenos's relationship with Ellos. That's all."

Blood trickles down my throat as the sword presses

into my skin. Rage contorts Omarion's face into an unrecognisable mask, but he's frozen in place. The other Arithean clasps Omarion by the shoulders and pulls until Omarion finally allows himself to be steered away.

Once Omarion has been escorted from the room, the Minister for Justice slowly emerges from behind the potted plant. He dusts non-existent dirt from his jacket and mutters to himself before regaining his composure.

"As I was saying, regardless of this new information, we advise that—"

"Wait!"

It doesn't take long for me to pick Uri out of the crowd. As she stands, a ripple of murmurs spread out from her like a stone thrown into still water. The sound does not hide the foul language that slips from the minister's mouth.

"The Arithean suggested that Nakoma should have a chance to defend herself, Your Majesty. May I speak in defence of her character?"

King Alessandro drums his ring-heavy fingers against the arm of the throne. The sound echoes in my ears, matching the thudding of my heart.

"Very well. Speak."

Uri curtsies in her place, the action stiff and awkward within the confines of the pew.

"My name is Lady Uri, and I shared a room with Nakoma during our time at the Pink Palace. I witnessed Nakoma during her times off from the Academy schedule. Not once did she act upon her training as a guardian while at the Academy."

Understanding dawns on me. Uri's following the steps of diplomacy that Olga taught us. A gentle, soothing tone that encourages friendship. A polite curtsey to demonstrate respect. Still, there is something missing.

"That is over six moons of abstinence from one's supposed occupation," Uri adds.

There it is. An implication supported by facts, so the listener feels as though they have come to their own conclusion. King Alessandro's lips twist into a wry half smile. Did he learn the same rules of diplomacy as a boy?

Calypso jumps to her feet. "Nakoma is also the daughter of a merchant!"

King Alessandro's eyebrows rise, but he makes no comment. The Minister for Justice does not show the same restraint.

"We have many merchants in our kingdom," he grumbles, "and I would not dream of referring to each of their daughters as ladies."

Calypso flips the tail of her braid over her shoulder and looks the minister in the eye. "I am the daughter of a merchant, and it was certainly enough to secure my position at the Pink Palace."

Red seeps up the minister's collar, and his mouth gapes like that of a fish out of water. I press my lips together and fight the urge to cheer. From the looks on Tia's and Hazel-Mae's faces, I'm not the only one.

"I'm told he is a merchant of wealth, and the finest of his profession in Arithenos," Calypso continues. "My father's pearl farm is the reason I was selected as the lady of Lake Lynton. I'm sure it's not so different for Nakoma."

"Is that all?" the minister drawls.

Harlow stands in her place. "Not yet. We have not addressed the accusation that Nakoma was on a sinister mission."

Her voice trembles as she speaks, and I wish I could comfort her. Still, there is something about her posture that reminds the room of her noble birth.

"Nakoma found me and ensured I returned to Ellos safely. Under her guidance, I gained the confidence to attend the Spring Ball as a lady of the Pink Palace."

Beads of sweat gather on the minister's wide forehead, and I wonder if he feels the same shift in the room that I do. Uri and Calypso spoke well, but Harlow commands the room's attention.

"If Nakoma's intention was to undermine the system of the Pink Palace or harm the royal family, why would she care who represents Unke?"

King Alessandro leans forwards and props up his chin on his fist. "The three of you create a strong defence for Nakoma."

Harlow curtseys elegantly at the king's compliment. Calypso is quick to follow her lead, but Uri hesitates. The corner of her mouth twists into the slightest frown. Without a verdict, the compliment is hollow. The only sound in the room is the shuffle of skirts against the pews as Uri, Harlow and Calypso resume their seats.

"Regardless of any late appeals," the minister says, "the council's recommendation still stands..."

King Alessandro regards the minister for a long moment. He squirms under the king's gaze, but his discomfort is nothing compared to my own. My stomach twists into tight knots, and I gnaw at the inside of my cheek.

"It is my understanding that guardians hold a position of power within the Arithean community. They're second only to the religious leaders. Is this correct, Nakoma?"

I wipe the blood from my throat and face King Alessandro. "Yes, Your Majesty."

"Even if this was not the case, Nakoma would still be an eligible representative for Arithenos."

The sound of my gasp is nothing compared to the collective outcry from the gathered court. The minister shouts for order. King Alessandro does not wait for silence.

"Nakoma's father, Barooch, is a merchant of considerable wealth, by Arithean standards. Reports suggest their family is one of the richest in the region."

My head snaps to attention at the sound of Papa's name. Omarion was wrong to assume this trial was a sham. Somebody made sure that King Alessandro did not rely on his ministers.

"However, Lady Nakoma *has* falsified information regarding her occupation. I find this crime insignificant in the face of her dedication to returning Lady Harlow to her father. For this reason, in relation to the charges of false impersonation and deception of the Crown, it gives me great pleasure to declare Lady Nakoma not guilty."

With his last two words, I deflate. My lips mouth a silent pray to the heavens for King Alessandro's mercy.

"The matter remains that Lady Nakoma's travel visa is false. She will have until sunset to gather her belongings and depart for Arithenos. If she wishes to return to Ellos, she must seek a new visa."

A gavel bangs and seals my fate. Relief floods my veins, but the smile I offer my friends lacks warmth. After my night in the dungeon, I have nothing left to give.

THIRTY-FIVE

I scrunch up another letter into a tight ball and hurl it across my bedroom. It lands with a soft thump against the wall, and I groan. Ever since I left Ellos, I've been trying to find the words to apologise to Lars, but every time I sit down with a quill, my thoughts become a jumbled mess.

I flop face first onto my bed and let the darkness envelop me. Lars deserves the full story this time, not the half-truths I fed him. My breaths come in shallow huffs as my nose squishes against my quilt. Doubt whispers in my ear that an explanation will never be enough. In the darkness, all I can see is Lars's disconnected court face – the stoic mask of the man who thinks I'm a liar, a savage thug who played him for a fool. The ache in my chest unfurls as memories of the ball dance before my eyes.

A soft knock at the door startles me midsob. I roll to my side, my face landing in the damp patch from my tears.

"Go away, Jakob."

Muffled sounds continue outside my bedroom door. I curl my legs into my chest. The added layer of defence does nothing to stop the door from looming before me. I can't go out there. Smiles in the marketplace, protruding bellies on once bone-thin beggars ... everything outside is a reminder that I should be happy.

"Seriously, Jakob. Not today."

The door clicks open, and I bury my head in my hands.

"It's not Jakob."

I peek out between my fingers. Warm, chocolate eyes lined with years of laughter gaze at me from the open doorway. Grey hair blooms from his temples and scatters throughout his once black curls, but Papa's face hasn't aged a day. I choke down a strangled cry and fling myself into his arms. Papa wraps me in his embrace, rocking us back and forth as gut-wrenching sobs pour out of me. He tucks my head under his chin and repeats the same five words until I can finally draw a steady breath. *It's going to be okay.*

PAPA STROKES MY GREASY HAIR AWAY FROM MY FACE AS WE SIT down on my bed. I lean into his touch, letting his gentle warmth fill the emptiness inside my heart.

"When did you get here?"

"Just now. I rode ahead of the party when we

received news of your early return. Stellan will arrive tomorrow with the silks from Sebba."

I glance at Papa from under my lashes. "Are you mad?"

"Mad? How could I possibly be mad? Your mother told me everything. Our darling girl, the hero of Unke."

I shake my head. "Mother said that? But I disgraced her."

"No, sweetheart. Your mother's the proudest of us all. She just doesn't want to smother you."

I pick at a loose thread in the patchwork of my quilt. Darkness threatens to overwhelm me once more. *Proud.* There's nothing to be proud of. Papa flattens the blanket and stills my hand.

"There's something else, isn't there?"

I sniffle. "I messed up. I wasted so many chances to tell Lars the truth. He should've heard it from me, not the palace guards. Now he hates me."

Papa rubs small circles onto my back. "You followed orders. That's nothing to be ashamed of."

"You didn't see his face."

Fresh tears slip down my cheeks and drip off my chin. Papa wipes them away with his handkerchief.

"If your training as a guardian is enough to scare him away, then he doesn't deserve you."

I pull away from Papa and kick at the scrunched-up balls of paper around my room. Silence stretches between us as the wall around my heart builds up again. He wouldn't understand. Love was too easy for my parents.

"I don't want to lose him," I admit.

"So, you've been trying to write to him?"

I gather the paper balls and toss them onto the bed. "Six times! But nothing sounds right. I try to explain my actions and end up with a pile of childish excuses."

"Nakoma, sweetheart, you're not presenting your case to the council of chiefs anymore. It has to come from your heart. Your Lars will appreciate honesty. Anything else will sound like a priestess wrote it on your behalf."

I perch beside Papa. Memories of the tea party spark the faint ember of hope left inside me. Uri insisted that Lars just wanted to know me as a person, without the formalities of the Crown. Omitting my role as a guardian is not so different.

"Thanks, Papa. I'll give it another try."

Papa pats my knee. His joints creak as he stands and stretches out his long legs.

"That's the spirit. Your mother and I will be downstairs if you need anything. You know, lend you an ear, or a second set of eyes for your letter."

Papa mimes plucking his ear off to leave on the foot of my bed. I roll my eyes at him and push him towards the door.

"I'll be ok."

Papa digs in his heels. "Are you sure? I make a great scribe..."

I groan and put my shoulder into shoving him out the door. Papa clings to the frame, a devilish smile in his eyes that reminds me of Jakob.

"Don't stay up here too long. We've got your sergeant's presentation tonight at the temple."

"I know. Now go. I'll be down soon."

Papa hovers for a moment longer before I slam the door shut. I listen until his throaty chuckle fades before I rush back to my desk. The fresh sheet of paper calls my name. Words flood the page as my heart pours out through my quill. I tell him everything from the moment we met to my promotion tonight.

I'd give it all up for another chance with you.

My quill freezes over the last line, but I don't blot it out. The embroidery I gain tonight won't make me any more capable of protecting people like Harlow. I blow the ink dry and seal the letter before I can second-guess myself. All that's left is to wait to send it off with Papa's pixie post.

THIRTY-SIX

The hard wood of the bedroom floor presses into my knees as I reach under my bed. Uri's scrunched-up letter mocks me, just out of range of my stretched fingers. I've read every word a dozen times to check for hidden meanings, but they're always the same – full of well-wishes, and not a word about Lars.

With a sigh, I slide onto my belly and retrieve the letter. I smooth it out against the floor and read Uri's latest correspondence again. My eyes skim over each line, but it's the same dull details. King Alessandro kept his word and held a hearing for a fairer share of tax for the outer provinces. He also reduced Arithenos's taxes. They invited Uri to the proceedings, and her letter describes the discussion in great detail, yet it's not enough.

I sit back on my heels and stare at the ceiling. My heart whispers to check one more time. Maybe I missed something. It'll have to wait. A quick glance out the window tells me I'm out of time. The sky has shifted from the pink of dawn to blue skies and sunshine. I carefully fold the letter, then drop it onto my desk and head downstairs.

Mother and Papa are up to their elbows in soapy water when I arrive in the kitchen. On the table is more food than even Jakob can eat, and he is nowhere to be seen.

I stop dead in my tracks. "What's all this?"

Mother glances over her shoulder, then keeps scrubbing the same bowl. She shrugs as if a full table this early in the morning is an easy feat. Papa points with his eyes to Mother and mouths something I can barely make out, yet the message is clear. The breakfast was Mother's idea.

"Just a little something to help you prepare for your first day back," she says.

I kiss her cheek. It's the only way I know how to say thank you without being awkward and emotional again. Plus, I can't handle Mother turning into a puddle of tears right before work.

"You know I can't eat all of this, right?"

"I'll have Jakob leave anything we can't finish at the temple for the priestesses to distribute."

As I help myself to the hot honey cakes, I smile at the thought of Jakob struggling to carry the leftovers to the temple. My mouth waters at the smell of grilled meats covered in rosemary and thyme, but I reach for the apple and pear crumble instead. The last thing I need is meat-sweats while I'm out riding. I finish the food on my plate quickly and kiss Mother on the cheek again before I leave.

I slip down the alley beside our house and follow it to the gated courtyard that Kato sleeps in. Thick green leaves crowd the space and provide ample shade. The exotic flowers aren't in bloom yet, but the air still smells fresh and fragrant. Kato neighs at me from his stable, and as soon as I'm in the saddle, Wish launches herself from Papa's mango tree.

The training fields are already a hub of activity by the time we arrive. My stomach twists with a prick of guilt. Most guardians have already worked up a sweat, but the High Priestess insisted on a lighter workload after my experiences in Ellos. The Chief of War tried to protest, but he quickly changed his tune once Omarion gave his full report of the court trial. I never had the chance to thank Omarion before he disappeared.

Ignoring the stares that follow me, I collect a standard issue bow and full quiver from a foot soldier. Kato prances to the start of the archery course, tossing his mane like a young colt. I press my palm against Kato's neck. Warmth soaks into my skin as I wait for the thump of his heart to sync with my own. My world narrows to the targets before us and the promise of endless blue sky beyond.

With the slightest command, Kato bursts into motion. My fingers fumble with the first arrow. It pierces the ground with a tiny puff of dirt.

I grit my teeth. Another arrow in the dust.

I breathe deeply and count the beats between Kato's pounding hooves. My heart sings as the next arrow meets its mark. I hit bullseyes on the last three targets and slow Kato into a trot.

Deep cerulean stretches into infinity at the end of the training field. An ocean of rose-tinted grass seeds sways on the breeze, beckoning us forwards. I ignore the call, steering Kato away. Racing at breakneck speeds won't allow me to escape my memories of Ellos.

A sharp sound from Wish draws my attention and pricks Kato's ears. The sound is halfway between a whistle and a shriek, enough to draw my attention without attracting the golden eagles. I spur Kato into motion, but he needs little encouragement to follow Wish.

Kato slows as we reach a crowd at the entrance to the training fields. Wish darts in and out of the group, earning curses from unsuspecting guardians. I stand in my stirrups and peer over the guardians as they shout and jostle each other.

"This is a private training field," one guardian yells.

"Only guardians or those in training may enter," another adds.

"I understand that, but I must speak with one of your guardians. It is a matter of urgency."

The third man's voice sends a trail of goosebumps racing down my arms. It can't be him. I dismount in one fluid motion and edge closer to the group. The first guardian continues to speak, his voice full of scorn.

"Even if it is urgent, only Aritheans can enter."

I squeeze my way through the cracks in the crowd. Younger men begin to curse me but catch themselves when they glance down and see the embroidered edge of my uniform.

"Can you at least let Nakoma know I'm here? I'm told this is where I'll find her."

My heart stops at the pleading tone of his voice. I chew my lower lip. The empty days without a word from Lars gave me ample time to accept that he didn't care to hear my side of the story, but it wasn't long enough. Just the sound of his voice turns my knees to jelly.

The guardian in front of me spits on the ground before speaking. "That's Sergeant Nakoma to you, commoner."

"That's enough," I shout, before any more guardians can make Arithenos look stupid by not recognising the Crown Prince of Patel.

The men in front of me flinch at the sound of my voice. They step aside quickly, muttering apologies. Lars stands in the centre of the group with his arms up in surrender. Sweat drips from his forehead, and his eyes dart between me and the guardians that surround him. Still, I have to fight to keep my breathing even as I drink in the sight of him.

I frown at Lars to mask the swirling mass of emotions he has stirred to life once more. The same butterflies from our first ride together are back, but this time, frustration and anger dampen them. I'm better than this. Lars made his choice, and it'll do me no good to indulge in hope.

"You've come a long way, Your Highness, to speak with me."

"I had to, Nakoma. I couldn't leave things the way I did."

The moment I meet Lars's green gaze, I know I can't keep up my mask of contempt. There are deep bags under Lars's eyes that speak of sleepless nights and deep remorse.

"I should have spoken up for you during that ridiculous trial."

"But you didn't."

"I know. I was hurt and wanted you to hurt as well."

I stare at the ground and hope my peers won't notice the heat that has risen to my cheeks or the tears that collect against my lashes. It's an impossible dream when Lars is speaking loudly enough for all of Arithenos to hear.

Oblivious to the crowd, Lars continues. "It's hardly an excuse. I acted like a fool. Nothing could have been more obvious the moment I faced the reality of choosing someone other than you."

I chew my bottom lip. My heart yearns to trust Lars again, but there's a voice that whispers what-ifs. I glance up at Lars. It's a long journey to travel to Arithenos just to break my heart again.

"I wrote to you last moon," I say. "You never replied."

Lars steps towards me, crouching so he can read my expression, even as I refuse to look him in the eye. "It must've gone astray. The pixie post is never reliable for travellers."

"You took your time to get here."

"I came as fast as I could, but I had to make sure Father would listen to the appeals from the outer provinces first."

Lars reaches for my hands, and I let him take them. The warmth I tried to forget radiates from his touch.

"Nakoma, I love you."

A choked cry escapes past the lump in my throat. "You hardly know me."

"I loved you as an Arithean lady, and I will continue to love you as an Arithean guardian. But I think I will love you the most as my wife..."

I gasp as Lars drops to one knee in front of me. He fumbles in his pocket for a moment before revealing a sapphire and diamond ring.

"We have the king's blessing to return to Ellos betrothed, if you'll have me? Nakoma Elainedaughter, I want to know the real you. Will you let me try?"

I wipe at my face, surprised to find it wet with tears. "That could take a while. You have a lot to learn."

Lars smiles up at me, and in his face, I see the dreams I never thought to wish for.

"As long as it takes."

My face splits into a giddy grin. Before Lars can say anything else, I throw my arms around him and kiss him with everything I am. Around us, cheers fill the air, but I can barely hear them. The only thing that matters is the crushing heat of Lars's lips, and his hands holding me steady. When we break apart, Lars wipes away the last of my tears with his thumb and slips the ring onto my finger.

My breathing ragged, I whisper the words that have been building within me since our first meeting in the royal stables.

"I love you too."

EPILOGUE

"Y ou're not dressed for tea with your grandparents."

I look up from my correspondence and shoot Lars a sheepish smile. He leans against the doorway to our study, ruggedly handsome in his formal embroidered doublet. The shadows beneath his eyes tell me everything I need to know about the latest council meeting.

"I've sent word that a headache will prevent me from attending this afternoon."

Lars shakes his head at me. We both know they won't believe me for a minute, especially not when half of Ellos has seen me striding around the royal chambers in trousers all morning, a team of youth ambassadors at my heels. Still, my grandparents are far too polite to say anything.

Lars crosses the room and presses a featherlight kiss against my temple.

"What were you reading?" he mumbles into my skin.

"A letter from Uri. She departs for Ellos soon to start an apprenticeship as a diplomat."

Lars finds the tight muscles in my shoulders and rubs the tension from them. I lean into his touch, the rest of Uri's letter almost forgotten. The new position is only half of her good news. Uri also shared that child abandonment rates have dropped in the marshlands of Froi since the lower taxes have made food more affordable for parents.

"It will be nice for you to have another friend close by," Lars says.

My only reply is a hum of pleasure as Lars's hands work their magic. Hazel-Mae moved into a town house last moon to be closer to the Minister of Food and Agriculture. Replying to their wedding invitation is on my current to-do list, along with an overdue response to my parents' most recent letter.

"Do you know of any other ministers or members of the court that need a wife?" I mumble.

Lars laughs. "I'll stay on the lookout for Tia."

I tilt my head back for a quick kiss, but Lars has other ideas. His lips trail my neck, his new beard tickling the delicate skin.

"I'll get the door," Lars murmurs into my skin.

I jump to my feet. "The door's still open?"

Lars kisses the inside of my wrist and pulls me towards him.

"A problem easily remedied."

"Later," I promise. "Kato is waiting for me. I asked

one of the stablehands this morning to set up a riding trail so I can practice my archery."

Lars sighs but releases me. "Try not to scare anyone today."

I grin but make no promises. If the new Princess of Patel galloping bareback on an Arithean steed under the shadow of an owl scares people, then so be it. A change of pace seems to be exactly what this kingdom needs.

Acknowledgments

From the earliest drafts to the final edits, my debut novel would never have seen the light of day without the support of my family, friends, and the writing community.

First, I want to give a very special thanks to my parents. Mum has been editing my writing for as long as I can remember, and Dad is always there to read my drafts (especially if there is a dragon). Your encouragement has allowed me to chase my dreams.

To Ian, thank you for your patience and unwavering faith in me. Your calm pragmatism helps me conquer my worst moments of spiralling doubt.

Third, I want to thank my beta readers Nicola, Jo, and Joanne. Your feedback has allowed Nakoma to shine and has given me the confidence to keep pushing through the drafts. Thank you also to the hive mind that is the Ipswich Writers group, the Lonely Writers Club, and the Springfield Writers Group. I have learnt so much from all of you.

And last, but certainly not least, thank you to my editor. Your flexibility and understanding have allowed me to finally finish Nakoma and the Prince.

About the Author

Monica Schultz is a high school mathematics teacher from Ipswich, Australia. She started writing fantasy when she got sick of waiting until she was asleep to spend time in her favourite fantasy worlds. Monica exists on a diet of Coke Zero and spends most afternoons surrounded by her menagerie of cats and dogs. Discover other titles by Monica Schultz at: https://monicaschultzauthor.weebly.com/

facebook.com/monicaschultzauthor

instagram.com/monicaschultzauthor